# Forget
# Me Not

# Books by Fern Michaels

Forget Me Not
The Blossom Sisters
Balancing Act
Tuesday's Child
Betrayal
Southern Comfort
To Taste the Wine
Sins of the Flesh
Sins of Omission
Return to Sender
Mr. and Miss Anonymous
Up Close and Personal
Fool Me Once
Picture Perfect
About Face
The Future Scrolls
Kentucky Sunrise
Kentucky Heat
Kentucky Rich
Plain Jane
Charming Lily
What You Wish For
The Guest List
Listen to Your Heart
Celebration
Yesterday
Finders Keepers
Annie's Rainbow
Sara's Song
Vegas Sunrise
Vegas Heat

Vegas Rich
Whitefire
Wish List
Dear Emily
Christmas at
    Timberwoods

## The Sisterhood Novels

Blindsided
Gotcha!
Home Free
Déjà Vu
Cross Roads
Game Over
Deadly Deals
Vanishing Act
Razor Sharp
Under the Radar
Final Justice
Collateral Damage
Fast Track
Hokus Pokus
Hide and Seek
Free Fall
Lethal Justice
Sweet Revenge
The Jury
Vendetta
Payback
Weekend Warriors

## The Godmothers Series

Classified
Breaking News
Deadline
Late Edition
Exclusive
The Scoop

## eBook Exclusives

Captive Embraces
Captive Passions
Captive Secrets
Captive Splendors
Cinders to Satin
For All Their Lives
Fancy Dancer
Texas Heat
Texas Rich
Texas Fury
Texas Sunrise

## Anthologies

Secret Santa
A Winter Wonderland
I'll Be Home for
    Christmas
Making Spirits Bright
Holiday Magic
Snow Angels
Silver Bells
Comfort and Joy
Sugar and Spice
Let It Snow
A Gift of Joy
Five Golden Rings
Deck the Halls
Jingle All the Way

# FERN MICHAELS

# Forget
# Me Not

**Doubleday Large Print
Home Library Edition**

## ZEBRA BOOKS
### KENSINGTON PUBLISHING CORP.

Zebra and the Z logo Reg. U.S. Pat. & TM Off.

ISBN 978-1-61129-191-9

Printed in the United States of America

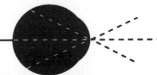

**This Large Print Book carries the
Seal of Approval of N.A.V.H.**

# Chapter One

Lucy Brighton sat back in her chair and looked at the array of drawings hanging on a wire with colored clothespins. Izzy, the fat little Yorkshire terrier; Bizzy, the equally fat white Persian cat; and Lizzy, the colorful red and green parrot. She laughed at her own artwork. IBL, as she called the trio, was her creation, and that creation had led not only to a seasonal line of greeting cards for children, but also to calendars, a comic strip, three books on IBL's antics that children clamored for, a cartoon that aired every day at ten o'clock in the morning, and a merchandising franchise. As far as she was concerned, she had it made in the shade and in spades, and she was only thirty-two. Thirty-two, and an old maid. No men in her life. How could there be? She worked virtually around the clock, but that was by choice.

Her friends, the few that she'd allowed into her inner circle, had long since vanished, either getting married or moving away in search of the perfect job—except, of course, for Angie, her best and only really close friend. At this point in time she had no interest in marriage, and she already had the perfect job. She knew she could retire right now, right this minute, as long as she was frugal with her money.

Her financial advisor had told her four months ago she was in the best position a thirty-two-year-old could possibly be in. Then the economy had started to tank, and she hadn't heard from him since. Well, that wasn't quite true. She had, in point of fact, heard from him, but he was singing a different tune and told her to keep working so she could make up for her losses in the stock market. She'd shrugged and thought to herself, **What goes down eventually goes back up.**

And her lifestyle required very little. Her house and this studio, where she whiled away all day and sometimes all night, had no mortgage, thanks to her parents, who had retired to Florida five years earlier. New Jersey was just too cold for them, they said. For some reason she thought that there was a lot more to it than that, but she'd accepted it and moved out of her cozy apartment and back into the house in which she'd grown up. Parents tended to be strange, and hers were definitely stranger than most.

Lucy tore her thoughts away from her parents and the colorful drawings and got up to walk over to the big picture window in the cozy four-room studio. She sat down on the window seat, pulled her legs up to her chin, and watched the autumn leaves swirling in the wind. Another week, and the leaves would all be down, and she'd have to go out and rake them unless she could hire someone to do it for her. She loved autumn; it was her favorite time of year. The pumpkins, the haystacks, the colored leaves, the brisk air, the local football games, pure apple cider, and, of course, a blazing fire in the hearth. What more could she possibly ask for? Perhaps someone to share it with? Then again, who would be foolish enough to put up with her weird hours, eating on the fly, playing wild music as she drew and sketched? Someday. Then again, maybe she was destined to go it alone and be a career woman. How bad could that be?

Lucy left her perch on the window seat, walked into the kitchenette, and made a pot of coffee. By the time she packed up her work and sent it off, the coffeepot would be empty, and it would be time to think about dinner. Not that there was anything to think about. She'd dumped some beans and vegetables into the Crock-Pot when she'd gotten up, so that was taken care of. She absolutely loved her Crock-Pots. She had three of them. One for the main meal, one for dessert, and one for soup. Because she'd read that beans were good for you, she made sure she ate at least a cupful every day in either the soup or her main meal. In some ways she was a health-food nut. Then she'd go and blow it by eating a pound of chocolate or a quart of ice cream while she watched television at night. As always, Lucy smiled as she slipped her one-of-a-kind drawings of the IBLs into individual plastic sleeves. Her agent was going to go over the moon with these. She dusted her hands dramatically. Six new greeting cards for Christmas. Check. Twelve drawings for next year's calendar. Check. Three months of the cartoon strip. Check. Book proposal. Check. A whole year's worth of work condensed into one FedEx package. She should celebrate. Like that was going to happen.

One last thing to do before heading up to the big house, the ugly big house, the hateful big house. The house in which she had grown up and the house that she hated with a passion. That house. Lucy clicked on her computer, brought up the FedEx Web site, and arranged for a pickup the following morning. She had had a special box built outside her studio, by her mailbox, where she left her packages for pickup so she wouldn't be disturbed while she was working. She looked around. Good to go. All she had to do was shut down her computer, turn off the lights, unplug the coffeepot, and lock up. Tomorrow she could sleep in. She was technically now off work, so to speak, until the first of the year. Not that that meant she wouldn't work—she would. She'd just not be on a schedule. Besides, Thanksgiving and Christmas were coming, and she really needed to think about either going away for a week or so to some exotic island or, horror of horrors, making plans to visit her parents. Even if it was only for a day or so. Maybe she could talk Angie into going with her, but Angie had a nine-to-five job with an ogre for a boss. Scratch that idea.

Lucy slipped on her Windbreaker, gathered up her package, turned off the light, then locked the door. She walked down the path to the mailbox, which sat between two cedar trees that she always decorated for Christmas. She opened the lid of the box, raised the red flag she'd screwed in as a joke, then dropped her package inside. She gave the bell a swat just to hear the sound that Toby, the driver, always made when there was a package. Done! Lucy gathered her jacket close around her neck; the wind had really grown strong, and the leaves were swirling like mad. She wasn't sure, but she thought she heard the phone ring inside the studio. No point in going back; by the time she got there and got the door unlocked, the phone would have stopped ringing. Whoever it was would call back sooner or later. She trudged up the hill to the big house and let herself in. She smiled at the pleasant aromas that greeted her, and realized how hungry she was. This was the moment when she always wished she had a real live pet instead of pets on paper to greet her. This was also the moment when she realized what a lonely life she led.

She hung up her jacket, washed her hands, and set her place at the table. If nothing else, she adhered to her mother's formal ritual at the dinner hour. Lucy removed the lid from the Crock-Pot and looked at the mess in the pot. She should give it a name. She went through this every night. Tonight, though, for some reason, it seemed important to give the contents a name. She looked down into the pot. Three kinds of beans and vegetables. Okay, Mess Number One. When she cooked soup, it would be Mess Number Two, and when she made dessert, it would be Mess Number Three. Done.

Lucy ladled out a generous portion onto her plate, grabbed a dinner roll from a bag on the counter, and set it alongside Mess Number One on the plate. Apple cider or beer? Or milk? Such a choice. She opted for the beer and reached for a glass. Since it was so quiet in the kitchen, Lucy turned on the television that sat on the counter just for sound. The early evening news. She flipped the channel, not wanting to hear or see the doom and gloom that seemed to make up the news these days. **Seinfeld.** Well, that was as good as anything else, even though she'd seen just about every episode at least a dozen times.

Lucy finished her dinner, scooped out a large spoonful of peach cobbler from Crock-Pot Number Three, and devoured it. She made a mental note to go to one of the roadside stands to get some nice juicy apples to make an apple pie. She could do that tomorrow since she was now technically not working. She cleaned up everything, transferred the leftover food to snap-on bowls, and set them all in the fridge for tomorrow's dinner. She looked around the neat kitchen. It was a beautiful kitchen, if you were into kitchens, which, unfortunately, she wasn't. Nor was her mother. Like the rest of the house, it was all for show. She out and out hated it.

I should have changed things, Lucy thought. But it had seemed sacrilegious somehow, and her mother probably would have pitched a fit, so it was just simpler to leave things as they were. It wasn't like she spent much time there in the big house; she didn't. All she did was eat and some-times sleep there. More often than not, she slept in the studio, on the couch, which was every bit as comfortable as her bed on the second floor.

She hated it when she let her thoughts take over like this. And why tonight? Maybe because she'd just finished up a long year's work and . . . And what? Now that she didn't have anything on her agenda, she had to think about her parents and this house. Maybe she needed another beer or a cig-arette. God forbid she smoke a cigarette in this house. Or have a drink, for that mat-ter. Well, no one was around to see her, but she knew cigarette smoke lingered or settled into the carpets and furniture, and if her parents ever came to visit, they'd surely smell it. Even if it was years from now. She didn't smoke, but once in a while, out of pure defiance, she fired up a cigarette, then almost choked herself to death as she puffed away. She wished again that she had a dog so it could poop on that fine Persian rug in the living room. A stain. She really wished there was a stain somewhere in this damn house. If she had a cat, it would probably claw at the custom draperies and shred them over time. If she had a parrot like Lizzy, it would fly all over the place and drop its feathers during molting season. More blights on the big house.

Carrying her bottle of beer and a stale cigarette she'd found in one of the kitchen drawers, Lucy marched into the family room, which was so well appointed, a person needed sunglasses. She moved over to the fireplace, threw in some logs, then turned on the gas starter. **Swoosh!** Instant fire. While she was growing up there, in that hateful house, the fireplace had never been used. Because . . . smoke escaped and settled on the furnishings, and one had to clean ashes out and carry wood in, and splinters fell all over, not to mention that sparks might escape.

"We have central heat, my dear, and Santa comes in the front door because he doesn't want to get all the white fur on his suit dirty." Even when she was a kid, she knew it was a crock. The phone rang just as Lucy was about to turn on the huge-screen TV above the fireplace. It was probably her artistic director, Henry, wanting to know if she had finished on time and if he could expect the results of her yearlong work the day after tomorrow. Good old Henry. She clicked on the phone, a smile on her face. Even before she could say hello, she heard a man's deep voice asking her if she was Lucy Brighton. She said, yes, she was, and listened.

"This is Detective Aaron Barkley of the Palm Royal Police Department. I'm sorry to tell you that I have some bad news. Are you alone, Miss Brighton? Would you prefer to call someone to stay with you, and I'll call you back?"

"No. I already know something is wrong, since you said you had bad news, so you might as well go ahead and tell me. I'll be all right. Please, just tell me whatever it is you're calling to tell me." Lucy sucked in her breath and waited.

"Your parents were killed two hours ago in a head-on collision. They died on impact. It's taken us this long to find you, or I would have called you sooner. A kind neighbor helped us."

Lucy's first wild, crazy thought was, **Now I can get rid of this house.** "How did it happen? You said they were killed. Who killed them?"

"A sixteen-year-old boy drunk out of his mind. He died in the accident, too. Your parents have been taken to the county morgue to await your arrival. Are you all right, Miss Brighton? I never like to deliver news like this over the phone, but you are out of state. I had no other choice, and I'm sorry, ma'am, for your loss."

"I'm okay, Detective. I understand about the phone and all. Thank you for calling me. I'll make arrangements to leave on the first available flight I can get for tomorrow."

The connection broken, Lucy stared into the flames as she fumbled around for the cigarette she'd forgotten to light up. She held the lighter to the tip of the cigarette with a rock-steady hand. She coughed; she sputtered; she swigged some beer, then took another puff and repeated the process until she felt like she had coughed out her lungs. **How do people smoke these things?**

Her parents were dead. D-e-a-d! She wondered if she was supposed to cry. Probably. She squeezed her eyes shut, but no tears nipped at her eyelids. Maybe it hadn't sunk in yet. Maybe she needed to think about her parents; then she would cry. She should feel sad. She didn't. She didn't feel anything. Just sort of numb. Now, if she had a dog, a cat, or a parrot, this would be the time to hug them, and they'd understand what she was going through. She didn't believe it for one damn minute. Animals, and probably birds, too, reacted only to their owners' emotions. And at that moment in time she didn't have any emotions.

Would the world miss Dr. Fritz Brighton, renowned heart surgeon, who, before his retirement, had traveled the world, operating on people who had money blowing out their ears? Would the world miss Dr. Helene Brighton, shrink to those same wealthy people, who couldn't wait to fatten up her bank account so that they could hear her words of wisdom that would make them mentally whole again?

The answer was, who cared? All she was interested in was why she didn't care. Why she didn't feel anything. Lucy finished her beer and trotted off to the kitchen for another one. She flopped down on a chair and watched the fire in front of her. What did the only remaining relative do when called in a situation like this? It wasn't that she was stupid. She had just never had death enter her life. She had no grandparents, no aunts, no uncles, no cousins. That meant she was all alone in the world. With her parents gone, so was the last and only buffer between her and her own mortality. That might be a good thing, she decided, to have all that open space around her, so she could spread her wings now that the buffer was gone.

The first thing she needed to do was plan a funeral. She wondered if her parents had a will. Didn't people who had wills state what they wanted done with their remains? Hadn't she read that somewhere?

She needed a black dress. A veil? On television the mourners always wore black veils. Black shoes and black gloves. Like that was going to happen. Not. People in Florida didn't wear black; they wore yellow, lime green, and white. At least that was what her mother had told her once. Scratch black. There was no one to call to announce the demise of her parents. Whoever had passed as their friends here in New Jersey were gone. At least she assumed they were gone, since no one had ever called or dropped by once her parents had relocated to Florida. Maybe she just thought there were friends, because for the life of her, she couldn't recall a single one.

A lawyer? Did her parents have a lawyer in New Jersey or in Florida? She realized that she hadn't a clue. There must be a lawyer in the background somewhere. How else had her parents deeded the house and studio over to her? A lawyer would have handled that. In order to find that out, she'd have to go to the bank and look in her safe-deposit box, where she kept the deed and the legal papers that came with it. Truth be told, she'd never even looked at those papers. The day she'd gotten her MBA, her parents had given her the news that they were moving and the house was hers. One week later, they were gone, and she was rattling around in a six-thousand-square-foot house that looked like no one had ever lived in it.

She hadn't cried that day, either, when she waved good-bye at the front door. When her parents didn't even look back, she had slammed the door and screamed, "Good riddance!" at the top of her lungs. Then she'd gone nuts and bellowed out the F word again and again as she banged on the door.

No one to call. Angie was off on an assignment; no sense in upsetting her when there wasn't anything she could do, anyway. Only the airline. Which she did call. She booked herself a first-class ticket on a one o'clock flight out of Newark Airport for the following day. Since she didn't know how long she'd have to be in Florida, there was no point in driving herself to the airport and leaving her car in the long-term lot. She called a car service, who said they would pick her up at eleven thirty the following morning.

With nothing else to do, Lucy banked the fire, closed the glass screen, turned off the television, locked the back door, and made her way up the long circular stair-case that resembled something in an ante-bellum Southern mansion. She made her way to her bedroom and, as always, was amazed at the lavishness of it. Everything was silk, satin, or brocade in champagne colors. The bed was a high riser, and she needed a step stool to get into it. Her bed-room had changed over the years from a little girl's pink palace to a teenager's do-main, then to what she was looking at that evening. She would come home from boarding school one day a month and see a brand-new bedroom, and no one would say a word. It was just there. More often than not, she found excuses not to go home, and her parents didn't seem to care one way or the other. Finally, she stopped going altogether. Everything was always neat and tidy, nothing, not even a piece of lint, anywhere to be found. She'd learned early on that nothing was negotiable with her parents. It just was.

Lucy sat down on a beige satin-covered chair and kicked off her sneakers. She leaned back and closed her eyes. She didn't hate her parents, but she didn't like them very much, either. Love simply wasn't in the equation. She couldn't really complain about her life. Her parents had been good to her. In other words, good providers in lieu of being loving parents. She'd wanted for nothing. In fact, she'd had more than most kids ever dreamed of having.

She had lived in a fine house full of people who saw to everything until she was ten years old. The things she yearned for the most, however, friends and a pet, had been denied. But her days were full at boarding school, with dance lessons, gymnastics, and piano lessons after regular classes. On the rare visits home, dinner was eaten alone in the kitchen with the housekeeper, whoever she happened to be that particular month. Breakfast was also with the housekeeper; then she was driven back to her boarding school by the chauffeur. Her mother looked in on her at night, usually around nine o'clock, for the obligatory kiss on the top of her head and a whispered good night during those rare visits. Sundays her father called her at school, usually at noon, from whatever corner of the world he was in that particular Sunday. The calls never lasted more than five minutes.

Boarding school was okay—she'd actually enjoyed being away from home and being with her peers. She remembered those days fondly. Then came college, where she'd made some good friends, specifically Angie, and had her first affair— which had turned into a disaster when she found out she was just one of a string of girls the jerk had been seeing. She had sworn off the opposite sex after that and had concentrated on her studies, graduating magna cum laude, to her parents' supposed delight. There had been no fanfare at her graduation. Her mother had attended, explaining that her father was in Germany, operating on the chancellor's daughter. She'd handed over a generous check and left.

Lucy had stayed on and gotten her master's, and that was when her life changed— her parents retired and moved to Florida. Funny how she remembered that and the white-haired guy sitting in the front row who had smiled and clapped when she walked across the stage to accept her diploma. She'd wondered at the time if he was a friend of her mother's, because he was sitting next to her, but she had never asked.

Time to get a move on. She hated it when her memories took her back in time. The past was past, and there was nothing she could do about it. So what if she didn't feel anything at her parents' passing? So what if she couldn't squeeze tears out of her eyes? So what! There was no one to care but her. Assuming she cared, which she didn't.

Pack. Good thing she hadn't packed away her summer clothing. She quickly emptied out a week's worth of clothing and slammed it all any which way into a suit-case. And there wasn't one stitch of any-thing that was black in the suitcase. All she had to do was pack her cosmetics and toi-letries in the morning, and she could be on her way.

Lucy brushed her teeth, stripped off her clothes, and pulled on her pajamas, certain she wouldn't sleep a wink and would end up staring at the ceiling all night, even though she'd consumed two bottles of beer.

She was wrong; the minute her head hit the pillow, she was out like the proverbial light and didn't wake till seven thirty the following morning. She showered, dressed conservatively in an olive-colored, lightweight suit, and headed downstairs, where she had coffee and a muffin. She watched television at the kitchen table while she waited for the car service to arrive. Her thoughts were everywhere and nowhere as she contemplated what lay ahead of her.

# Chapter Two

Lucy let herself into her parents' house, or, as she thought of it now, the other hateful house. She thought at that moment that the house was giving off vibes that the people who had lived in it were gone. Gone as in never coming back. She dropped the house keys, her mother's keys, in a little crystal dish that sat on a table in the massive foyer. She knew they were her mother's keys because they were in the purse the police had given her. Everything had been in a sealed clear plastic bag. A purse whose contents were sparse: a package of Kleenex that hadn't even been opened, a cell phone, the keys, a small wallet with two credit cards, a driver's license, an insurance card, and ninety dollars in cash. A small coin purse had $3.47 in change in it. In a smaller plastic bag inside the police-tagged bag were her mother's earrings, her watch, and her wedding ring. All that was left of Helene Brighton.

There wasn't even that much in her father's police bag. His wallet with two credit cards, his insurance card, his driver's license, along with the car registration; a cell phone; and $451.00 in bills, plus ninety-four cents in change, which must have been in his trouser pocket at the time of the crash. His watch, his tie clip, his wedding ring, and his car keys barely filled the little bag. It was all that was left of Fritz Brighton, the world's most respected and renowned heart surgeon. How sad that her parents had been reduced to two small plastic bags. Right now, right this moment, she couldn't even remember where she'd put the two plastic bags. Probably in the kitchen, which looked like it had never been used.

Lucy looked at herself in the foyer mirror. She didn't look like she'd just come from a funeral. To her eye, she looked the way she always looked. She had pulled her hair back in a bun; she was wearing makeup, something she didn't normally wear during the day. Her dress was simple, a beige, sleeveless A-line dress with a pair of pearls. Her shoes and handbag were a darker beige. She kicked off her shoes and padded barefoot out to the kitchen, where she brewed a pot of coffee. While she waited for the coffee to run through the filter, she stared out across the deck, which was empty of furniture or flowers. The day was gray and gloomy, and if she was any judge of the weather, it would rain before the day was over. Funeral weather.

Now, where did that thought come from? What she knew about funerals and weather would fill a thimble. Must be from television shows. Or perhaps she'd read it in a book? That was the best she could come up with for an answer.

Lucy poked around in the refrigerator, thinking she should eat something, but she wasn't hungry. Maybe later. Instead, she thought about the funeral, which wasn't really a funeral—only a service, since she'd had her parents cremated. She hadn't been able to find a will in the house, which would possibly have stated her parents' burial wishes. So she'd gone ahead with the cremation since, according to the police, the bodies had been so mangled during the accident that identification was all but impossible. The detective had gone on to tell Lucy it would be better to remember her parents the way she'd seen them last and not the way they'd died. She remembered nodding as she agreed with the detective.

Lucy sipped at her coffee, wishing she could cry or feel something. When no tears or feelings emerged, she sighed and looked around the marvelous kitchen, which had every right to be featured in **Architectural Digest.** Everything looked bright and shiny new. Barely any staples in the butler's pantry, little to nothing in the refrigerator. Did her parents eat out every day? Her mother had never been a cook, and her father had teased her about burning everything, which was why they'd always had a cook while she was growing up. Did her parents have a cook here? A housekeeper? If so, where was she? Maybe she needed to talk to the neighbors, ask a few questions about her parents.

It was odd, Lucy thought, that none of the neighbors had stopped by to offer their condolences. Neighbors did things like that back in New Jersey. And no one had been at the service except for herself, the pastor, and someone named Lucas Kingston, who, the pastor told her, was the developer of Palm Royal, the enclave where her parents lived. An elderly couple, perhaps her parents' age, had sat in the last pew, but when the service was over and she turned around, they were gone. They could have been neighbors, for all she knew, or they could have been strangers who just attended services because they had nothing better to do with themselves.

How could her parents have lived here in Palm Royal for five years and not have friends who would attend their funeral service? It was all so weird that she didn't know what to think. But thinking wasn't going to get her anywhere; she knew that for certain. Just then, though, she needed to get off her duff and dive into what needed to be done until she could figure out if her parents had an attorney, a will, or where they kept their records. And she would have to make a decision if she was the one who needed to do all the work about putting the house up for sale, checking to see if any bills were owed, things of that nature.

Maybe what she should do was engage the services of a lawyer and let him handle it all. That way, she could simply pack up her parents' things and put them in storage or take them back to New Jersey. She could pack a lot in her father's Range Rover in the garage and drive back instead of flying. Maybe she could sell the house furnished. Then she wouldn't have to worry about donating or selling off the furnishings, since they were new and looked new. The Mercedes her parents had been driving at the time of the accident was, of course, totaled. That meant she'd have to deal with the insurance company as soon as she figured out who that company was. Best-case scenario, three more days before she could leave. Worst-case scenario, at least a week to tidy up all the loose ends and be on her way.

Lucy almost jumped off her chair when she heard a boom of thunder. She finished her coffee and made her way to the second floor, stopping just long enough to pick up her shoes in the foyer. It took her just ten minutes to pack up her dress and shoes and put on a pair of faded, comfortable shorts and a T-shirt. She tied the laces of her sneakers and headed back to the first floor. **Start at the bottom and work your way to the top,** a niggling voice said. That meant the garage first.

**No one has a garage like this,** Lucy thought as she turned on the overhead light. There wasn't so much as an oil stain on the off-white concrete. Her father's Range Rover sat silent, its doors locked. There was nothing on any of the shelves, no jars of nails or screws, no tools, no gas can, no boxes of anything. No lawn equipment. There wasn't even a trash can. She frowned as she tried to remember if there was one outside. Didn't people here recycle? Well, if they did, her parents weren't among those who did their duty for the environment. She made a mental note to check the Rover later, although it was doubtful anything of any importance would be in the truck.

It took Lucy two full hours to check all the rooms on the first floor. All she could do was shake her head at what she didn't find. The drawers in the hutch and buffet server were empty. Every single drawer on the first floor was empty. The kitchen drawers held nothing but one notepad, one pen, a screwdriver, a small hammer, and eight slim candles still in the box they came in, along with a pack of matches tucked inside the box. The candles must have been her parents' idea of a hurricane package.

Back in the kitchen, Lucy washed her hands and poured a second cup of coffee. Her hands hadn't even been dusty, which meant someone had cleaned this house at some point. That someone definitely was not her mother. Not only didn't her mother cook; she didn't clean, either. Maybe the house cleaner came only once a week and didn't even know about her parents' death, and she'd show up on her assigned day. Anything was possible, she thought fretfully.

Lucy watched the rain slashing at the windows. Off in the distance, she could see lightning as it danced and zipped across the sky to the tune of the wild thunder. She did take a moment to wonder if a rainstorm like this was normal for the time of year. In the end, however, she didn't really care, so she finished her coffee and headed back up to the second floor.

Lucy started with her parents' bedroom. It was lovely, she thought, white wicker with bright accents of color. It made her think of sunny days and lush gardens. She couldn't imagine her father sleeping in such a room, but she had to admit that she really knew virtually nothing about his likes and dislikes. The monstrous walk-in closet was a puzzle, though. It was screamingly neat. Everything, and there wasn't much of everything, was neatly arranged. For some reason it all seemed staged, and that was the only word that came to mind. Seven suits, seven pairs of shoes on her father's side. Dress shirts, all white and seven in number; a heavy parka in a clear dry cleaner's bag; two casual jackets with leather patches on the elbows; a Windbreaker; and three zippered heavy sweat jackets with hoods, seven in number again. A pair of stout cold-weather boots. Seven sweaters in the gray and beige line. A rack with seven ties and seven belts. That completed her father's side of the closet.

Her mother's side of the enormous walk-in closet held seven pantsuits, seven dresses, seven skirts, seven blouses, and seven pastel cashmere sweaters. A heavy outdoor jacket and two long coats were hanging side by side next to two raincoats, one gray, one black, and two evening wraps, one black velvet and one a champagne color. Again, seven in number. She counted sixteen pairs of shoes, from flats to mid-heel to spike heels. Jimmy Choo and Ferragamo. A lone pair of snow boots sat in the corner. Two pegs held seven scarves, seven belts, and one umbrella with a jewel-encrusted handle. The top shelf assigned to her mother held designer handbags: Chanel, Prada, Gucci, Fendi, Louis Vuitton, Givenchy, and Bottega Veneta. All of them were empty and appeared to be new. And even if not new, then barely used.

A frown built between Lucy's brows when she realized that there were no suitcases or even duffel bags anywhere to be seen. And yet her parents traveled constantly. Scratch that thought: They used to travel constantly, before they retired five years ago. She had no idea what they had done these past years.

Lucy continued with her search and walked next to the room that had been used as an office. The desk was a custom rosewood affair, extra long, with two beautiful burgundy ergonomic chairs side by side. Two laptop computers, a fax machine, a copy machine, and a printer. All separate units. An eighty-six-inch plasma TV hung on one wall. The other walls were bare. Did her parents sit in the ergonomic chairs to watch TV? She tried clicking on the laptops, but everything was password protected. She'd need a hacker to get into either one of them.

Lucy looked around. Every office had filing cabinets. This home office did not. The desk drawers were empty, with the exception of a box of paper clips, several gel pens, sticky notepads, a calculator with big numbers, a large box of staples, and a stapler. The closet was just that, a closet. But instead of a rod to hang clothes, there were shelves, which held boxes of copy paper, file folders, and mailing envelopes. The phone was black and was just an ordinary landline. The fax machine was also black.

"Well, this is a bust," Lucy muttered out loud. As if her outburst needed an exclamation point, a roar of thunder shook the house. Lightning must have struck something close by, she thought, as the lights flickered once, then again, but remained on. Lucy walked from room to room on the second floor. She'd already checked out the bedroom she had slept in, and it was just a room, with nothing hidden or stuck anywhere. The other bedrooms and connecting baths were just as bare. All were furnished, but that was as far as it went. No clues, no scraps of paper, no hidden messages. Neat and tidy.

Now what was she supposed to do? Where were her parents' medical files on their patients? Where were their banking records, their brokerage accounts? What was she going to tell a lawyer? "Hey, guess what, my parents died, and I can't find their paperwork?" Were her parents paranoid? Did they hide stuff? And if so, why? "I guess I never really knew my parents," she murmured as she walked back to her folks' bedroom. She looked around again. Where was her mother's jewelry box, her perfume? All women, even young girls, had a jewelry box, even if it was nothing more than a cigar box. Where was the box her father kept his cuff links in, the dish where he put his change when he emptied out his pockets? She remembered seeing those things when her parents lived in the New

Jersey house. The tops of the dressers were bare. The drawers didn't give up anything but sleepwear and underwear and socks and, in her mother's drawer, hosiery.

Next came the his-and-her bathroom, two of everything, even two bidets. Lucy's eyebrows rose at the sight. Her father's shaving kit and toothbrush were neatly placed on his sink. Her mother's sink held a little more—a blow-dryer, curling iron— but they were set into a niche in the ceramic wall. Night cream, day cream, a toothbrush, a comb, and a brush. In the shower she found ordinary shampoo and conditioner, Dove soap. A back scrubber that looked like it had never been used hung from the showerhead. Anyone's bathroom in the good old US of A. Just like her own back in New Jersey.

Then something came like a bolt out of the blue. A safe! There must be a safe somewhere in the house. But where? Lucy looked at her watch. It was almost three o'clock, and her stomach was rumbling. She tried to remember when she'd eaten last, and the best she could come up with was early yesterday morning.

Back in the kitchen Lucy fixed herself a

dry-as-dirt cheese sandwich. She finished off the rest of the coffee and promised herself that she'd go out to dinner at the first restaurant she could find when the rain finally stopped. If it stopped. As she sipped and chewed, she asked herself, knowing what she knew about her parents, where they would install a safe. Did her father install it himself? Unlikely, since he never used his hands for anything except his miracle surgeries. Her mother? Ridiculous. Maybe the house came with a safe. Highly unlikely. She'd have to search the rooms again. Wall safe? Floor safe? She just didn't know. And there was no one to ask. Still, she couldn't put the house up for sale if there was any possibility there was a safe for the new owners to find.

She remembered a mystery novel she'd read not too long ago, where one of the characters wanted to hide something. In plain sight was what the character had decided, and in the book it worked for him. Maybe her parents had read the same book. Or else they were smarter than the character. Plain sight? Lucy walked over to the door and looked out at the driving rain. "I just want to go home," she murmured over and over. "I hate this house, just the way I hate that big house back in New Jersey."

She made a mental note to think about going to a shrink to find out why she couldn't cry, why she didn't feel anything, and why she hated both of the houses her parents had lived in. Why? Why? Why?

Her shoulders stiff, her face set in grim determination, Lucy started again on the ground floor, this time to search for a safe. She knocked on walls, looked for recessed buttons that would possibly open a cleverly disguised safe. She got down on her hands and knees to inspect any irregularity in the floorboards but found nothing. She even checked the fieldstones in the fireplace. She went so far as to poke through the artificial ash on the floor of the firebox. She found nothing.

Tomorrow she would tackle the upstairs, because at that moment she was tired, and she was hungry. She raced upstairs, removed her shorts, and pulled on a pair of jeans. Even though it was still raining, she got into her rental car and made it as far as a Burger King, where she ordered two grilled veggie sandwiches, a milk shake, and a large french fries. She devoured it all in the parking lot, then headed back to Palm Royal. On the ride back, she came to the conclusion that her parents must have had a safe-deposit box somewhere in town, at one of the many banks. There were no safe-deposit keys on either her mother's or her father's key rings. She groaned when she thought about looking under all the different drawers in the house. In a movie she'd seen once, someone had duct taped a key to the bottom of a drawer. Checking each drawer and recessed cabinet could take her hours and hours, if not all day. Her departure time was going to have to be extended to possibly ten days rather than a week. She groaned again as she swerved into the driveway.

The house was just as silent as it had been that morning, after the funeral service. She should have left the TV on or the stereo unit. She shivered. Now she knew what it felt like to be in a mausoleum. She walked through the rooms, turning on lights, the different TVs, as well as the Bose system for sound. It hit her then, right between the eyes. There wasn't even one picture of her anywhere in the whole house. Parents always displayed pictures of their children, usually candid shots taken here and there. Back in New Jersey, when she was growing up, there had been a few. One of her on her first pony ride, another with her father, sitting side by side on a bench in some park. They had been on the piano, in shiny silver frames. Where were they? Hadn't her parents cared enough about her to put those same pictures on the piano in the living room in this house? The thought that they hadn't hurt her heart.

Lucy flopped down on the sofa, which felt stiff and unyielding, as if no one had ever sat on it or broken it in, and drew her legs up to her chin. She stared at the television screen, listening to Charlie Sheen bantering with his costar, but she didn't really hear the words. Her thoughts took her back in time to a fond, treasured memory of her father as he played with her on the floor in her room before bedtime. She was around five, and he was giving her a ride on his back as he made whistling sounds like he was a train engine. She remembered how she'd laughed and giggled and how her father had kissed her on the cheek and had told her she was his fairy princess. Her mother had stood in the doorway, a huge smile on her face. And then the hateful words every child detested hearing. "Time for bed." Her father had read her a story, kissed her good night. Then her mother had read her a story, and she had hugged her and kissed her and wished her sweet dreams. She smelled so good; her perfume was light and pleasant. She didn't know what the scent was at the time but later on realized it was lily of the valley.

At some point in time over the years, her mother must have changed her scent to one Lucy didn't really like—it was musky and heavy, like a winter scent. Even now, when the lily of the valley flowers bloomed back home in the flower beds, they reminded her of that particular night and her smiling mother when she hugged her good night. It seemed like a hundred years ago, but the memory was still fresh and had never been forgotten. The big question now was, why did she have just that one treasured memory? Did she just forget the others? Because surely there had been others. And had she kept this one because it was so special? She'd never found the answer, even though she'd asked herself the same question hundreds of times over the years. She didn't have an answer now, either.

Lucy yawned. Time to go to bed. But first she decided to make a list of things she had to do in the morning, after she continued her search to find a safe, if there was one. An hour later she looked at the list in dismay. So many phone calls to make. So much to do. Well, she'd just have to tackle it the best way she could and hope for the best. She wanted to berate her parents for putting her through this. She wanted to wail and screech and pound her fists on something. Dammit, why hadn't they trusted her, their own daughter, to tell her what to do in case anything ever happened to them?

Why? Why? Why?

# Chapter Three

Lucy woke to monsoon rain pelting the bedroom windows. She groaned. What happened to sunny Florida? She looked toward the nightstand and squinted at the portable clock she'd brought with her. Seven ten. She lay quietly, listening to the driving rain and staring through the windows at the gloomy day outside. **Should I go back to sleep? Will I even sleep if I try? Probably not.**

So she swung her legs over the side of the bed and headed for the shower. But first she looked in the mirror. Who was this person staring back at her? She shook her head and turned on the shower.

Fifteen minutes later, she was downstairs, scooping coffee into the pot. While she waited for the coffee to drip into the pot, she munched on doughnuts she'd picked up on her way home from Burger King the night before. Less than fresh now, but she didn't care. She just wanted something in her stomach before she got on with her search for a safe. She turned on the counter television just to have sound. She half listened to the global doom and gloom, which seemed to match the day. Didn't those made-up mannequins who spewed the news ever have anything good to report? Something warm and fuzzy, feel-good news? She couldn't remember the last time she'd heard anything that brought a smile to her face.

As she sipped at her coffee, she thought about her pleasant life, her successful life, back in New Jersey. She had Angie and other friends, neighbors, and a guy she saw off and on. She was close enough to New York that all she had to do was go to Metropark, hop on a train, and be in New York in forty-five minutes when she needed what she called a New York Fix. Of course, she had demons; everyone did. But her life was way too busy to worry about something over which she had no control. Then she remembered the promise she'd made to herself the day before to consult a shrink to find out why she couldn't cry or feel anything over her parents' deaths. And, of course, why she hated this house and the big house back home. Well, she would do that. In fact, she could search out a good qualified shrink from here and even make an appointment she would keep as soon as she returned home.

Lucy finished her coffee, closed the doughnut bag, and let loose with a loud sigh. Time to start her search.

By three o'clock Lucy was so frustrated that she wanted to scream. She was sitting cross-legged in the massive walk-in closet, staring at the assorted clothing hanging on the rods. Such precision, almost military looking, one inch apart for each garment hanging. She thought about her own closet, which left a lot to be desired as she just tossed and jammed things in any old which way. She did not like regimentation of any kind. She also hated rules and regulations. "Guess that makes me a free spirit," she muttered to herself. "I just give up!" she muttered again as she untangled her legs and, in doing so, slumped sideways, her shoulder hitting the far end of the wall. "Ouch!" She maneuvered around to see what it was that was digging into her shoulder. And there it was, in plain sight, so to speak.

Lucy looked at what she thought was a walking stick but was more like a cane, actually. But on closer inspection, it turned out to be a man's black umbrella, which only appeared to be leaning against the wall but was actually mounted, the brackets undetectable unless you were on your knees and looking right at them. In plain sight. A man's cane, a short man's cane. A short man like her father. But it wasn't a cane; it was an umbrella. She sucked in her breath again and started to press and prod and squeeze until she found the button that would normally release the umbrella. The umbrella didn't open up. Instead, the floor right in front of her started to slide toward her mother's section of the closet. The safe. Lucy sat down and hugged her knees.

**So,** I was **right, after all,** she thought as she looked at the safe in the floor. **This has to be the queen mother of all safes.** Some engineer somewhere, she opined, must have designed this particular safe, because it looked so unusual, at least to her eyes. She'd seen safes, all kinds, in movies, on television, and she'd read about safes in novels. None were anything like this one. It was almost as long as two yardsticks end to end, or seventy-two inches long. While it looked to be a one-piece unit, it had three doors and three keypads. "And what is behind Door Number One?" Lucy said out loud. Then she went off on a rant that only frustrated her more. Right at that moment, at that precise moment in time, Lucy knew that her parents were involved in something other than being retired. Why would two retired doctors need a safe of this magnitude, hidden away like this?

Lucy continued to hug her knees as her mind raced. Houses that didn't look lived in. Clothes that appeared brand-new, never worn. Staged. But for whom? Certainly not for her, because she never came here. Who then? Her parents didn't know they were going to die in such a tragic accident. Were they in hiding in plain sight? Doctors had an inside track to drugs. Were her parents involved in something like that? Where did they go when they traveled? Where did they actually live? Anyone who was reasonably intelligent would figure out sooner rather than later that this house and everything in it was for show. She was positive now that her parents had not lived in this house on a daily basis. Maybe they came and went, but they sure as hell didn't live in it. That was one thing that she was absolutely certain of.

Lucy continued to stare at the state-of-the-art safe in the floor. Three keypads. Three different combinations, and she had no clue what they might be. The keypads were digital.

By four thirty, Lucy was ready to go nuclear. She'd tried every sequence of numbers she could possibly think of, house numbers, birth dates, special dates, random numbers, anything she could think of, but absolutely nothing had worked. She was angry at herself, but angrier still at her parents. What was she supposed to do if she couldn't figure out how to open the safe? Was she supposed to walk away and forget about all of this? Whatever the hell **this** was? Was it possible that the first keypad had to tie into the second, then the third? More than likely. If that was the case, she might have to blow the damned thing up before she could get it open. Or, magically, come up with a safecracker out of nowhere. That, in itself, would open up a whole other can of worms.

Lucy was back to hugging her knees, her eyes narrowed as she ran through numbers in her head. Outside, the monsoon rain continued to lash at the windows. She could hear the winds howling. She shivered and almost jumped out of her skin when the doorbell rang. She realized how vulnerable she was, all alone in this big house, even more so now that she'd actually found the safe. She got up and ran to the window but realized it overlooked the side of the yard and not the front of the house. She ran down the hall to the second empty bedroom and looked out the window. With the pouring rain, all she could see was a person—she assumed it was a man—holding an umbrella and punching the doorbell. She craned her neck to see if there was a vehicle in the driveway, but it was too gray and rainy to see anything.

The house was locked up tight, so she wasn't worried that anyone could break in. The doors were stout and solid mahogany. The locks and dead bolts were top of the line. She knew she was safe as long as she didn't open the door. She'd had the good sense to park her rental car in the garage, so anyone coming to the door would assume no one was home. She clearly remembered turning out the kitchen light that morning, when she'd come upstairs to start her search. That meant the house would appear dark to anyone just looking or attempting to visit.

"Go away, whoever you are," Lucy whispered to herself.

The doorbell rang one last time, a long peal that didn't let up, as if the person was pressing the button and holding his thumb on it. And then the house went silent again.

Lucy watched as the figure turned around, walked a few steps away, and stood staring up at the second floor. Unless the person down below had X-ray vision, Lucy knew he couldn't see her in the darkened room. Still, she shivered. She remained where she was until she saw the lights of a vehicle spring to life. She watched until she couldn't see the lights anymore before she left the room and barreled down the steps and into the kitchen, where she made a fresh pot of coffee and scarfed down the two remaining doughnuts from the bag on the counter. She hadn't realized how hungry she was until just that moment. If nothing else, the doughnuts took the edge off her hunger.

Lucy carried her cup of coffee back up to the second floor, where she made her way into the walk-in closet again. She sat down, her back to the wall, and stared at the safe. She needed to think about the phrase "If you want to hide something, hide it in plain sight." Well, that was how she'd found the safe, so now she had to find the combination in the same way. **Think, Lucy. If this were you, where would you hide the combination?** When nothing came to her, she continued to sip at her coffee as she stared at the contents of the closet. **Seven!** Without stopping to think, Lucy leaned forward and started pressing the number seven, hoping against hope the red armed light would turn green. It didn't.

Lucy squirmed farther back and stared again, going from left to right, then from right to left, the way the old-time safes used to work. Seven was the key number; she was sure of it. Four times to the right, three times to the left, then two times to the right again. She'd seen that in a movie once. She realized then that she'd watched an awful lot of movies to have retained this kind of information. She tried again and again and still again, growing more frustrated as she went along. Seven. But . . . there were sixteen pairs of shoes on her mother's side of the closet, plus each of them had a pair of snow boots. One pair each. Could that be a two? If you added the two numbers that made up the sixteen pairs of shoes, you got seven again. She was onto something; she could feel it. Then if you took that seven and added two, it would make the last number nine, or if you subtracted it, it would make the last number five. Or possibly the last number was just a two.

Lucy pressed the numbers at the speed of light, but nothing happened. **Plain sight.**

**Think plain sight.** She'd exhausted every combination but one, so she flexed her fingers. If this didn't work, she would simply close the safe back up and walk away. She pressed the number seven three times on the first keypad; then she pressed it three more times on the middle keypad. When she got to the third keypad, she hit the seven, then the one, then the six. She held her breath and almost fainted when the red light turned a bright emerald green. She was so shocked, she didn't know what to do. She forgot the storm outside, forgot how hungry she was, forgot the stranger who had knocked on her door. She focused only on the three keypads and the heavy iron handles that would open the doors. She crawled on her hands and knees over to the first one and opened the door. **Slick as a whistle,** she thought.

Lucy opened the second door just as easily, then the third. She stared down inside the square compartments that made up the three safes. Things looked tidy, and everything was neatly bundled. She started with the first one and gave the contents a cursory inspection. Deed to the house, no mortgage; titles to the two cars, the wrecked

Mercedes and the Range Rover. Both paid in cash. Insurance papers, homeowners', car, and life insurance. Two policies for ten million dollars each with the beneficiary either her mother or her father, and if both were deceased, then she became the beneficiary. Two wills in blue covers, the same as the insurance policies: if both died, she was the sole beneficiary. There were bequests to people she didn't know and had not ever heard of. The dates on the wills, as well as the insurance policies, were the year she turned ten and was sent off to boarding school.

Lucy frowned at the thought. Her parents had sent her off to a boarding school and out of their lives, then had taken out enormous insurance policies and made a will. Why? It didn't make sense. A yellow folder held brokerage statements from Wells Fargo, current as of the last quarter. Lucy blinked. She had no idea being a doctor could yield the kind of money she was looking at. Astute investing? An itch settled between her shoulder blades and worked its way up to her neck. There was something wrong here. She could feel it. A small check register, the kind you could carry in your purse, was current for the year, with the entries clearly legible. Household expenses, utilities, and entries she didn't understand. Later, she could try to figure that out. The current balance was $17,866.03. January's balance had started with $67,000.00, with a check written to a name she didn't recognize for $50,000.00. Other than that one check, there were just ordinary expenditures.

Lucy replaced everything the way she'd found it and moved on to the second compartment of the safe. Three ordinary cigar boxes were nestled inside. Not exactly ordinary. They were Cuban cigar boxes. She could smell the faint scent of tobacco. She opened the first box and stared down at what seemed to be dozens of passports. Mostly blue, but some were other colors. She looked through them. Different names on each of them, but all the pictures were of her mother and father. All the passports were heavily stamped from all their travels. Why did her parents need other identities? She started to feel sick to her stomach, and it wasn't from lack of food.

Lucy opened the second cigar box and saw credit cards, Visa, MasterCard, American Express, and at least a dozen different driver's licenses, with names that matched the names on the passports. Aliases. Most of the licenses were international; only four were American. The names matched the passports and credit cards. Were they all forgeries?

Getting sicker by the moment, Lucy reached for the third box. This one had two thick rubber bands around it. She removed them and gasped. She looked down at stacks of thousand-dollar bills. A hundred to a pack. **Rainy-day money?**

"My ass!" The words exploded from her mouth like gunshots. Getaway money? Take-it-on-the-lam money? At the bottom of the box was a small envelope, the kind a party invitation might come in. Inside was a slip of paper with nothing but rows of numbers. You didn't need to be a rocket scientist to know these were numerals for numbered bank accounts somewhere in the world, thanks again to her movie knowledge.

Lucy rocked back on her heels as she tried to fathom what she was seeing. She packed up the money and put the rubber bands back on the cigar box. She eyed the third compartment of the safe and cringed, but she knew she had to open it. Steeling herself for what was to come, she gingerly opened the door of the safe, almost expecting a bomb to go off. She looked down into the depths of the compartment and wanted to scream. Six guns. Two Glocks. Two SIG Sauers. Two Berettas. This time, her movie knowledge didn't help her. She could clearly identify the makes of the guns because they were carved into the handles. Boxes of magazines—**bullets** were her words—completed the contents. Dear God, were her parents terrorists, mercenaries? She slammed the door shut and scooted back to the wall.

She had to think. **Think!** her mind screamed. She felt numb, unable to think. All she could do was test the safe doors to make sure they were locked. And then she pressed the button on the umbrella. She watched, her eyes as big as saucers, as the floor slid back into place. She started to hyperventilate then. She dropped her head between her knees and struggled for air. That was when she realized there were no income-tax records in the safe. She bolted upright and ran from the room, down the stairs to the kitchen, where she grabbed her purse off the counter and ran out to the garage, where she raised the garage door and backed her car out. She had to get out of there right now.

She drove through the pouring rain until she saw the garish lights of a steak house on the right, an eighth of a mile in the distance. She put on her blinker and drove into the lot, where she sat in the car and cried.

Lucy had no idea how long she sat there; a long time, she was sure. Finally, she dried her eyes, blew her nose, smoothed down her hair, and got out of the car. She ran through puddles up to her ankles. She was soaked. People were staring at her. She stared back. A hostess offered a towel. She realized she couldn't sit and eat in soaking-wet clothes with the air conditioner going full blast. For sure, this was no time to catch cold or, worse, pneumonia. She ordered a steak, a baked potato, and a garden salad to go. She stood dripping by the front door, hoping against hope that she didn't look as deranged as she felt.

She shoved bills into the waiter's hands, knowing she was paying too much for the food she had ordered, but she didn't care. Minutes later, after she'd slogged her way through the parking lot, she was back in her rental car and headed back to her parents' house.

Her parents' house!

# Chapter Four

Lucy chomped her way through her dinner, barely tasting it, her head buzzing with her newfound discovery. Her head felt like an overactive beehive, her thoughts buzzing every which way as she finished her meal. She reached into a fresh doughnut bag. Knowing what a terrible sweet tooth she had, on her way home from the steak house she had gone past the drive-through and stocked up on chocolate-covered doughnuts, some for that evening and some for the morning.

When she finished eating, she tidied up

and carried the take-out containers to the trash can, which she had finally noticed beside the garage. She took a moment to wonder what day the trash pickup was. Back in the house, Lucy started to pace. She always paced when she couldn't make sense of something that was troubling her. Her thoughts kept taking her back to the strange-looking safe in the floor of the walk-in closet. Where were her parents' birth certificates, their IRS records? Another thing that bothered her was the lack of a calendar anywhere in the house. Everyone had a calendar. She herself had three back in New Jersey. A person needed a calendar. Had her parents spent the last five years of their lives living in a bubble, a cocoon of some sort, where dates and times had no meaning? God, she was getting a headache just thinking about all the odd and disconcerting things she had learned since she had arrived in Florida.

"How could you do this to me? How?" she wailed. "I can't do this. I don't want to do this. This is above my pay grade. This isn't fair!" she screeched at the top of her lungs. **This is good,** she thought. **Let it out. Don't bottle it up. Scream till you're hoarse, if it will make you feel better.**

Which was precisely what she did. But it didn't help; she didn't feel any better than before. Then she cried. Not for the death of her parents, but for the ugly position she found herself in.

Satisfied that the kitchen was tidy and the doughnut bag closed tight, Lucy turned off the lights and made her way upstairs. Sometime during the past hour, her chaotic thoughts had led her to a decision to go on the Internet and see if she could take care of matters that way. She remembered the name of the lawyer who had drawn up her parents' wills, so she could Google them, then e-mail and fax them copies of the wills, although she was sure they had copies of their own. If she could get all of that out of the way that evening, she would be able to pack up her parents' belongings and head for home at some point the next day. The rest of whatever she had to do she could do from New Jersey. She could get boxes from The UPS Store, load up everything, and, with any luck, be on the road by noon. First, though, she'd have to open the damn safe again to get out all the papers.

But that left a great big question: What should she tell the lawyer about the contents of the second and third compartments? Maybe that was something she should keep to herself. As to the arsenal in the compartment . . . was it actually legal to transport six guns, plus ammunition, across state lines? Maybe she could pack them in the clothes in the boxes she got from UPS. The ammunition could go in another box. When she got back home, she could decide what to do with the guns and ammunition. Just the thought made her shiver.

Lucy opened the safe, took out the papers she needed, then made her way to the room her parents had used as an office. Since she still couldn't use the desktops, she flipped open her own laptop and went to work. First, she Googled the law firm of Schwager, Schwager, and Schwager. Robert Schwager, Stuart Schwager, and Sara Schwager. A family firm. That was good. All three looked like serious, no-nonsense lawyers. Between them they had a lot of years of experience, and Robert, also known as Bob, had taken a case all the way to the Supreme Court and won it. Another plus. At six hundred dollars an hour, they had better be good, she thought.

She scrolled down until she found an e-mail address. She fired off a message, short and to the point. Her bottom line was for the firm to get in touch with her after she returned to New Jersey. She looked for a fax number and immediately faxed copies of her parents' wills, along with a copy of her own driver's license and voter registration card, and a copy of one of her credit cards, together with her address and phone number back in New Jersey. Death certificates. She sent off another e-mail to the law firm, saying she would fax them copies in the morning, after she picked the certificates up from the funeral home.

Her third e-mail went to the Dial Funeral Home, asking them to have a dozen copies of both parents' death certificates ready for her first thing in the morning.

The next thing Lucy did was Google the insurance companies that had written the astronomical policies her parents had taken out years and years ago. She photocopied the benefits page, sent her pertinent personal information, and promised them copies of the death certificates in the morning. She informed them in the same e-mail that she would be leaving Florida the next day and to contact her in New Jersey.

Lucy decided she could wait until she returned home to deal with the wrecked car and the Department of Motor Vehicles. Dealing with the DMV was a pain in the neck, as she knew from personal experience, so why put herself through more stress any earlier than she had to? The cars were undoubtedly part of her parents' estate, so maybe the law firm could handle that end of things. She made a mental note to ask that very question when she e-mailed and faxed the certificates in the morning.

Finally, she was left with the big question, What should she do with the money, the forged passports, and all those forged credit cards and driver's licenses? **Let sleeping dogs lie, at least for the moment,** she decided. Obviously, no one knew about them, so for the present, lying low was likely the best course of action. Why look for trouble when it might be avoidable?

Lucy turned off her laptop, returned all the papers to the safe, then pressed the button on the crazy-looking umbrella. She couldn't help but wonder what genius had come up with that. Pure James Bond.

It was too early to go to sleep, but Lucy decided to take a nice hot shower, crawl into bed, and watch some television until she fell asleep. But before she did that, she had to call her best friend, Angie, and tell her what was going on. She'd first met Angie in college, where they were roommates. She was from New Jersey, too, lived in Ridgewood, twenty-five miles from where Lucy lived. They spoke daily, e-mailed and sent each other text messages, and tried to meet up every other weekend for girl time. Of late, though, Angie had been spending more and more time with her on-again, off-again boyfriend when she was not traveling on her job. At last word, they were on, or at least they had been before Lucy had made the trip down to Florida. Lucy hauled out her cell phone, only to find that the battery was dead. No bars. And she had forgotten to bring the charger. At least there was a landline she could use. She thought about going back downstairs and getting her parents' cell phones, but she remembered that when she had tried to turn on the strange-looking phones, she'd had no luck. They had just looked at her, as if to say, "Who are you kidding?" Probably more James Bond gizmos.

Angie picked up on the third ring. She didn't even give Lucy time to say anything other than hi. "Where are you? I've been calling you for days. I even drove down there, and you were gone. You had a ton of mail, and I took it into the studio. There was a bunch of FedEx stuff in your box, so I took that in, too. Why haven't you called me? I was worried sick. You always tell me when you're going out of town. We agreed, Lucy, that we would always tell each other when we would be out of touch. Well? Say something!"

"My parents died, Angie. I'm down here in Palm Royal. I'm sorry I didn't call. It was such a shock, you know. And my cell phone is dead, and I forgot to bring the charger. I have been . . . busy. God, have I been busy." Suddenly, Lucy stiffened. What if this phone was bugged? She told herself to stop being so overly dramatic. Still . . .

"Oh my God! Oh my God! Do you need me to come down there? I can get a flight out first thing in the morning. Oh, Lucy, I am so sorry. What can I do? I feel so bad about not being there for you. And all I'm doing is bitching at you. . . ."

"I know. It's okay. I think I'm still in shock. I can't believe it. They're gone, Angie. I'm leaving tomorrow. I'm going to drive my father's Range Rover home. I can't leave it here. I think I have just about everything under control. All I have to do is pack up their clothes and personal items first thing in the morning. Then I can start out."

"That has to be at least a fifteen-hour trip, and you won't have a cell phone. Don't try to do it all in one day, okay? Can't you pick up one of those throwaways and charge it in the cigarette lighter?"

"Good thinking, Angie. I will do that before I start out, and I'll call you with the number and we can talk while I drive. So, how's things?"

"Well, that's one of the reasons why I was trying to call you. I finally took your advice and kicked Brad out. He went kicking and screaming, but he went. I caught him with another girl at Starbucks day before yesterday. They were all kitchy koo. When my blood started to boil, I just booted him and all his designer clothes out of my place. My job sucks, and they're talking layoffs. I'm low man on the totem pole, so I'm getting my résumé together. I don't fancy myself standing in an unemployment line, I can tell you that."

"Stop right there! I have the perfect job for you. I want to hire you. Or, rather, IBL wants to hire you. Pack up and leave all that behind you. I would have made the offer to you sooner, but you were so wrapped up in that go-nowhere guy, I knew you wouldn't take me up on it. We can be partners in all but name. Officially, you will be my director of graphic arts. I'll pay you three times what you were making at your company, and with me, you will get to use your talents. Naturally, your compensation package will have generous stock options.

"The board of directors wants me to expand IBL. You know, coloring books for kids, stickers, storybooks, a whole bunch of stuff. I know you like the cartoons, so you could head up that part of the operation. You're a great graphic artist. I've also got something in the works, but I don't want to talk about it just yet so I don't jinx myself. We'll have to hire a few assistants if you sign on with me. So, what do you say?"

"I'm throwing stuff in my suitcase as we speak. I'll head out first thing in the morning and be there before you get home. Shoot! I have four more months to go on my apartment lease. I don't have eight grand to pay it off."

"I'll pay it. Stop worrying. We can take care of that when we get together. Just give them notice in the morning. What about your furniture?"

"It's all secondhand IKEA, so, no, I don't want it. I'll tell the property management company. Maybe they know someone who will want it, or they can rent it furnished. Lucy, I don't know what to say. This is so beyond generous. I will pay you back if you pay off my lease. That's a promise."

"Would you do the same for me?"

"Well, yeah, I would, but still. . . ."

"Do we have a deal, then?"

"Lucy, we do indeed have a deal. Thanks.

Question. Am I going to live with you in the big house, or should I start looking for an apartment?"

"I'd like it if you moved in with me, Angie. You know how I hate that house. I was thinking today that I'm going to donate all the furnishings and redo the house to the way I would like it to look. The first thing I'm going to do is go out to the farmer's market and buy a boatload of pumpkins and stuff and decorate the front porch for Halloween. How about it?"

"I'm in. We can recapture our youth."

"What youth?" Lucy asked, bitterness ringing in her voice.

Without missing a beat, Angie responded, "The childhood you missed. We'll make up for it. Hey, let's dress up in costume and stand on the porch when the kids come trick-or-treating!"

"Sterling idea. That's a plan. Okay, listen, I'm going to take a shower and go to bed. I'm sorry it didn't work out with Brad."

"Liar!"

Lucy laughed as she replaced the phone in the case. She sat on the edge of the bed, staring at the phone. If anyone was listening, she hadn't said a word to give anything away. **God, I am paranoid. Yeah, well, false identities, guns, and ammunition in a crazy-ass safe the likes of which I've never seen would make anyone paranoid, not to mention that equally crazy James Bond umbrella, plus the weird cell phones.**

Lucy hugged her arms across her chest as she wondered what the next days would bring and, whatever it turned out to be, whether she could handle it. Like she had choices blowing out her ears. She had to handle it, and she had to move on.

Lucy was up, dressed, and out of the house by seven o'clock in the morning. She did everything she had promised herself she would do. She even stopped at a service station, topped off her father's gas tank, and had the tires and oil checked. All good. At eight she picked up boxes at The UPS Store; by eight thirty she was at the funeral home, waiting for the doors to open. She thanked Mr. Dial for the certificates and turned to leave.

"Miss Brighton?"

"Yes?"

"Didn't you forget something?"

"I don't think so. I just wanted the certificates. I paid for the cremation the other day. I have my purse. No, I'm good to go, Mr. Dial. Oh, you must mean the remembrance cards. I thought you said you would mail those to me."

The funeral director stared at her. "I was referring to your . . . ah . . . parents. Their remains. They're ready."

**Sweet mother of God! My face must be apple red,** Lucy thought. She turned around. And lied. "No, Mr. Dial, I didn't forget. I was going to go back, pack up the truck, and come back. I wanted to make sure I could secure them safely in the cargo hold."

Even to her own ears it sounded like the lie it was. She could tell by the look on the man's face that he wasn't buying it, either. She had forgotten. That was the bottom line, which didn't say much for her.

"I can take them now, if it's a problem. Actually, sir, I should take them now, as it will save me coming back this way. Are they in boxes or urns?"

Mr. Dial sniffed. "You specified urns, and urns are what you're getting. I wrapped them in bubble wrap."

"Bubble wrap?" Lucy said inanely.

"You said you would be taking them with you. The urns are sealed, but one can't be too careful with the remains of loved ones."

"Oh, I absolutely agree," Lucy said. "Where are they?"

Mr. Dial pointed to a table in the foyer. "I had my assistant set them out when he opened at six this morning. Travel safely, Miss Brighton."

Lucy licked at her dry lips as she marched over to the table and picked up the box in which the urns rested. She hadn't expected it to be so heavy. She nodded to the director, who was holding the door open.

Lucy almost ran to the truck, but she knew that the man was watching her. So she opened the cargo hold and plopped the box on top of the boxes she'd picked up at The UPS Store.

A splatter of rain hit the windshield as Lucy climbed into the driver's seat. When she had awakened that morning, she'd thought the rain was over. But the sky had turned almost black. Not good weather to be traveling up I-95. She might have to wait till the storm passed before she started out. Ordinarily, driving in the rain didn't bother her, but she'd never really driven a big SUV like a Range Rover on a major highway. Driving around, doing errands, wasn't quite the same thing to her mind.

Lucy made it home just as the sky opened up. The first thing she noticed was that her rental car had been picked up. The waterfall of rain was so heavy, she couldn't see the house across the street. She pulled into the garage, turned off the engine, closed the garage door, and popped the cargo trunk. She grabbed the urns and ran into the house and up to the second floor, where she set them on the floor and pressed the switch on the crazy umbrella. In the blink of an eye, she had the third compartment open and was pulling out the guns and ammunition. In went the urns, and then she slammed the door shut and pressed the keys. Locked. As in forever. That was when she noticed she was drenched in sweat. She felt so dizzy, she had to close her eyes and will herself to calmness. When she felt stable enough, she peeled off her clothes, headed into the bedroom she was using, opened her suitcase, and pulled out fresh clothes. She dumped the clothes she'd been wearing on top and zipped up her bag. She longed for Valium.

**Get ahold of yourself. Go downstairs, make some coffee, eat the last of the doughnuts, and shift into a neutral zone,** she told herself. **Ha!** Easier said than done. But she did just that, and within twenty minutes she felt normal enough to go out to the garage to take the boxes out of the cargo hold. She carried the boxes upstairs and started packing up her parents' belongings. She was glad she'd picked up the packing tape at the same time. She hustled then as she folded and jammed as much as she could into each box. She ripped off tape and sealed box after box, doing her best not to stare at the guns and ammunition on the closet floor. She labeled each box neatly with a Magic Marker from her purse. MOTHER'S PURSES AND SHOES. MOTHER'S SCARVES AND BELTS. MOTHER'S SLEEPWEAR, MOTHER'S SUITS. MOTHER'S JACKETS.

Lucy started on her father's boxes. In between each suit, she wrapped a gun in a towel, then layered the box. She picked it up to make sure it wasn't too heavy. It wasn't. She repeated the process until all the guns were safely packed in thick, thirsty towels. She sealed up the box and wrote on the outside with the same Magic Marker. Finally, she slipped the ammunition into the toes of the shoes and used three different boxes to pack them up, until she'd used up all the face and hand towels from the master bath.

Time for a break. Lucy headed downstairs and out to the kitchen, carrying one of the boxes with her. In the garage she pulled out the manual from the rear pocket of the Range Rover and flipped to the page that gave instructions on how to fold down the backseats. That small feat accomplished, she shoved the box as far forward as she could push it. She crossed her fingers that all the boxes would fit. If not, she would have to go back to The UPS Store and mail them. But not the ones with the guns and ammunition, in case they scanned packages.

Lucy drank another cup of coffee, her gaze on the windows. It was still dark, it was still pouring rain, and she could hear the rumble of thunder. So much for Florida's boast of being the Sunshine State.

It was almost eleven o'clock when Lucy shoved the last box into the cargo hold. Somehow, she'd made them all fit. She felt like cheering. All she had left to do was fax off the death certificates, pack up her parents' personal papers from Compartment Number One, and decide what she was going to do about the contents of Compartment Number Two.

Thankfully, she'd gauged right, and she still had one box left. That one she could set on the floor or on the seat of the passenger side. She frowned. There was nothing left to wrap the cigar boxes in. Unless . . . she could use the sheets and towels from the guest-room bath. At that moment, she couldn't decide which was more dangerous to travel with, the guns or the cigar boxes. What she did know was that the combination of the two was a lethal mix if she got stopped for speeding or she broke down or got robbed in a parking lot. Well, she'd just have to make sure that didn't happen. She'd drive the speed limit all the way. The Rover was new, so she seriously doubted it would break down. If she didn't stop along the way, she couldn't get robbed. So much to think about and worry about.

Back on the second floor, Lucy gathered up sheets and a few matching decorator towels and carried them into the walk-in closet. She looked down into Compartment Number Two and cringed. She pulled out the three Cuban cigar boxes. Then she started to layer the sheets and the towels, wrapping the cigar boxes in fancy lace-trimmed towels with her mother's initials on them. She yanked at the packing tape and wrapped the boxes so tight, a flea couldn't have gotten into them. She was breathing like a long-distance runner when she reached for the Magic Marker to mark the box. In neat script she wrote: QUEEN-SIZE MIST-GREEN SHEET SET, CHAMPAGNE-COLORED KING-SIZE SHEET SET, MATCHING TOWELS, PALE BLUE QUEEN SHEET SET WITH MATCHING TOW-ELS, ONE LIGHTWEIGHT CHAMPAGNE AFGHAN. She put the same amount of tape on this box as she had on the others. A pattern, so to speak, in case anyone were to look in or want to search.

"I think I might have the makings of a criminal," she muttered to herself, "because I'm starting to think and act like one."

Lucy carried the box and the big manila envelope in which she'd sealed her parents' personal papers back downstairs. On the front of the envelope she had written, MOM'S AND DAD'S PERSONAL PAPERS. The envelope went in the passenger-side door, and the box was placed on the floor. That left the seat empty for her purse, soft drinks, coffee, and whatever she bought for the trip before she got onto I-95.

The only thing left to do was to pull out all the plugs from the appliances, then make sure the fridge was empty and no trash remained. She walked from room to room and managed to get it all done in fifteen minutes. She found a stray bag under the sink, into which she put the contents of the fridge. All that was left to do was go back upstairs, make her bed, be sure her wet towel was hanging so it would dry out, open the safe, take out the urns, close the safe, and get rid of the umbrella.

In the walk-in closet, Lucy stared down at the three-compartment safe, then pressed the button on the umbrella. There were no answers there. She realized that there would probably never be any. She picked up the urns and the umbrella, walked out into the hall, and pressed the button. She dropped the umbrella to the floor and ran back to see if the floor had slid back. It hadn't. That had to mean the umbrella needed to be in the closet so it could connect with some unseen eye to make the safe open. Lucy looked down at the urns and said, "Bye, Mother. Bye, Daddy," as she walked out of the room for the final time.

Back in the kitchen, Lucy looked down at the umbrella. What to do with it? Should she take it? What was the point? She'd cleaned out the safe. Her parents were sealed away for eternity. Better to destroy the umbrella. She ripped at it, pulled the wires from the core, and stuck them in her pocket. She did her best to crunch up the umbrella, then stomped on it.

The clock on the Wolf range said it was twelve o'clock on the nose. Outside she could hear the deep rumble of thunder and see lightning zipping and cavorting across the darkened sky. Rain continued to come down in torrents. Lucy finished her coffee, rinsed the cup, and unplugged the pot so she could be on her way. If she didn't leave immediately, she could end up getting stuck all day, and there was no way she was going to spend one more day in that house. Not even one more hour.

Lucy reached for the trash bag, the remains of the umbrella, and her purse. In the garage she locked the door leading to the kitchen and pressed the remote for the garage door to slide open. If she stayed under the overhang, she wouldn't get too wet. She had reached the opening of the garage when she noticed a car's headlights coming down the street and a big brown UPS truck right behind it. Both were merely crawling. Lucy raced for the trash can. She had the metal lid in her hand just as a bolt of lightning zigzagged downward, and her world went all black.

# Chapter Five

Lucy tried to open her eyes, but she couldn't. There seemed to be lead weights on her lids. Then she tried to work her arms, but they felt heavy, too. She struggled to talk, but her mouth was dry, as though she were sucking on cotton balls. And she felt pain. Where? Pain in her foot. She needed to tell someone.

Then she heard a gentle voice saying, "Wake up, sleepyhead."

She tried and finally got her eyes open, but she couldn't focus at first. She blinked, the heaviness receding. She licked at her lips. "Water." She felt ice chips—at least she thought they were ice chips—pass between her lips. Her tongue moved. "Hurt," she managed to say as more ice chips passed her lips. A thin stream of water trickled down her cheek, but she couldn't make her hand move to wipe it away.

Lucy felt panic then, as she struggled to move. Strong arms held her down. "Easy now. I want you to stay calm. Everything is fine."

The voice was so soothing, so gentle and kind, Lucy immediately calmed.

"It hurts."

"Yes, I'm sure it does. Getting struck by lightning will do that to you. Do you remember what happened? By the way, I'm Dr. Lyons. My friends call me Jim. And this is Nurse Franks. Her friends call her Margie."

Lucy shook her head. "Am I in a hospital?" she managed to croak. More ice chips found their way to her lips. This time they didn't dribble down her chin. "How did I get here?"

A neighbor and a UPS driver saw what happened, and they called EMS. Your neighbor came with you in the ambulance.

You were very lucky they saw what happened and got you immediate attention.

"Why does my foot . . . my leg hurt so bad?"

"Because your foot was burned. It appears you were holding the metal lid of a trash can when the lightning hit the ground and your foot. You have third-degree burns on all of your toes and the top of your foot, down to the arch. It will heal, but you'll have discomfort for a while. We have pills for that. And we've been giving you shots for the pain. You're going to be fine."

Lucy worked her tongue again as she tried to focus on the fatherly-looking doctor standing at the side of the bed.

"How long have I been here?"

"Today is the third day. I can discharge you if you think you're ready to leave, but if you feel you need another day, that's fine with us. I have some questions I need you to answer. Are you up to it? If not, I can come back later, now that you're fully awake."

"Sure," Lucy mumbled.

"What's your name?"

Lucy made a snorting sound in her throat.

Such a stupid question. "My name is . . . is. My name is . . ."

She felt a flutter of panic rush through her. She should know her name. Why didn't she know her name? If she didn't know her name, they would keep her there. "My name is . . . Is it Angie?"

"Nope, wrong answer. Want to try again?" the soothing voice asked.

"I think it's Angie," Lucy said fretfully.

"Where do you live?"

Another stupid question. Or was it stupid? "In a house, I guess."

"What's the address?"

"I . . . I can't remember. An apartment?"

"Do you know what state you're in?"

Lucy let her gaze go to the window. She saw tall palm trees outside. "Someplace warm, I guess. Palm trees are outside. I don't know. You're scaring me. Why don't I know the answers?"

"Short-term memory loss due to trauma in cases like yours. Unfortunately for you, you had what we call a twofer. What that means is, the neighbor who came here with you told us what she knew. She said your name is Lucy Brighton, and you live in New Jersey. You came here to Florida for your parents' funeral. There's no way to soften this for you, so I'm just going to tell you what she told us. Your parents were killed in a head-on crash. She and her husband attended the service you held for your parents. She told us where they lived in Palm Royal. Does that ring a bell?"

"No. My parents are dead?"

"I'm sorry, but yes, they are. Do you remember anything about the service, your parents, anything at all?"

Lucy squeezed her eyes shut. "This is terrible. My parents are dead, and I can't even remember who they are. Can I talk to the lady who came here with me?"

"Absolutely. She's come by every day to see you, but you were always sleeping. She volunteered to take you back to your parents' house when I discharge you. Her name is Adel Longhurst, and her husband's name is William, but she said everyone calls him Buddy. They seem like very nice people. Does that help?"

"No, it doesn't help. I can't put a face to them, and the names mean nothing. Can I sit up? I want to see my foot. Can I walk? How long will it take for my memory to come back?"

The nurse pressed a remote dangling off the rail of the bed.

"Is that better?"

Lucy nodded as she tried to look down at her foot. A massive bandage covered her entire left foot, but her toes were exposed. They were red and raw looking, and they looked greasy.

"I suppose you could hobble around if we fashion a heel of some sort on your foot. For now, crutches or a wheelchair will be best. The dressing has to be changed four times a day to ward off infection. You're in luck, Ms. Brighton, because Mrs. Longhurst is a retired nurse. She said she would be glad to help you out until you can do it yourself. If you are agreeable to all of this, I can go ahead and sign your discharge papers and call Mrs. Longhurst to come and pick you up.

"As to your last question, I can't answer it. It varies with patients. Your memory could come back in an hour, a day, next week, or a month from now. What I'm hoping for is, if you are in familiar surroundings, among familiar people, your memory will come back sooner. You could wake up tomorrow morning and remember everything. I just don't have a pat answer. I do have some advice for you, and that is, don't rush it. Don't try to force it. The brain is a very challenging organ. It will happen. The worst thing you can do is agitate yourself. Try to stay calm. I'm going to be discharging you with several prescriptions, and I want you to take them religiously."

Lucy nodded.

"Does that mean you want me to call Mrs. Longhurst? Or do you want to stay one more day?"

"I want to go . . . wherever it is she's taking me. Did you say I live in New Jersey?"

"That's what Mrs. Longhurst said. When I asked her how she knew you lived in New Jersey, she said that the funeral director told her. She said she lives on the street behind your parents' house."

"Well, then, I would appreciate it if you called her and asked her to pick me up. I don't think I like hospitals. I don't think I've ever been in one."

The doctor chuckled and patted her on the shoulder. "Nurse Franks will help you get dressed. I'll have someone come in and fashion a heel for your foot, but please, try to avoid walking as much as possible.

We will be sending you home with crutches but ask that you return them when you no longer need them."

"What about my bill?"

"You'll have to take that up with the billing office. I'm sure you have insurance and can settle up when you know what's what. You didn't come in with a purse, so I assume billing has nothing on you."

"So I'm in Florida," Lucy said, her eyes on the swaying palms outside the window.

"And it's eighty-five degrees today with no humidity, and just for the record, it is thirty-eight degrees in New Jersey and New York. I heard the weather on the radio on my way to the hospital this morning." The doctor chuckled on his way out of the room.

"I'm scared," Lucy said to the nurse. "What if I can't remember my life?"

"Don't think like that. You heard what the doctor said. Don't agitate yourself. My guess is two days. I've seen my share of patients who have gone through this. Take the sedatives the doctor gives you, sleep as much as you can, drink a lot of fluids, and let nature take its course."

"Easy for you to say," Lucy grumbled.

The nurse laughed as she rummaged around for Lucy's clothes. "Oh, now I remember. Mrs. Longhurst took your clothes home and said she would launder them and bring them back, so you won't be able to get dressed till she gets here."

"That was nice of her."

"Yes, it was, and that's why the doctor is discharging you. He knows you will be in good hands, and she was a nurse before she retired. I'm going to leave you now and see what I can do about expediting that heel for your foot, and I also need to rustle up some crutches for you. I'll turn the TV on. I can get you some coffee or juice if you like."

"Thank you. I would like some coffee. I think I like coffee. Not decaf, though."

The nurse laughed as she walked out of the room. Within minutes a candy striper carried in a tray with a steaming cup of coffee, a doughnut on a plate, and some orange juice.

Lucy didn't drink the coffee right away, afraid she'd burn her tongue. She closed her eyes and tried to think. **Who am I? Why can't I remember? How can the death of both parents not be bothering**

**me?** She bit down on her lip. **Why did I say my name is Angie? Do I know someone named Angie? What are my parents' names?**

She wanted to cry when she couldn't remember. "Don't force it," the doctor and nurse had said. Easy to say, hard to do. How was she going to take a shower? A bath? Hang her foot over the tub? Not. One leg outside the shower? Not. Sponge baths? Absolutely not. No way in hell was she going to go through her days with sponge baths. **A crisis. Stay calm. Don't get agitated.** Lucy closed her eyes and tried to bury herself in the pillows behind her. Did she have any money? How was she going to pay for all of this? She had to eat, too. Eating cost money. Strange that she would know that but not know her own name. Childishly, she crossed her fingers that she had a bank account somewhere that she could draw on.

Lucy dozed then, the coffee forgotten, and didn't wake until she felt a gentle nudge to her arm. She opened her eyes to see a little gray-haired lady wearing a huge smile.

"I'm Adel Longhurst. I've come to take you back to your parents' house. There's a man waiting outside the room to fasten a heel onto your foot. I brought your clothes back. I washed and ironed them, so let's get you dressed. And then the man from the lab can go to work on your foot. I already took your crutches down to the car, where my husband is waiting outside. You'll go down in a hospital wheelchair. I took the liberty of ordering one for you, and it will be delivered this afternoon. It's just a rental and will have to be returned, but it is electric, so that will make it easier for you to get around on the ground floor."

Lucy felt her heart start to race. "Ground floor?"

"Yes, ground floor. Your parents' house has two floors, and the staircase is quite long. I think you'd be exhausted if you had to go upstairs. Their house is the biggest one built in Palm Royal. I think it must have around six thousand square feet. It's just big is all I know. I was never inside. For now, the first floor will work, don't you think?"

Her heart still racing, Lucy nodded. **Second floor, ground floor.** Just the words were having an effect on her. What did it mean? She needed to say something to this kind lady. "I appreciate your helping me like this. You don't even know me. Did you know my parents?"

"That's what neighbors do. They help one another. No, I didn't know your parents."

"The doctor said you were at the funeral service. If you didn't know them, why did you go?"

"Because it was the right thing to do. Why don't we talk about this later, when you're back home, in a more comfortable setting?"

Lucy nodded, wondering what that meant. If she couldn't remember the house, what made this nice lady think she'd be comfortable there? When no answer came to her, Lucy allowed herself to be helped getting dressed. She smiled as she watched her benefactor slip on her sneakers and tie the laces.

"Reminds me of when my children were little, and I had to put their shoes on. That was such a long time ago, but some things you just never forget, especially the pleasant memories."

"How many children do you have?"

"Five, scattered all over the country, and one lives in London. I haven't seen him in years. I also have four grandchildren I rarely get to see. To be honest with you, Buddy and I don't even know what they look like these days. Everyone has their own life, and there's just no extra time for us old fuddy-duddies. They do call from time to time, and when they think about it, they might send an e-mail. Buddy and I used to stay at home and wait so we wouldn't miss it if they called or e-mailed, but eventually we had to come to terms with the fact that it wasn't going to happen the way we wanted, and the kids had set their own priorities. And we weren't anywhere near the top of the list," she said sadly.

Lucy didn't know where the words came from. They just flew out of her mouth.

"Well, I could use a mother. Do you want the job?"

Hands on her plump hips, Adel looked at Lucy, trying to decide if she was joking or not. Whatever she saw in her expression worked for her, because she said, "I accept, but it has to be a package deal since I have a husband. His real name is William, but I call him Buddy. His poker pals call him Bud."

"I could use a father, too," Lucy said seriously.

"Then it's a deal."

For some reason, Lucy suddenly felt on top of the world. She had parents again. When she got her memory back, Adel and Buddy would be there for her, and she wouldn't be devastated at her loss. At least that was how she hoped it would work out.

Forty minutes later, Lucy was being helped into a sleek-looking Jaguar by Buddy, who could have been a stand-in for Santa Claus. She said so, to his delight.

"When should I start calling you Mom and Dad?" Lucy asked, straight-faced.

"How about right now?" Buddy chuckled. He turned to his wife, smiled, and said, "You never cease to amaze me, darlin'." Then he leaned into the backseat and gave Lucy a sweeping hug.

Startled, Lucy blinked at the suddenness of it all, but she had to admit, she felt warm and safe all at the same time. Such nice people.

Settled in the front seat, Adel turned around to talk to Lucy in the backseat. "If you give me your prescriptions, Buddy can stop at the drugstore, and I can run them in. They'll deliver them when they're ready. Is that okay?"

"Yes, of course. You two are being way too kind. Thank you," was all Lucy could think of to say.

"That's what parents do, dear. They help their children. Besides, we love having something to do besides looking at each other twenty-four/seven. Buddy stopped playing golf because he has a bad hip, and I was never one for arts and crafts at the clubhouse, so we just kind of stay home for the most part. We have talked about moving back to Texas, where we were both born and raised, but we also talked about moving to the Carolinas. In the end, we'll probably just stay here."

"You should go wherever you think you will be the most comfortable. They told me I live in New Jersey. You could go there. I'll be going back there as soon as I remember where I live. I wonder what it's like there."

"Do you have a computer, darlin'?" Buddy asked.

"I don't know. Probably. Why?"

"That's okay. I can bring our laptop over and do a Google Earth quest and show you where you live in New Jersey. It might help you jog your memory."

"You can do that?" Lucy asked in amazement.

"Buddy is a computer fool. He can do anything on a computer. He loves it. I just know how to do e-mail. I'd rather sit down and read a good book," Adel said. "Ah, here we go. I'll just run in your prescriptions. I'll be right back out."

Adel was as good as her word; she was back within minutes. "Home, James!" she said imperiously.

"Yes, darlin'," Buddy said, leaning over to give his wife a smooch on the cheek.

In the backseat, Lucy grinned. She liked her new parents. They might be elderly, but she could tell they were young at heart. She'd made a good choice.

Ten minutes later, Buddy swerved into the driveway of a monstrous-looking house.

"This is your temporary home, Lucy," Adel said. "If you notice, you packed up your father's truck there. I know it's his truck because I've seen him driving it. Your mother used to drive a Mercedes sedan, but it was totaled in the crash."

"How are we going to get inside? Do I have keys?"

"You did, dear. Buddy said they were in your purse in the garage. He had to go in and look for them so we could lock up behind you. While this is an ultrasafe neighborhood, you can't leave things to chance, and we didn't want to leave the packed truck in the open garage. We also put your purse on the kitchen table. We didn't think we had a choice. I hope that was all right," Adel said.

"Of course. So then I must have money in my purse. And credit cards, maybe a checkbook."

"I'm sure you do, but neither of us looked. I just took the keys. Buddy has them. We also left some lights on in the house at night."

"I appreciate that."

"You just sit tight there, darlin', and I'll lift you out of the car while my sweetie opens the door for us."

Lucy stared at the Range Rover. She knew what it was because she could see the block letters on the back. She could also see boxes and boxes piled inside.

Her heart kicked up a beat, then another beat, and her hands started to shake. She seemed unable to take her eyes off the Range Rover.

"Ready, little lady?" Buddy asked, opening the door wide. "What's wrong, darlin'? You look like you've just seen a ghost."

"Is that . . . is that my father's car? Am I the one who packed it up?"

"Well, Adel said she saw your father driving it, so I guess so. I also guess you were the one who packed it up. I imagine you were going to drive to New Jersey. We'll be able to tell if that's the case when we get you inside."

Inside the sterile-looking kitchen, Buddy bellowed to his wife. "Tell me where to put our new daughter, darlin'."

"Here on the sofa in the family room. There's a TV in here. I think she'll be the most comfortable here, and there's a powder room off to the left, so she won't have too far to walk."

Buddy settled Lucy gently on the sofa and looked around for the remote control. He clicked it on, and nothing happened. He spied the electrical cord lying on the floor. "I think you must have disconnected all the appliances since you were leaving," he said as he plugged the cord into the outlet on the wall.

"Yes, everything has been disconnected, and there's no food in the refrigerator," Adel called from the kitchen.

"Well, then, why don't I go to the grocery store and get whatever you think she's going to need for now. You two can chat it up till I get back. What about dinner, darlin'?"

"It's not even lunchtime yet, Buddy. Bring something back for lunch and whatever else you want. I can cook here and get Lucy settled before we go back home for the night. Oh, and pick up some bandages and everything I'll need to change Lucy's dressing."

"Wait, wait! Take the money out of my purse. Please, I can't let you pay for all of this."

"Just you never mind, little lady. We can settle up later."

And then Buddy was gone. Adel settled herself in a chair across from where Lucy was sitting. "Does anything look familiar to you, dear?"

Lucy looked around. "No. Everything looks new."

Adel followed Lucy's gaze. "It does, doesn't it? I don't think your parents spent much time here. Sometimes they were gone for months at a time. At least it seemed that way. What I mean by that is, there were never lights on in this house at night for long periods of time. I remember seeing someone who looked like you out on the deck once a year or so ago. You were just sitting there, staring across the yard. You weren't reading or anything."

"I don't remember ever being here. From what I've seen of this house, it's not to my liking. It's cold and formal. I wish I could remember what they were like. I don't even know if I have sisters or brothers or aunts or uncles."

"Well, if you do, they weren't at the funeral service. The only people there were Buddy, myself, Mr. Kingston, and, of course, yourself. He's the developer who built Palm Royal. You had your parents cremated. The minister said that at the service."

"No one came to the service? Didn't my

parents have any friends? The neighbors didn't attend?"

For the first time since setting eyes on Adel, her new mother, Lucy noticed how uncomfortable she suddenly looked. "Did I say something wrong?"

"No. I guess you had . . . have no way of knowing, but you're right. No one else attended. There was an episode a while back, two, maybe three years ago or so. One of the residents of Palm Royal was playing golf, and he had a heart attack. This house backs up to the hole he was playing when he collapsed. Jason Wyler ran over here to get your father to come and help him, but your father refused. He offered to call 9-1-1, but one of the other golfers had already done that. Carl—that was his name—Carl Palmer died right there on the ground before the EMS people could get there. No one understood why your father, a world-renowned heart surgeon, refused to help a man suffering from a heart attack. The enclave here turned on your parents, I guess you could say. The next day your parents were gone. They didn't return for almost a year."

"My father was a heart surgeon?" Lucy asked, a stupefied look on her face.

"Not just a heart surgeon, a world-renowned heart surgeon. When Buddy comes back, he can show you on his laptop. Your mother was a doctor, too."

"And he refused to help that man?"

"I'm afraid so. No one knows why. After they did return, the people here just shunned them."

"And my mother was a doctor, too?"

"Yes. And she was not social at all. Neither was your father. They kept to themselves. They never went to any of the affairs at the clubhouse. They refused to put out the candle bags at Christmas. To be honest, Lucy, I don't know why they moved here. Buddy and I have thick hides. We tried several times to interact with them. I even baked an angel food cake and brought it over. Your mother thanked me, but Evelyn Donner, who lives across the street, told me she saw your mother dump it in the trash can. Buddy wouldn't let me come back after that. I didn't want to, either."

"I don't think I knew any of that. If I did know it, hearing you talk about it should be ringing bells inside my head, but I don't hear any bells. That's just awful, Adel."

"Yes, dear, it is. I'm sorry I had to be the one to tell you."

"I wonder what else I don't know. Things like that, I mean."

"I am more than confident your memory will come back soon, Lucy."

Both women jumped when the phone in the kitchen rang. Adel hustled out to the kitchen and picked up the phone. In the family room Lucy could hear a conversation going on but couldn't make out the words.

"That was a young lady named Angie from New Jersey. She said she's your best friend. She said she's waiting at your house for you, and you were supposed to be there the day before yesterday. She said she's been calling here every ten minutes. I explained what happened to you, and she said she is taking the first flight she can get and will be here as soon as possible."

"That's where I got the name Angie from. She's coming here? She must really be a good friend to do that."

"I'd say so. I'm also betting when you

see her, that memory of yours is going to come roaring back."

"I hope so. She must know my parents if she's my best friend. Maybe she can tell us some stuff that will make sense."

"If you think you'll be okay till Buddy gets back, I'm going to scoot home and fetch some things so I can make dinner for us. I know you must be starved. I love, just love to cook things in a pressure cooker, and I didn't see one in the kitchen. Is it okay if I leave you for half an hour at the most? I just have to cross your yard and mine. Then I'll be right back."

"Of course, go. I'll be fine. I want to sit here and think a bit."

"I won't be long. Don't try walking till I get back, even though the crutches are there by the couch. They take some getting used to."

"Yes, Mom." Lucy giggled. Adel beamed as she heard the most loved word in the English language.

# Chapter Six

It was eight o'clock when Lucy's new mother called a halt to the evening. "You look exhausted, Lucy. Buddy and I are going to go home, but we're just a phone call away if you need us. The dressing on your foot will be good till morning. Are you sure you don't want Buddy to carry you up to the second floor so you can sleep in a bed?"

The look of panic on Lucy's face at her words was enough to cause Adel concern. She looked over at her husband and motioned for him to check out the upstairs.

"Is there something about the upstairs that bothers you, dear? Every time you look toward the stairs, you get a strange look on your face."

Lucy shrugged. "I don't know. When I look at it, I get this . . . really creepy feeling. That's the best way I can explain it. Maybe because my parents slept on the second floor." She shrugged again.

"All clear on the second floor, girls. Adel found a charger at home that fits your cell phone, which is charging right now on that table next to you. I programmed our number so we're first on your speed dial. Just hit the number one if you need us. Now, is there anything else we can do for you before we leave?"

"No, I'm good. Thank you so much, and, Adel, I think that was the best pot roast I've ever eaten. I must love mashed potatoes, because I sure ate a lot of them. This couch is wide enough that I know I'll sleep okay. I've taken all the pills, so I'll sleep when I get tired of watching television. It's okay for you to go."

"We'll be over first thing in the morning to get you ready for the day. Remember, now, Buddy and I have our physicals tomorrow, so that will take up most of the morning, but we'll be back by lunchtime.

Then we'll head to the airport to pick up your friend."

Lucy nodded.

When the door closed behind her new self-proclaimed parents, Lucy leaned back and closed her eyes. The house was so quiet, it felt like a tomb. An uneasy feeling settled between her shoulder blades. She looked toward the staircase and shivered. Buddy had said there were no bogeymen up there. Then why did just looking at all those steps make her heart race? **If I could only remember.**

Lucy clicked off the MUTE button, and sound from the television invaded the family room. She looked at the blond personality on the screen and knew who it was— Nancy Grace. If she knew that name, she must have watched her show. How could she know that and not know where and how she saw the show?

She thought back to the earlier hours of the evening, when Buddy had shown her the house she lived in back in New Jersey compliments of Google Earth. She hadn't recognized it. Then he'd gone to Facebook and shown her a picture of her friend Angie, but she hadn't recognized her, either.

When the picture of the smaller structure on the property where she lived came up, Buddy had homed in on it and the box and bell and a sign that said IBL. She'd gotten excited then. "I know those letters. I do."

"What do they mean, dear?" Adel asked.

"They mean . . . I know what they mean. . . . I just can't remember them right now. Do you know what they mean?"

Adel and Buddy nodded. "Izzy, Bizzy, and Lizzy."

Lucy shook her head. "Doesn't ring a bell. Clever, though. They rhyme. What do they mean?"

"They're animals. You created them. Izzy is a dog, Bizzy is a cat, and Lizzy is a parrot. You're an artist."

"I am!" Lucy said in stunned surprise. "I must like animals, then."

So much to think about.

As hard as Buddy tried, he couldn't come up with any pictures of her mother, but he did manage to pull up on his laptop several articles that had been written about her famous father. He was a stranger to her.

"He doesn't look like he has much of a

bedside manner," Lucy said as she eyed the professional pose. "Kind of like this house. Cold and empty. I wonder if I liked him."

"I'm sure you did, dear. He was your father. Don't judge your father by a newspaper picture."

And that had been the end of that conversation, which only meant she didn't know one thing more now than she had when she woke in the hospital.

Lucy lowered the volume until the sound was just a murmur on the television, then curled up on the sofa. She closed her eyes and said a prayer that when she woke, she would have her memory back.

Lucy slept soundly until three thirty. She woke with a start. And knew instantly where she was and what had happened to her during the past week, indeed, during her entire life.

She struggled to sit up, careful not to let the light blanket touch her injured foot. She clenched her hands together into tight fists when she started to shake. Her thoughts were jumbled with memories and the situation she was in. Her memory had returned at three thirty in the morning. How strange was that? More like how weird was that?

Lucy hobbled to the bathroom, taking her thoughts with her. From there, she went to the kitchen and poured a glass of iced tea Adel had left for her. The delicious angel food cake she'd brought over—which, she said, won prizes at the State Fair of Texas—sat on the counter. She ripped off a chunk and scarfed it down. Delicious. A sharp pain shot up her leg, reminding her she wasn't supposed to be walking around. She looked down at her toes peeking out of the heavy-duty bandage and winced.

Carrying her iced tea, Lucy made her way back to the sofa and her made-up bed. She took a pain pill and unplugged her cell phone from the charger. She didn't care what time it was or if she woke Angie. She had to talk to her, and she had to talk to her immediately.

Lucy wasn't surprised when Angie answered on the second ring. She didn't sound like she'd been sleeping. "I remember everything, Angie." She babbled on for a full five minutes before she ran out of breath. "I can't wait for you to get here."

And then it was Angie's turn to babble on, which she did nonstop. At four thirty, Angie called a halt to the conversation, saying she had to shower and drive to the airport. "My flight leaves at seven, and I have a ninety-minute layover in Atlanta. I'll call you from there. See ya, friend."

Lucy's mind started to race. She prayed then, thanking God for returning her memory. Then she cried, great hacking sobs that shook her whole body, which required another trip to the bathroom for tissues. She was exhausted when she returned to the sofa and within seconds was sound asleep again and didn't wake until Adel shook her arm and smiled down at her.

"Oh, you are not going to believe this. I woke up at three thirty to go to the bathroom, and I remembered everything. Everything. I know who IBL is. I draw them every day. I don't have to work until the first of the year. I hate this house. I hate the one in New Jersey, too. I couldn't cry at the service, because I didn't feel anything. That picture in the paper, that's how my father looked all the time, except that one time when he gave me a ride on his shoulders when I was five. He pretended to be a train, and he whistled. They were cold people, but they were good providers. I liked them, but I didn't love them. Isn't that terrible? I love Angie, I love Izzy, Bizzy, and Lizzy, and they aren't even real. I need to talk to a shrink when I go home."

"Well, now, that's something," Adel said as she struggled to keep the surprise she was feeling under cover.

Buddy just stared at his new daughter. "Darlin', you've had a terrible shock. Your parents died. Then you got hit by lightning. Your body is out of kilter, and your thoughts . . . well, they're just sort of jumbled right now. You need time to come down to earth, and when the dust settles, things that appear now . . . Well, they won't be like that then. Adel, explain that for me, will you, honey?"

"She doesn't have to, Buddy. I understand what you're saying and why, but you're wrong. I know what I feel, and I remember everything. Nothing is going to change. It's okay. I got this far in my life basically on my own. Honestly, these past few years, months would go by, and I wouldn't hear from my parents. They were pretty much strangers to me. Please, don't look at me like that. I'm okay with it. Angie is moving in with me, and she's going to help me run my business. It's gotten too big for just me to handle."

Adel looked down at her watch. Just when she had found someone to love again, she was going to go off and leave her and Buddy alone again. She felt tears prick her eyelids. "Come on, dear. Let's get you into the shower so you're all nice and spruced up for your friend when she gets here. Where is your suitcase, dear? Buddy will fetch it in, and we can get you some nice clean clothes."

Lucy felt a wave of panic skitter through her. **Where is my suitcase? Buried under all the boxes in the Rover? Where?**

"It's in the Rover," Buddy said.

"That reminds me, Lucy. When I took your clothes home from the hospital to launder them, I found some strange wires in your pocket. I didn't know what they were, so I saved them. Buddy put them on the counter in the kitchen."

"Thanks. Yeah, I need those," was all Lucy could think of to say. Adel gave her a strange look but didn't say anything more.

\* \* \*

An hour later Lucy was back on the sofa, her foot dressed in a clean bandage. She had on clean but wrinkled clothes, and her hair was still damp. But she felt so good, she wanted to sing. Adel and Buddy were gone, and she was alone with a cup of coffee.

She felt terrible at how devastated her new friends were. Happy, truly happy that her memory had returned, but terribly sad that she would be leaving them. For a short while, just hours, really, they had felt like they had a real daughter to help. Now they were going to go back to their uneventful lives, hoping she'd invite them to New Jersey so they could stay in touch. They hadn't really carried on a conversation during her shower, while her dressing was changed, and when she got dressed. In fact, both Adel and Buddy had been pretty much silent the whole time.

They weren't words! They were **thoughts.** Adel's and Buddy's thoughts. She knew what they were thinking. How could that be? Lucy looked over at the pill bottles on the table by the sofa. It must be the pills.

That was when it hit her like a pile driver. She'd traded in one problem for another.

**Now I can read minds. Dear God! Don't let this be real. Please don't let this be real.**

She started to shake then, and she felt so light-headed, she had to lie down. When she felt more clearheaded, she bolted upright. She looked at the warning labels on her medicine bottles. Take with food, don't drive or operate machinery, and sleepiness can occur. Standard warnings. It had to be some trick of her imagination. A fluke of some sort. People couldn't read other people's minds. It all came down to energy, electricity. She'd been struck by lightning. Did that make her a candidate to be a mind reader? That was just too stupid for words. Wasn't it? She'd talked to Angie, and she hadn't been able to read her mind. **Stupid. Really stupid, Lucy. The person has to be near you for that to happen. Not a thousand miles away.** What if it was true, and suddenly she could read minds? What would her life be like? No one would want to be around her. Maybe she should call the doctor and point-blank ask him. He had said to call him if her memory returned.

Lucy's hands were shaking so badly, she could barely dial the number of the hospital. She asked for the doctor, and she was surprised when he picked up the phone. She identified herself and explained how her memory had returned.

He sounded happy for her, admonished her to take the pills until they were finished. "Is there anything else I can help you with today? How's the pain?"

"Not as bad as yesterday. It's itching slightly. There is one thing I'd like to ask you. You'll probably think this is silly, but I'd really like to know the answer."

"Try me."

"I vaguely remember reading, or maybe it was a movie, about someone who got hit by lightning who ended up being able to read minds."

"There are case studies on that very thing. I personally never treated anyone like that, but yes, it has happened. Are you afraid that's going to happen to you, Miss Brighton?"

"No. Yes. I don't know. I just feel peculiar. I can't put my finger on it precisely. I do have my memory back and . . . I'm sorry. I'm probably just being a worrywart and borrowing trouble."

"Well if anything like that should happen, call me."

"Yes, yes, I will. Thanks for the good care. I plan on going home tomorrow."

"Have a safe trip."

"You bet," Lucy mumbled to herself. So, she wasn't nuts, after all. Shoot, why hadn't she asked how long something like that would last? Was it like memory loss, which could be temporary, or was something like that permanent? Her brain had short-circuited. Amazing.

The doorbell rang. More curious than anything, Lucy got up and hobbled to the front door. She opened it to see one of the best-looking men she'd ever seen in her life standing there. **Nice.**

"I'm Lucas Kingston, but everyone calls me Luke." He looked down at her bandaged foot. "That has to hurt. I just wanted to stop by to offer my condolences on your loss. I was in Miami, working on a development that my father and I are building there, and I couldn't get back in time for the funeral service. My father told me that he attended, and he also told me about your accident. I came by the other day, before your accident, but I guess you were out. Again, I'm sorry for your loss. Is there anything my father and I can do for you?"

**What's wrong with her? She looks like she's seeing a ghost. Maybe I have a big piece of spinach stuck in my teeth.**

"Thank you. My foot does hurt. I don't see a ghost anywhere, do you? And rest easy. There's nothing stuck in your teeth," Lucy blurted out.

"What?"

"What **what?** Is there anything else, Mr. Kingston?"

**Shit, she's just like her weird parents. It must be true that the nut doesn't fall far from the tree.** "Well, as a matter of fact, there is one other thing. You do know that if you put this house up for sale, Kingston and Kingston will be the ones to sell it. It's in the contract and the covenants, as well. You cannot use an outside real-estate agent. Your parents signed the agreement, and you're bound to it as next of kin."

"You know what, Mr. Kingston? I haven't decided what to do with this property. I am leaning more toward taking a wrecking ball to it than selling it. My weird parents would probably approve of that. But, then, I'm not weird like they were, and I know all about nuts not falling far from the tree."

She had to get rid of him. **Just shut the damn door so you don't have to look at his horrible expression. You had to do that, didn't you? Why, why, why?**

"What? You're some kind of mind reader?"

"Why would you think something like that?" Lucy said. She wondered if she looked as frazzled as she sounded. **What is going on here? Why am I being so ugly to this good-looking guy?** "You delivered your message. I get it. Is there anything else?"

Luke Kingston backed off a few steps as he stared at Lucy. How could someone so pretty be so . . . ornery? "Well, if there is, I'll be back," was all he could think of to say.

**He thinks I'm pretty. Imagine that.** "Well, guess what, Mr. Kingston. I won't be here. I plan on leaving tomorrow, so if you need me, you'll have to come to New Jersey."

**Like that's going to happen.** "I hate this house. Just so you know. I think it's an abomination. Maybe instead of a wrecking ball, I'll just burn it down."

"What? An abomination! This is the best-built house in Palm Royal. It was featured in every building magazine in the world, and it was also in **Architectural Digest.** They don't just put any old house in **AD.** It's worth over ten million dollars. It was built to your parents' specifications, and let me tell you, they were hell on wheels to work with. Everything is top of the line. The best materials money can buy were used to build this house. It's against the law to burn down a house."

**Damn, just what I need, another loony tune.** Still, curiosity got the better of him. "What, specifically, do you hate about it? Seriously, I'd like to know. You could invite me in, you know. I never saw the inside once your parents moved in. As a builder, when someone tells me they hate something I poured my heart and soul into, I want to know why."

He did have a point. Lucy thought about it for a few seconds. He was rather cute, and if she could read his mind, all the better. "All right, but don't take all day. I have things to do."

She held the door open wider, and Luke Kingston walked through. Lucy walked back to the sofa and plopped down. Her foot was killing her. She propped it up on the coffee table while her guest meandered around the house. She took a deep breath when she noticed him going upstairs at a good clip, taking the steps two at a time. He was back down within ten minutes.

Luke stood in the doorway to the family room. "I guess I can see now why you hate this place. It's cold and sterile. I could never live in this house. When your parents came to us and we worked on the plans, I had this vision of a big family with lots of grandkids visiting, hence the layout. I guess that was my mistake. The house is sound."

Lucy strained to hear or see or feel his thoughts, but nothing came her way. Or maybe the person had to be very close to her. "Yes, I'm sure it is. Sound, that is. My parents were not into green plants and cozy anything. As you can see, there are no . . . personal touches at all. I packed up their personal belongings, but they were just clothing, shoes, that kind of thing."

"Everything looks like it just came out of a furniture showroom."

"Yes, it does," Lucy agreed. **What an inane conversation**, she thought.

"How are you managing? Do you need any help?" Luke asked as he advanced into the room.

"I'm good. Mr. and Mrs. Longhurst have been helping me."

"Nice people. My dad likes them a lot. You couldn't have anyone better helping you."

He was close now, only a foot or so away. **That explains it,** Lucy thought. **The person has to be that close for me to feel what they're thinking. God, that foot looks beastly. It must hurt like hell. And all those pill bottles. Guess she has a right to be snippy.**

Lucy looked up and smiled. "It doesn't just hurt. It hurts like hell. I'm sorry for being so snippy."

Luke chewed on his lower lip. He looked like he wanted to say something but couldn't get the words out. "So, where should I send the rules and regs of Palm Royal? I want you to have a copy of the covenants."

**Maybe I'll head up to New York over**

**the holidays and stop in to see her. Jersey is just across the river from Manhattan. Won't she be surprised! I can always say that I'm going to meet up with two old friends if I need an excuse.**

Lucy grinned. This was almost fun. "Tell you what. Send everything to the Schwager law firm here in Palm Royal. Now, should you find yourself in New York over the holidays, just pop on over and surprise me. Jersey is just across the river from Manhattan."

Luke dropped to his haunches. He was less than a foot away from her. "How do you do that?"

Lucy played dumb. She stared at him. His eyes were magical in their intensity. "Do what?"

"You know, read my mind. I think something, and you say it out loud."

"Now, that's just silly. Coincidence."

"There's no such thing as coincidence. You were hit by lightning. It could have left you with extraordinary powers. I saw a movie once about that very thing. It was a curse."

Lucy laughed out loud. "You mean like Superman?"

**She's making fun of me. Reducing me to a stammering fool. Who is this person?**

Lucy laughed again. "I think you think I'm making fun of you. I'm not. Not really. I'm just enjoying your little joke. In the end, I'm just me, Lucy Brighton, who came to Florida to bury her parents and managed to get hit by lightning as I was preparing to leave to return home. I'm just your normal get-hit-by-lightning kind of gal."

Luke stared at the tiny bridge of freckles marching across Lucy's nose. That was how close he was. She had the clearest, greenest eyes he'd ever seen. Those green eyes were laughing at him. In spite of himself, he grinned. "I think I've worn out my welcome. Have a safe trip home. Don't get up. I can see myself out."

"Don't forget to stop by if you make it to Manhattan."

"Count on it, Miss Brighton."

**You know it, Mr. Kingston.** Now, wouldn't that be something if he really did show up at her door during the holidays? **Ah, the stuff dreams are made of.**

# Chapter Seven

Luke Kingston opened the kitchen door of the house he shared with his father. It smelled good, which meant his father was cooking again, trying to recapture the recipes his beloved wife had left behind some ten years ago. Since his father's stroke two years earlier, there wasn't much else for him to do, according to Lucas Kingston Sr.

Kingston and Kingston. Father and son. Florida's top builder of one-of-a-kind houses. They'd made their mark, all right, with the construction of Palm Royal. They'd made enough money that neither of them would ever have to work again, but building was in their blood. At least it was in young Luke's blood these days. He loved looking at a blueprint, loved spilling coffee over it, loved pounding nails. He was hands-on, just like his father was. Luke Sr. still offered advice, still listened, still peered at blueprints, but then he went back to the kitchen to peruse his wife's collection of cookbooks.

Today lunch was going to be vegetable soup and ham sandwiches. When he got up at five this morning, the ham was already in the oven, proof that his father had had another sleepless night. By the time he finished his homemade bagel, which left a lot to be desired, and his coffee, the vegetable soup was simmering in a giant pot on the back burner of the Wolf range.

He was early for lunch. And he was antsy. All he could think about since leaving the Brighton house was how green Lucy Brighton's eyes were. He shivered at the pain he knew she must be enduring from her burned foot. Sassy, too. He liked sassy. His mother, God rest her soul, had been the feistiest woman he'd ever met, not that he'd met a lot of women, but he relied on his dad's opinion of his mother. For sure, there was no one walking the planet like his mother. That much he knew as well as he knew his own name. His father knew it, too, another reason why this kitchen was a shrine to her, the place where she had spent all her time. He had to correct that thought. He and his father had built this house just for her. And it was a work of art, especially the kitchen. And they had not duplicated any areas of this particular house in the buildings they put up in Palm Royal.

Shortly before his mother's death, he had, with the help of his father, built his own house one street away. He hadn't even moved into it when his mother passed away in her sleep. And then he couldn't bring himself to leave his father, who was so lost without his wife that it made Luke Jr. cry. He remembered those early years so vividly; he still cringed when he thought of them. It was touch and go there for over a year. His father lost interest in everything and just sat for hours, staring at nothing. He took all the pills the doctors gave him for depression, but nothing worked.

Then one day, by pure accident, Adel

Longhurst stopped by with an angel food cake, her specialty. His father forced himself to come out of his cocoon of misery to talk about his wife's cooking, which was also a passion of Adel's. Before he knew it, his father was cooking and baking and going through every cookbook his mother had owned. He made himself eat everything, and his comment to his father when he was done was, "You almost got it, Pop, but Mom's was better." Which pleased his father to no end. He constantly teased his father that he should look into getting a cooking show and give Paula Deen a run for her money. That also pleased his father to no end, and he said that one of these days he just might do that.

Luke looked across the kitchen at his father, who was clad in his red chef's apron that said he was the NUMBER ONE CHEF, a gift on Father's Day two years ago. He saw that the table was set for four. Guests?

Luke Sr. was a tall man with snow-white hair, eyes the color of washed-out denim, and a winsome smile. He had big hands, carpenter's hands, just like his son. He stayed in shape by walking five miles in the morning, usually when it was still dark.

Then he'd do another five miles before dinner. It didn't matter if it was raining or the sun was boiling hot. The residents of Palm Royal said you could set your watch by Luke Sr. The bottom line to all the residents of Palm Royal was that Luke Sr. was a good man, just like his son, Luke Jr.

"So, Pop, who's coming for lunch?" Luke asked as he hung the baseball cap he was never without on a Peg-Board next to the kitchen door.

"Bud and Adel. She's torturing me again with that angel food cake she's known for. She said in a million years, I could never duplicate it. I hate fighting with her, because I can never win."

Young Luke laughed as he moved off to the laundry room to wash his hands. He sniffed appreciatively. He did love the smell of freshly baked bread. Fresh bread for the ham sandwiches. "Eat your heart out, Paula Deen," he muttered.

"So, son, how did it go over at the Brightons'?" his father asked. Luke grinned at the expression on his father's face. Anytime the Brighton name came up, his father looked like he had bitten into a sour lemon.

"Well, Miss Brighton looked to me to be in pain with her foot. She has a huge bandage on it. Guess she was burned pretty good. She looked tired, and she was cranky. I think I was the last person on earth she wanted to deal with. I probably should have waited a few more days before I paid a call. I offered up my condolences on the loss of her parents, explained why I wasn't at the service. She didn't seem to care.

"Oh, and did I tell you she can read minds? Jesus, Pop, she knew every damn thing I was thinking. She's sassy, that one. And, Pop, she has the greenest eyes I've ever seen. Greener than the grass at the golf course. Like emerald green, and those eyes were shooting sparks at me. She didn't like me, but she invited me in to look at the house. Made my blood run cold. It was like a mausoleum. She didn't know anything about the covenants or the bylaws, none of that."

"I can see how much you liked her," Luke Sr. drawled.

"Actually, Pop, I did like her. I'd like to see her in a more . . . social setting. Reminded me a bit of Mom. Sharp-eyed, sharp tongue, a no-bullshit kind of gal."

"Guess she didn't like you all that much, eh?"

"I think you got that right. She just wanted me out of there, and to be honest, I couldn't wait to leave. That damn house gave me the creeps. She said she might want to take a wrecking ball to it or burn it down. She couldn't decide. I think that means she doesn't like the house, either. She lives in New Jersey."

Further discussion came to a halt when Adel and Buddy Longhurst burst into the kitchen like a whirlwind.

"Aha, vegetable soup, fresh bread, and baked ham. And my prizewinning angel food cake for dessert. If you don't mind, I'd like to take some to go if you can spare it. For Lucy Brighton. I hated leaving her alone, but her friend's flight was delayed two hours, so that's why we're here. Otherwise, I would have had to cancel."

"How did your physicals go?" Luke Sr. asked.

"Good. Let's eat," Buddy said. "This one," he said, pointing to his wife, "needs to get back to the Brighton house so she can fuss and fret over that young lady, who, by the way, is as sweet as honey."

Young Luke rolled his eyes. He recounted his visit with Lucy Brighton.

"Fire and water," Luke Sr. said as he ladled out soup into colorful soup bowls.

Conversation was sprightly as Adel and Buddy passed remarks on Luke Sr.'s culinary efforts. For the most part, young Luke inhaled his food, savoring each mouthful. Adel summed it all up the way she always did, and the reason her response was always the same was so Luke Sr. wouldn't give up and revert to being a walking, talking vegetable with no interest in life.

"You almost got it this time, Luke, but something is missing." She looked at young Luke, who pretended to think.

"Too much parsley?" asked Luke Sr.

"No, I know what it is," Adel said. "You used water instead of stock. I keep telling you, Luke, you can't start off a soup with water."

Then they went at it again, but it was all friendly and full of laughter.

"Luke was just telling me about the

Brighton house. He said it gave him the creeps," Luke Sr. said.

"I'd have to second that," Adel and Bud said at the same time.

"There's just something about that place that . . . I can't explain it," Bud said. "Reminds me of a movie set or something, where the actors are standing in the wings, waiting to make an appearance. Adel and I talked about it ad nauseam, and we both agreed. Lucy is not comfortable there. That much is obvious. That house is going to go up for sale the minute she returns to New Jersey. That young lady has everything pretty much under control. Like I said, she's sweet as honey."

Young Luke snorted. "I guess you got to see the best side of her. What I saw was a buzzing bee, a hornet, if you will. Nice smile, and those green eyes of hers are like emeralds."

"And he noticed all of that while she was being ugly to him," Luke Sr. volunteered as he cut into Adel's angel food cake. He ate a snippet, then said, "I think you put too much vanilla in it this time, Adel."

"Ya think, Luke?" Adel said, rolling her

eyes for everyone's benefit, especially Luke Sr.'s.

"I never liked the Brightons. They were a strange couple. Never once in the entire year that I dealt with them did they mention that they had a daughter. They never talked about anything. All they wanted to discuss was square footage, flooring, and completion dates. They paid in full at the closing, signed their names, and off they went. I've never had a client pay that kind of money in cash. By cash I mean a cashier's check. An hour after they moved in, they had new locks installed on all the doors. A day after that, a furniture truck arrived with enough furniture to fill the whole house. The day after that, the Brightons left town. They were the most polite, unfriendly couple I've ever met. There was something very strange about them from day one. Artie, the mailman, told me no mail ever came to the house. Everyone gets mail, even if it's junk mail. He said they didn't even get occupant mail. Tell me that isn't weird."

"Guess they were private people," Luke Jr. said.

"There's private. Then there's private,"

Adel said as she got up to help clear the table.

"There was that episode on the golf course," Bud said. "You tell me what kind of doctor would refuse to help someone who had just collapsed and ended up dying."

"He called 9-1-1," Luke Sr. said.

"Well, all I can say is, it's a good thing they skedaddled the next day, because I think this enclave was about to form a lynching party. Sorry, Luke, but Bud and I have to leave now to pick up Lucy's friend at the airport. Lunch was great, as always. My turn next time. Try the stock next time you make soup. I'll call you," Adel said breezily as she shooed her husband out the door ahead of her. She turned back to young Luke and winked. "You know, Luke, that young lady is one of a kind. I can actually close my eyes and visualize you two together." Adel laughed out loud when Luke Jr.'s face turned bright pink. "See ya."

Luke Sr. looked at his son. "Adel is never wrong. You know that, right?"

Luke Jr., his face still flushed, nodded.

"So how is that going to happen if she lives in New Jersey and you live here?"

"When I figure it out, I'll let you know,

Pop. Look, I gotta go now. I have some stuff I have to do in the office, and I want to get a copy of everything for Miss Brighton so she knows the rules and doesn't do something she'll regret later that will cost all of us some money. I'll drop everything off in the morning, before I head down to Miami. Why don't you come with me, Pop? I hate leaving you here by yourself."

"Stop worrying about me, son. I'll be fine. By the way, your sister called me this morning and invited us to spend the holidays with her and the kids. I said I wanted to talk to you first. I don't want to leave you alone during the holidays if you don't want to go to Seattle. I know you hate it there. You and I always put the tree up together, and I make that big turkey for Thanksgiving. Marie has been pestering me for over a month now, and today she got the kids to weigh in before they left for school."

"You should go, Pop. In fact, I insist. I was thinking maybe I'd head up to New York this year. I haven't seen Jack and Dave in over a year."

"Your best friends for forever. You should go, Luke. Friends are like gold. You need to treasure them. You like to ski, so let's both decide to go our separate ways this year."

"That sounds kind of . . . strange coming from you, Pop."

"It does, doesn't it? I want to see my grandkids. Haven't seen them since last year. I don't want to miss out on these growing years. Before you know it, they'll be in high school and won't want to spend time with their old grandpa."

"Then it's settled."

"It's settled," Luke Sr. said.

Luke Jr. slapped on his baseball cap and walked out into the Florida sunshine. He started to whistle. Inside the house, standing at the kitchen window, Luke Sr. smiled. Then he crossed his fingers that Adel Longhurst was right. It was time for Luke to settle down. He just hoped that Lucy Brighton was the one to make that happen for his son.

Angie Powell bolted from the Longhurst car and flew up the walkway to the front door of the Brighton house. She opened the door, screeching Lucy's name at the top of her lungs.

"No, no, don't get up!" She flopped down

on the sofa and almost bounced a foot high as she threw her arms around Lucy's shoulders. She smacked her with kisses, then reared back to look at her. "You look good, friend. The foot looks like a sorry mess, that's for sure. Ooooh, I hate this house already. Bad vibes. Really bad vibes. When are we leaving? Isn't this the same sofa you have in the house in Jersey?" She finally ran out of breath and just stared at her friend. "And then, to top it off, you get hit by lightning and lose your memory. How cool is that? Or hot, as the case might be. Wow! This is really strange. I'm right. This is the same damn house as the one in New Jersey, just different colors. Does your foot hurt, burn, or sting, what? I bet it itches!"

"We can leave now, if you're up to driving after the trip here," Lucy said. "The truck is packed up. We just have to decide." **Please, please, say yes, Angie.**

Angie looked around, saw Adel and Buddy coming into the house. "Just give me time to go to the bathroom and to wash my hands, and we can leave."

"Seriously?" Lucy gasped.

"Are you kidding me?" Angie said, looking around. "This place creeps me out. I'm your gal. Do what you have to do, and we can be on our way. Where's the bathroom? Never mind," Angie said, closing her eyes. "I think I can find it." And she did.

"Oh, dear, did I hear that right?" Adel asked as she set Angie's small carry-on bag on the floor by the sofa. "You're really going to leave right now?"

Lucy nodded. Tears puddled in her eyes as she realized she could read Adel's mind and the thoughts coursing through that very same mind.

"I understand. I really do. Buddy and I are sorry to see you leave, and we promise to head north to see you as soon as we can. But right now I'm going to dress your foot. I want to show Angie how to do it so she can do it for you. She's a sweetheart. It's easy to see why you two are such fast friends. How's the foot feeling?"

"It's starting to itch, but it doesn't feel right."

"You know, I'm from the old school of medicine, so if it's okay with you, I'd like to try my way. I think I can guarantee that your foot will feel almost normal by this time tomorrow if you agree."

"What?"

"Honey. It's the best thing in the world for burns, especially serious burns. I had Buddy stop at the farmers' market, and I bought some really good honey with the honeycomb still in it. Shall we give it a try?"

"Absolutely."

Angie returned and was instructed to watch, which she did. When Lucy's foot was rebandaged, she said, "Okay, I can do that. Four times a day, you said."

"Yes, and by tomorrow that foot should really be on the mend. I'll take all the trash out to the can. What else do you want us to do, honey, before you leave?"

Lucy smiled and shook her head. "Just give me a big hug, and we'll be on our way. If we go out through the garage, we won't have to worry about locking up. I don't know how to thank you two. I don't know what I would have done without you."

"That's what neighbors and friends are for, to help one another," Buddy said.

Fifteen minutes later, Angie Powell was behind the wheel of the Range Rover and, with Buddy's help, Lucy was settled in the passenger seat. There were more kisses, more hugs, and then Angie backed the

Rover out of the garage. The garage door slid down.

"You ready, Lucy?"

"Hit it, Angie, and let's get out of here."

"You don't have to tell me twice. You want a sing-along?"

"No, but I do want to talk to you. I can read minds now, so be careful what you think about."

"Holy shit!"

# Chapter Eight

Luke Kingston parked his utility truck in the lot of the Kingston and Kingston construction company. He looked up to see that the sunny sky of a few hours ago had disappeared and turned overcast and gloomy. Unpredictable Florida weather for this time of year. In other words, it sucked. He wondered if the weather was any better in Miami, but didn't care enough to check it out.

Luke banged through the door the way he always did. "A bull in a china shop" was the way his father described all of Luke Jr.'s entrances. As always, the staff looked up and grinned. There was Debbie, who was in charge of mortgages; Stephanie, who was in charge of finances; Allison, who showed the properties and drafted contracts; and the office manager, named Tillie. All of them were young, late twenties and early thirties, and Luke, unlike his father, was able to relate to them. It was not lost on him that there were no other males in the office. There were days when the four of them were like hissing felines. When those days occurred, Luke made himself scarce.

"Good afternoon, ladies!" Luke said cheerfully.

"Tell me one thing that's good about it, Luke," Tillie snapped. "Look at the sky! I was supposed to go to a garden cocktail party at five."

"Boo hoo! I need all the paperwork on the Brighton house. Chop-chop, ladies. I don't have all day. How old is this coffee?" Luke yelled from the kitchen.

"Fifteen minutes old. It's safe to drink, and it's hazelnut, your favorite," Debbie called out.

"Oooh, I'm excited, Luke. Does that mean the house is going up for sale?" Allison said as she calculated her commission on the sale. If she sold it for the full amount, she'd be able to pay off her Boston Whaler.

"At some point. We have to wade through probate. The new owner, or I should say heir to the estate, says she wants to take a wrecking ball to it or else burn it down."

Allison, a stunning blonde with pearly white teeth, put her hands on her hips, a frown digging in over her eyebrows. "That gorgeous house! Why? She can't do that, can she?"

"Not on my watch. I have to get all these papers to her before she leaves in the morning. She lives in New Jersey. She's the one who got hit by a lightning bolt. It was in the papers."

"Yes, I read about that but didn't tie the house and her together. I'd say that's enough reason to want to put some distance between her and the house. By the way, Luke, there is an association meeting tonight at eight at the clubhouse. Should I pencil you and your dad in or not?"

God, how he hated those boring meetings. "Pops is iffy, but I'll be there. Where are those papers?" he bellowed.

"Right here, Mr. Kingston," Stephanie said, handing him a thick, stapled, bound batch of papers. You want a folder with that or an envelope?"

"That would be really nice, Stephanie, since I am going to be dropping these off for Miss Brighton to peruse. She knows nothing about how our association works. You know how those Yankees are. They always want to do things their way."

The four women laughed.

"Guess she told you a thing or two to get you so riled up, eh?" Tillie said. "Those Yankees will tell you right where it's at, and if you miss it, woe to you."

Luke rubbed at the stubble on his chin as he made his way to his office. "She was feisty, but I'm putting that down to the pain she was suffering because of the lightning strike. You all know women can't resist me!" He slammed the door to his office, then flopped down on his swivel chair. "Feisty, my ass," he muttered under his breath. "And what's up with that mind-reading act?"

Luke leaned back in his chair and closed his eyes. He hadn't been lying when he said women couldn't resist him. For some damn reason, every woman he met wanted to walk him to the altar. It wasn't that he was opposed to marriage—he wasn't. He did want to get married, but so far, the right girl hadn't found him. On more than one occasion, his mother had told him not to fret, the right woman would find him. Then she'd laugh and tell him to stand still. He thought about Lucy Brighton's green eyes and how they seemed to see right through him. Not to mention reading his mind. Was she pulling his leg, teasing him, or could she really read his thoughts? He cringed at the possibility. That would certainly be a game changer if he had romantic intentions, which, somewhere deep inside, he knew that he did. It was those green eyes.

Luke clicked on his computer. He was by no means a wizard when it came to computers, but he could navigate the Internet and do e-mails. He was pretty good with Google, almost as good as his father was. He snorted at that thought as he bellowed for more coffee.

Luke typed in Lucy Brighton's name and was stunned when he saw how much information there was on the green-eyed beauty. He started to read, his eyes almost popping out of his head. IBL! Everyone knew about IBL and the skyrocketing success of the fledgling company run by a lone young woman. Lucy Brighton was the lone young woman. For crying out loud, he'd bought a thousand shares when the IPO came out. His father, at his and his sister's urging, had bought another thousand. Then, that first year, he and his father had bought an additional three thousand shares for Marie's kids.

Here he was, busting his chops building one-of-a-kind houses, and there she was, drawing pictures of a dog, a cat, and a parrot, and she was making tons more money than he was. Unbelievable! Luke was so engrossed in what he was seeing and reading that he didn't even notice Tillie set his coffee cup down.

Within sixty seconds the office staff was buzzing like a beehive. The boss was smitten. He was checking up on Lucy Brighton.

"Good thing you have great vision," Allison said to Tillie, who grinned from ear to ear.

Oblivious to the office gossip, Luke was trying to comprehend what he was reading.

Lucy Brighton was financially loaded. What would she want with a nail-banging carpenter like him? She'd never consider him a good catch, a term his mother used to use when she referred to her only son. But was he a good catch for someone like Lucy Brighton? Assuming he was even remotely interested in being caught. A soft groan escaped Luke's lips. No sense in lying to himself. He did want to get caught, and if it was someone like Lucy Brighton, all the better.

Satisfied that the rearview and side mirrors were to her liking, Angie Powell looked over to see that her passenger and best friend in the whole world was buckled in properly and that her own seat belt was attached securely. Satisfied that everything was copacetic, she hit the gas and was stunned at the pickup on the Rover. **This is like being king of the road,** she thought.

Lucy laughed. "How does it feel to be king of the road?"

"Oh, my God! You really can read my mind! You weren't kidding, were you?"

"Apparently, it works only when you're close to me, like you are right now. I thought, when I couldn't remember my name, that it was bad, but this is so much worse. I don't want this . . . this . . . mind-reading ability. This is a curse!" Lucy said vehemently.

"Wow! Maybe you could turn it somehow to your advantage, you know, get a bead on things. Like when you negotiate contracts and such with the companies you deal with. I'd say that was a definite advantage."

"Angie! That would be dirty pool. I would never do something like that. I'm just hoping this mind-reading thing is as short term as my memory loss turned out to be. My brain just short-circuited. It's bound to change, like when I couldn't remember things. God, I hope I don't have to live like this for the rest of my life. It's a curse. It really is."

"Okay, now that that's out of the way, tell me everything that has happened since you got to Florida, and don't forget the part about that good-looking guy Adel was talking about. I want to hear all the details, every last one of them. Oh, oh, it's starting to rain. I thought you said we would have a clear day to drive."

"That's what the weatherman was saying this morning. It's rained practically the whole time I've been conscious in this state. Those weather people down here aren't like the ones up north, where they get it right 90 percent of the time. Here it's a crapshoot. Okay, here goes. Just listen and don't interrupt me."

"Okay. Does this vehicle have cruise control?"

"I don't know, Angie. I only drove it once. Just drive and listen. God, I have to tell someone about all this craziness before I lose my mind. What's left of it, that is."

Angie listened as Lucy droned on and on about her parents' house, the strange assortment of clothing, the funeral service, the cremation, and how she almost forgot to pick up her parents from the funeral home.

"They're in the cargo hold! You put your parents back there with all those boxes! We're driving with two dead people! Oh, my God!"

"They're in an urn and wrapped in bubble wrap," Lucy said through tight lips.

"They're still there. Here in the car. With us," Angie gasped.

"I know. It creeps me out, too. That shouldn't be, you know. If anything, it should be a comfort knowing I have my parents with me. At first I put them in that . . . that . . . coffin-like safe. Then I took them out. The reason I took them out was that I made a promise to myself that I was never going back to that house, so I couldn't leave them in the safe for all eternity. My God, Angie, what if I had left them in the safe and the new owners found them? Think about that! That's the reason they're with us in the car. I have them wedged in good and tight."

Angie clenched her teeth. "You know what, Lucy? Hearing you say that doesn't make me feel one bit better. We are still transporting two dead bodies to New Jersey."

"Not bodies, Angie. Ashes. In urns. In bubble wrap. They cannot spill out. The urns are sealed. Look, I don't like it any better than you do, but think about it. Did I really have a choice? I have to . . . find . . . you know, a final resting place for them. How else can I get them from point A to point B unless I transport them myself, which I am doing with your help?"

"Couldn't you have packed them in a wooden box and sent them by FedEx? You have an account with them."

"We need to move on here, Angie."

"Yes, we do, and I would like to hear about that coffin-like safe. You were kidding, right?"

"I wish I was, but I'm not. Wait till you hear this. It's going to blow your mind."

Angie sniffed. "My mind is already blown, but go ahead."

Lucy took a deep breath and explained about the walk-in closet, the arrangement of the clothes, and, finally, finding the safe.

"Were your parents paranoid or what?"

"You know what, Angie? I'm not even sure those people were my parents. There, I finally said it out loud. This is all way too weird for me. But I haven't even told you the best part. The part you aren't going to believe, because I'm still having trouble believing it myself."

"Hit me, girlfriend."

"What would be your guess as to what would have been in that safe, Angie?"

"You're asking me something like that! I

have no clue. Jewelry? Money? That's what people usually keep in home safes."

"Stretch your mind further. Think unbelievable," Lucy said tightly.

"Okay, birth certificates for other children you never knew about. They hid a winning lottery ticket for three hundred million and were keeping it safe until they could figure out the best way to beat the taxes. Just tell me already!"

"Guns! Ammunition! False identities, passports, credit cards, and driver's licenses with their pictures on some of them. Money, somewhere between three hundred thousand and half a million dollars. And, of course, all the other paperwork, titles to the cars, insurance policies, the deed to the house, and a will they made out when I was ten years old and sent off to boarding school. Insurance policies for twenty million dollars. Now you can say something."

Angie took a deep breath. "I would if I could think of something to say. Unfortunately, I can't right this second. I do have a stupid question, however."

"What?" Lucy almost screeched.

"Would I be wrong in assuming all those

things you just mentioned are in the back of this vehicle, along with Mom and Dad?"

"You would not be wrong at all. For God's sake, Angie, I couldn't leave that . . . that stuff there. I wish you could see that safe. I think it's safe to say I was in shock for a good ten minutes when I found it. There were three separate compartments."

"How'd you get it open? Did they leave you a combination?"

"No. That safe was never meant to be found. You know how people always say when you want to hide something, hide it in the open. That's what my parents did. The clothing, the shoes, that's what gave me the combination, and, of course, the umbrella had this very James Bond gizmo on it that opened the safe. I threw the umbrella away, but I have all the wiring. I'm thinking, Angie, that there is a safe back in Edison, in the big house, just like the one in Florida.

"As far as I can remember, there was no umbrella in the closet. I never touched anything in their suite of rooms after they moved away. I just closed the door and never went inside. Well, I'm going inside that suite the minute I walk into that house.

My parents, or whoever they were, were into something, and I don't think it was good, either."

"What . . . what do you think they were into, Lucy?"

"Think Occam's razor."

"Meaning the simplest explanation is usually the correct one. Which would be . . . what?"

"That my parents were some kind of terrorists. Spies perhaps. My father certainly had the credentials for something like that. He traveled all over the world just about every other day. Maybe he was a courier of some kind. The fact that all this stuff in the back was hidden, and hidden so well, has to mean whatever they were doing was illegal."

"And now you have it all."

"Yeah, now I have it all. I picked up one of the Glocks, and it felt like it was molded to my hand. The balance was dead-on, Angie. Remember when we decided in our junior year at college to join that gun club to learn to shoot because we thought we'd meet some good-looking guys?"

"Yeah, so what?"

"I remember my instructor showing me

his own gun and explaining how the stock was molded to his hand and how the balance was dead-on. Only people who use guns and know how to really use them, like that instructor, would have guns like that. I wonder if my parents ever shot anyone. Like in killing them. My parents might be murderers. Think about it, Angie. If this ever got out, IBL is down the tubes. I could never survive a scandal like that. No one could if they deal with children. I'm just sick over this."

Angie was silent for so long, Lucy prodded her to say something.

"A while ago you said you didn't think those people were your parents. Why did you say that?"

"Because I don't want my parents to be terrorists, spies, or murderers. It's easier to say they couldn't possibly be my parents. I'll never know, Angie."

"Why not? You could check their DNA."

"I had them cremated. The only way we could possibly get DNA is if some of the . . . some of the teeth survived the . . . the furnace. I checked on the Net."

"Their toothbrushes or their hairbrushes."

"Didn't you hear me? Everything was new. Brand-new. As in never used. The whole scene was staged. For whose benefit, I have no idea. The Longhursts said they were never there. Well, hardly ever there. They never got any mail at the house. None came while I was there, because I checked."

Angie waited for a break in the traffic before she moved to the center lane to get away from a slowpoke in the right-hand lane. She gave a soft tap to the horn in case the driver was elderly, and sped up. Seconds later, she was back in the right lane and cruising at a sedate seventy-five miles an hour.

"So what are we going to do, Lucy?"

Lucy was so grateful to hear the "we" in Angie's statement, she wanted to hug her friend. "I don't know, but what I do know for sure is that I am scared out of my wits."

"That makes two of us," Angie said.

"Maybe we'll be able to decide if we find a safe in the house in Jersey. If we do, I might go to the FBI."

Angie pondered the statement. "I don't think I'd be too eager to do that. Maybe between the two of us, we can figure something out. You could hire private detectives, for one thing. A reputable firm."

"Now, that's a thought."

"This might be a stupid question, but do you think those guns you found are legal?"

"The serial numbers were filed off. I checked. So, my answer is **no.**"

"That's not good."

"No, it isn't," Lucy said quietly.

# Chapter Nine

Luke Kingston felt like a teenager getting ready to go out on a first date as he peered at himself in the mirror. Unruly dark hair properly tousled; shaved, cheeks smooth as a baby's bottom, just a dab of after-shave. A woodsy, manly scent guaranteed to have women drop at his feet, according to his sister, Marie, who had given it to him as a gift. So far, no woman had dropped at his feet. Maybe today Lucy Brighton would be the very first. He winked at himself in the mirror, then made a growling sound deep in his throat. Like that was going to happen. Ah, those green eyes. He couldn't get them out of his mind, or that slight smile that had tugged at the corners of Lucy Brighton's lips.

Luke stood back a little farther to get the full effect of his attire. White shirt, open collar, sleeves rolled up to mid-arm. His deep tan obvious. Starched and pressed khakis with a crease so sharp, he was surprised it didn't gut his legs. Docksiders.

His game plan was to drop off the file of papers for Lucy Brighton, then get in the truck and head to Miami. Luke closed his eyes as he imagined the hooting and hollering his crew would give him when they saw what he was wearing. On the job, he wore baggy cotton cargo shorts, sleeveless muscle shirts, his baseball cap, and work boots that came up to his ankles, with cotton socks sticking out at the top, a utility belt hanging down over his hips. All the guys dressed the same way. Even though he was their boss, he never tried to stand out.

Luke took a deep breath and let it out slowly. He wondered what his father would say when he saw him duded up like a lovesick teenager. Plenty was the answer he came up with. The time was 10:45, and he still hadn't eaten breakfast. He'd dawdled long enough; he'd grab a cup of coffee and a muffin and be on his way. Maybe he should forgo the muffin—the bran might stick in his teeth. How would that look to those magnificent green eyes?

Luke Sr. blinked, then playfully shaded his eyes. "You going on a date this early in the morning, son?"

"No, Pop, I'm just dropping off the covenants to Miss Brighton, and then I'm heading to Miami. I'll be back on Saturday, and we can watch football all weekend. Did you forget?" Luke asked anxiously. He hated it when his father got what he called his blank looks and couldn't remember things.

"I was just funning with you, son. That's why I didn't make breakfast."

Young Luke relaxed. False alarm. His father was okay. As antsy as he was to be on his way, he sat down at the table to drink his coffee. "So, Pop, what's on your agenda today?"

Luke Sr. pretended to think. "Well, I'm going to watch a few cooking shows. Then I'm going to take some of my soup and the ham to a few friends." The **few friends,** young Luke knew, meant the widow Barbara Axelrod and Calvin Sandler. "I'll visit with them for a while, then take my daily walk. I might head over to the clubhouse to have a beer with Tom and Alvin. Haven't done that in a few days. Then it's back home to make dinner. Same old, same old."

"Why don't you invite the guys over for a poker game tonight?"

"You have to stop worrying about me, son, and let me do things my own way. I don't mind being alone at night. I can watch a movie or do any number of things. I plan to call the grandkids, and they like to chatter for an hour or so. Like I said, I'll be fine. More coffee?"

"Nope. Gotta run. I'll call you when I get to Miami. Answer the phone, Pop."

"Don't I always?"

"No. That's why I'm reminding you."

"I hate that damn cell phone."

"I'll call you on the house phone, so pick up when I call."

"All right, Luke. I will pick up the phone if you call."

Young Luke laughed. He hated leaving his father, he really did, but the old man insisted and reminded him that he wore a medical alert bracelet and Adel and Bud checked on him regularly.

Father and son hugged. Luke hated feeling his father's bones through his baggy shirt. "Don't go getting into any trouble with the widow Barbara while I'm gone."

"You'll be the first to know," the old man cackled. "Shouldn't I be saying that to you about Miss Brighton?"

"No, you shouldn't." Young Luke grinned. "See ya, Pop."

Luke was in the car, the engine running, when he realized he'd forgotten the folder on the kitchen counter. He was about to open the car door to go and get it when he saw his father walking toward him, the folder in his hands, grinning from ear to ear. "Thought as how you might need this, son. And you worry about me forgetting things." He guffawed.

Luke reached for it, a sheepish grin on his face. **Yep, one sick, sorry, dopey teenager going on his first date.**

Five minutes later, Luke was ringing the doorbell of the Brighton house. When there was no response, he rang it a second

and third time. When there was still no response, he peered through the long windows on the sides of the door. There were
no lights on, and the house looked deserted. Maybe Lucy Brighton was sitting
out on the patio. He walked around the
back, only to see that the patio looked just
as deserted. He walked up to the kitchen
door and peered into the glass portion of
the door. Everything was neat and tidy,
and there was no sign that anyone was in
the house.

Luke's shoulders slumped as he walked
back to the patio and sat down on one of
the wrought-iron chairs. When he heard
his name called, he looked up to see Adel
Longhurst crossing her yard to enter the
Brightons' yard. Luke waited.

"Lucy left yesterday, Luke. She was gone
within an hour of Buddy and me dropping
off her friend Angie. I showed Angie how to
dress Lucy's foot, and off they went. Buddy
tried to talk her out of leaving until today,
but she was adamant about not spending
another night in . . . that house. Might I say
you look particularly handsome this morning, Luke."

Luke forced a grin. "What do you think I

should do with this, Adel?" he asked. He'd long ago given up calling Adel and Buddy Mr. and Mrs. Longhurst, at their insistence.

"What is it?"

"Copies of everything, along with the covenants. I guess I could mail them, but I don't have her address. Do you have it?"

"I do. Walk home with me, and I'll give it to you. I suppose you could drop it off at the law firm she hired to handle the probate."

"I could do that, but I told her I would drop it off to her. I'm thinking she should be the one to decide if she wants to turn it over to the lawyers or not. Don't you agree?"

"You have a point, Luke. Come along. Have you had breakfast yet?"

Now that he didn't have to worry about food sticking in his teeth, Luke admitted that he hadn't eaten.

"Then it would be my pleasure to rustle up some pancakes for you. Why are you dragging your feet, Luke?"

Luke looked over his shoulder at the Brighton house. He told himself it was just a house. A house he'd built for people he didn't know. "Even though I built that house," Luke said, pointing to the house behind him, "and I was damn proud of it, I don't like it now. Not at all. There's something not quite right back there." He jerked his head to the side to make his point. "Bad vibes, and I know that sounds silly as hell, but it's what I think and feel."

"No, it's not silly at all. Buddy and I felt . . . feel exactly the same way, and I think that's why Lucy was so eager to leave. Actually, Luke, it isn't the house. Like all houses, it's just bricks, mortar, and timbers. The house itself is beautiful, no one can deny that. It's the people who lived in the house who left their bad vibes behind. To be perfectly honest with you, Buddy and I stopped sitting out on the terrace because we didn't like looking at it. That's why we planted all those oleander bushes that we allowed to grow wild. Another year's growth on those bushes, and we won't be able to see the house at all. Coffee, darlin'?" Adel said as they entered her house.

"Sure." Luke settled himself on a chair next to a round white table. He loved Adel's kitchen. Everything was sunshine yellow, bright and cheerful, like the kitchen's owners. It was the kind of kitchen his mother had decorated and basically lived in when they resided up north. Except his mother's kitchen was full of brick, green plants, over-head beams, and red crockery. He really missed the hominess of it all, especially the one-of-a-kind fireplace in the kitchen, with the two rocking chairs next to it, where his mother liked to have her afternoon cof-fee. He felt his eyes start to burn at the memories.

Adel placed a comforting hand on Luke's shoulder. Just the way his mother used to do. His world was suddenly right side up at her warm touch. "Let me get you Lucy's address and phone number. Then I'll whip up those pancakes."

"If you don't mind, Adel, I think I'll skip breakfast and get an early lunch on my way to Miami. I'm not all that hungry right now, but I'll take you up on your offer when I come back up for the weekend. You'll keep your eye on Pop, right?"

"Darlin', of course we will. Buddy finds four or five excuses a day to go see your father. That's not going to change. Here it is. Lucy said the house number is unlisted, so you better not lose it, and she also said she's not big on answering her cell phone. I also put her e-mail address on there. She called last night. Did I tell you that?"

Luke did his very best to appear nonchalant, but he wasn't really sure if he had managed to pull it off. "No, you didn't tell me that." He made a big production of pulling out his wallet and stuffing the small piece of paper in it.

"They called when they got to Virginia. Lucy said Angie was tired, and Lucy's foot was itching pretty bad. Once Angie changed the dressing, she was okay. The plan was to leave at five this morning, and she said that would get them home just about right now. I think I would wait a while and let her get settled in before you call her. That's just a piece of motherly advice, darlin'."

"When I get to work, I'll package this up and put it in the mail. I'll give her a call tomorrow if I have time. Thanks for the coffee, Adel. Don't forget to check in on Pop."

Adel gave the tall young man, who was like a son to her, a bone-crushing motherly hug. "You behave yourself now, Luke, and drive carefully. Send me a text when you get there so I won't worry."

"Don't I always?" Luke said, enjoying every second of the warm motherly hug.

*    *    *

Just as Luke pulled into the Miami construction site, Angie Powell swerved into the
driveway that led to the back of the Brighton
house and the garage. She hopped out of
the Rover and pressed the security code
Lucy called out to her. By the time she got
back into the truck, the garage door was all
the way up. She drove in, set the parking
brake, and turned off the engine.

"Home sweet home." She giggled. "I am
tired, Lucy. How about you? And how's
your foot?" Neither one got out of the truck
until the garage door slid all the way down.

"I'm just as tired. My foot is itching, but
the pain is totally gone. I can't wait to take
a shower and put on some clean clothes. I
can't remember the last time I slept in my
clothes, got up, and went somewhere at
five in the morning. We didn't even brush
our teeth. How gross is that?"

"Who's going to know that unless we tell
them? So, do we shower first, and then I
fix your foot, or the other way around?"

"Right now all I want is a good cup of
coffee. You go ahead and take your shower.
And then I'll take mine. I have to put a
plastic bag over my foot and use duct tape

to seal it around my ankle. I'll get all that ready. Take whatever room you want upstairs."

"I put all my stuff in the powder blue room on the left. You sure you can manage till I get back down?"

"Of course I can manage. I'm not helpless. Listen, Angie, thanks. I really appreciate your flying down to Florida and being such a good sport about driving all the way back here."

Angie made a face. "That's what friends are for, you dodo. Make the coffee strong, okay?"

"Will do."

Alone in the kitchen, Lucy fixed the coffeepot. Then, with the aid of the rolling heel on her foot, she scooted over to the window seat and looked out at the backyard, which was full of colorful leaves swirling in the strong wind. Typical harvest weather, with Halloween just a few days away. She thought about the promise she'd made to herself to decorate the wide front porch. She wasn't sure now if she even wanted to do that, or if Angie would mind tromping through a pumpkin patch up on Route 206.

And if she didn't decorate the porch, so what? She knew that the sky wouldn't come tumbling down.

As hard as she tried, Lucy couldn't keep her gaze from the kitchen door that led to the garage. **What am I going to do with all the stuff in the Range Rover?** As soon as the question surfaced, she revised it. **Where am I going to hide all the stuff in the Range Rover?**

She also had to make a decision as to what to do with the two urns in the Rover. Should she put them on a shelf in a closet upstairs? Or should she take them to a mortuary or mausoleum and let them keep her parents? She wished she knew what her parents wanted done in terms of their remains. **What if I choose the wrong thing?** she thought as perspiration beaded on her brow. **What if my parents wanted to be buried?** "Well, then, dammit, you should have let me know. I'm sick and tired of all these secrets," she mumbled through her clenched teeth.

"Hey, who you talking to, girl?" Angie asked, looking around. "No, no, don't get up. I'll get the coffee. Damn, that shower felt sooooo good. What did you decide about your foot?"

"You can change the bandages after I take my shower. I was talking to myself. No, that's not true, Angie. I was railing at my parents for not . . . Why didn't they trust me with their wills, to let me know what they wanted done just in case . . . you know?"

Angie brought her cup to her lips. "Some people don't even make wills, Lucy, because they don't want to think about their own demise. Then there are those who are prepared. They pick out their own cemetery plots, plan the eulogy, let it be known what kind of flowers they want, the particular prayers they want said. And they prepay everything so their kids won't have that burden. I read about that all the time in the paper. Look, stop torturing yourself. You can't unring the bell, and you did the best you could under the circumstances, so stop beating yourself up."

"Easier said than done. I'm going upstairs to take my shower. Poke around in the freezer and see what you want for dinner. I have tons of food in there."

"Can you make it up the steps by yourself?"

"Did you forget the chair rail? The one my father put in when he broke his leg?"

"I did forget, and I did see it at the bottom, but I wasn't really paying attention to it. It was just there. You know what I mean?"

"Okay, I'll be down in a bit. Hey, do me a favor, Angie. Go out to the studio and turn on the heat. I set it at fifty-five when I left."

"Okay. Take your time and be careful."

"Always."

At the top of the stairs, Lucy stood still for a moment, looking at the closed door to the room that had been her parents' when they had lived in this hateful house. She was tempted to turn the knob and walk in, but she fought the impulse. When she entered that room, she wanted Angie with her, because she knew what she was going to find. She could feel it in every bone in her body. She marched on down the hall to her own room and started to shed her clothes.

**Think about something pleasant for a change. Think about something happy. Think about Lucas Kingston, the good-looking dude who built your parents' house and who has a killer smile.** She wondered if she could come up with some reason to call that good-looking young guy.

**The covenants.** He said he was going to drop them by this morning. She wondered if he had tried. Well, that was reason enough to call him, to tell him she'd left and to mail everything to her and to also send a copy of everything to the Schwager law firm. She frowned as she tried to remember if she'd already told him that or not. She'd been so busy reading his mind, she just couldn't remember exactly what she had said. Well, mind reading was certainly worthy of a ten-minute phone conversation.

Her foot wrapped in a double plastic bag and secured with duct tape, Lucy stepped into the shower, where she blissfully allowed the steaming spray to pound at her body. She washed her hair and lathered up twice. She didn't get out until she felt her skin starting to pucker.

In her opinion, a nice hot shower was the cure-all and end all to any and all of life's problems. At least on a temporary basis.

# Chapter Ten

Angie poked her head in the door. "You decent, Lucy?"

"I am now. You ready to do my foot?"

Angie held out the packet of bandages and the honey mix Adel had sent home with them. She peered down at Lucy's charred foot. That was how she thought of it, charred. "I think it looks good. It's healing. That's obvious. How does it feel?"

"Good but itchy. No pain. That's a plus. Not to worry. I will take the meds until they run out as per the doctor's orders. Hey, is it my imagination, or is the temperature dropping?"

"You are spot-on. I turned the heat up downstairs. It's getting dark out. Looks like a typical New Jersey snow day. And all the leaves aren't even off the trees yet. You sure you don't want to move back to Florida? You could see that good-looking guy you told me about every day. Don't start reading my mind now. Promise, Lucy!"

Lucy laughed. "I promise to do my best not to read your mind. Hold on, hold on! Quick, Angie. Toby is ringing the bell. Go get my FedEx. Explain who you are, and he should give it to you. Hurry, before he leaves!"

"Lucy Brighton, you are absolutely shameless."

Lucy cackled to herself. She just knew, knew that Toby Nesbit and Angie Powell would make the perfect couple.

Lucy hobbled over to the bedroom window that overlooked the studio and the mailbox outside. She smiled as she watched the couple talking. Even from the second floor, she could see that shy Toby was finding Angie interesting. Now, if Angie didn't frighten Toby off with her forthrightness, they might get something going. She crossed her fingers that it would happen as she made her way back to the chair she'd been sitting on.

Lucy passed the time waiting for her friend's return by staring down at her sticky, black, ugly foot. It was enough to scare anyone, she thought. Yes, the doctor had told her, her foot would be scarred, and it would remain pink for a very long time. Well, wasn't that why they made bronzers that you could spray on? In the scheme of things, her foot was the least important on her list of problems.

Twenty minutes later, just as Lucy was dozing off, Angie bounded into the room, her cheeks flushed, her hair looking like a haystack. "How come you didn't tell me he was such a cutie?"

"Since when are you into red hair and freckles?" Lucy teased. **Yessssss.**

"I gave him my phone number, and he gave me his."

"No kidding?" Lucy said in pretended amazement.

"Yeah, no kidding," Angie drawled. "Listen, girlfriend, don't for one minute think you are fooling me. You sent me down there just so I could meet him. The good news is, it worked. Okay, let's get that foot dressed so we can . . . what, Lucy?"

"Check out that damn closet, that's what. I need to make decisions here, get some kind of game plan in place. You have to have a game plan if you're going to accomplish anything significant."

Angie nodded as she got to work. She half listened as Lucy picked up the phone on the little table next to her chair to check her messages. When she felt Lucy go still, she looked up, concern etched on her face. "What?"

"What's your feeling about moving to Freehold?"

"Like pack up and move all our stuff, that kind of move? Why not?"

Why not indeed. "Months and months ago, I took a virtual tour of a horse farm down there in Freehold. You know how much I've been wanting to get away from this . . . this house. I just didn't know where I wanted to go, and one day, on the Internet, I saw this advertisement about a farm in Freehold. I called a broker, and he told me that when the owner's estate was settled, it would go up for sale. What I really liked about it was, there is a four-bedroom bunkhouse, a log cabin of sorts, that would make a perfect studio for us. The farmhouse is all wood and cozy, with big, old fieldstone fireplaces. I gave him the go-ahead to make an offer if and when it went on sale, and the estate accepted my offer. We can move the first of the year. Actually, he said I could be in before Christmas if I went through with the deal. What do you think, Angie? Now that you're IBL's director of graphic arts, I have to consult with you."

"Where does Toby live?"

Lucy started to laugh and couldn't stop. She continued to giggle as she gasped out that Toby lived in Hazlet, which was just a hop, skip, and a jump from where they would be living. "Actually, Angie, Toby will be closer to us in Freehold than he is here."

"Then let's do it! Call your guy back, and I'm all for being in before Christmas. Oh, we can put up a real tree and the whole nine yards! Outstanding, Lucy!" Angie said, giving Lucy a high five.

Lucy's fingers moved at the speed of light. Her voice was just as fast and as breathless. "We have a deal, and I'd also like to be in before Christmas."

The two young women looked at one another and burst out laughing at the same time. Then they hugged each other.

"All we have to pack up is the stuff from the studio and my clothes from this room. I don't want anything from this house. I can call a moving company, and they can pack up everything. That's probably the better way to go. Then we drive down there and move in. See how simple that is?" Lucy said nervously.

"What about this place?"

"I can answer that better after we check out the master bedroom. If we find what I think we're going to find, then, no, I am not going to put it on the market. Besides, the housing market is so dismal, I wouldn't get half of what it's worth. I'll just pay the taxes and insurance and close it up the way I did the one in Florida."

Angie stared at her friend for a full minute.

"It's okay, Angie, and yeah, I am scared. That's another reason I want to get out of here. Yes, yes, I read your mind. Doesn't take a rocket scientist to know I'm edgy about all of this. Before, when I didn't know anything and was too stupid to be afraid, was one thing, but now . . . someone, somewhere is going to want all . . . all that money and those fraudulent passports and identities. And the guns. The guns are what scare me. What were my parents into?"

Angie held out her hand to pull Lucy from the chair she was sitting on. "Let's do it, Lucy. Better to know, then go to plan A, B, or C."

"You're right. We need to know. If things go . . . you know, south . . . do you think anyone will believe I didn't know about all of this?"

**Of course they'll know. What's wrong with you, Lucy?** "Of course not."

"Liar!"

Lucy didn't pause at the door that led to her parents' room. She grabbed the doorknob and thrust the door open. She walked as fast as she could across the room to the huge walk-in closet.

"This room is as big as my whole apartment was," Angie said in a squeaky voice.

Lucy turned on the light switch. The massive walk-in closet came to life. "It's just their winter clothes. They left them behind because they moved to Florida and wouldn't need them. And they would be here if they came back to visit in the wintertime, which they never did, of course. Do me a favor and bring in the footstool so I can sit on it."

Lucy couldn't ever remember being so jittery. Even her voice sounded strange to her ears. "Angie, push the clothes along the rod. See if the outfits number seven. Do my mother's first, then my father's. Is there an umbrella there somewhere? I seem to vaguely remember an umbrella."

Angie followed instructions. "Nope, it's just a jumble of clothes. Winter boots, heavy coats, and no umbrella. Are we relieved or not?"

"Do you remember where I left my purse?"

"On the kitchen counter, I think. Why?"

"Because the wires from the umbrella are in there. The umbrella in the Florida house. Can you fetch it, Angie?"

Angie literally flew out of the room and down the steps. She was back within minutes, a tangle of wires in her hands. Lucy didn't know whose hands were shaking more, hers or Angie's.

The moment she untangled the wires in her hand, Lucy looked up at Angie, her eyes full of concern and fear.

"Just do it, Lucy, and put us both out of our misery. We have to know one way or the other."

"Get behind me. The floor slides all the way to the end. Okay, here goes!"

Lucy jammed her finger against the button that would have opened a normal umbrella. She didn't realize she was holding her breath until she heard and saw the floor start to move away from the wall. "I knew it! Oh, God, Angie, what does this mean?"

"I don't have a clue, Lucy. I honestly don't. I don't think I've ever seen anything like this. It looks like it belongs in a bank or some outer-space place. Would you look at that!" she said, awe ringing in her voice.

"Yeah, I know. That's the first thing I thought of when I saw the one in Florida. This looks to be an exact duplicate."

"Do you think the combination is the same?"

"Let's see," Lucy said, sliding off the footstool, careful to stretch out her bad foot. "Oh, God, this can't be good." She pressed in the digits of the code she'd used in Florida, then waited. When she heard the audible click of the gears engaging, she said, "You're closer, Angie. See if you can open any of the compartment doors."

Angie clenched her teeth. "Lucy, are you sure you want to do this? All you have to do is close this thing up, and we can pretend it isn't here. Once you open the doors, it's a whole other ball game. I'll do it if you want me to. I'm just saying . . ."

"I have to know. Not knowing, suspecting, worrying, that's worse. Just open the damn doors, okay?"

Angie had to use both hands but was finally able to open what she called Door Number One. "I guess you want what's in here, right?"

"That would definitely help, Angie."

Angie withdrew a thick bundle of papers and handed them to Lucy.

"Legal papers. Just like in the other safe in Florida. Okay, open the next one."

"Cigar box, credit cards, different driver's licenses and passports, and a whole lot of money. A whole lot of money. More money than I've ever seen in my whole life," Angie said in awe.

"Same as Door Number Two in Florida. Open Number Three and there will be guns in there. I'm almost sure of it."

"And you're right, Lucy. With what you said you have out in the car plus these, you have a good arsenal here. I'm not touching those guns. Do you hear me? I'm not touching them."

"I heard you. Okay, put everything back, and let's close this up and decide what we're going to do."

Angie couldn't comply fast enough. She was breathing hard and hugging her knees when the floor slid closed. She put her head between her knees to ward off the dizziness she was feeling.

"This is spy stuff, Lucy. Nothing else makes sense. This is getaway loot. You always read about stuff like this or see it in James Bond movies. The good guys, and I stress, the good guys, always have to have a safe haven in case their cover is blown. You know, time to fall back and regroup before they go on their next mission. That's the only thing that makes sense to me, unless you can come up with something different."

"Yeah, well, does that mean my parents were the good guys or the bad guys?"

At the torment she was seeing in Lucy's eyes, Angie said, "Look, Lucy, your parents were respected doctors. Whatever this . . . ," she said, waving her arms at the floor, "is about, I'm not thinking they did bad things. Just the opposite. I don't have a criminal mind, so just because all this stuff is here doesn't mean they were directly involved. Maybe this house and the one in Florida were, like I said, safe houses, and your parents, for whatever reason, helped other people. Always the good guys, okay? I refuse to think otherwise until you can prove they were not."

"We need to tell someone," Lucy whispered.

"Who?" Angie dithered.

"We should have looked at the bundle of legal papers. I'll bet you five dollars, there are many, many more properties just like this one. When I went through the papers from the Florida house, I saw deeds to other properties, but I just thought they were real-estate holdings, and didn't pay attention to them. If we go to the authorities, this will go public. I don't hold out much hope that IBL could survive that kind of scandal. Even if my parents turn out to be the good guys. If we don't go public, that means someone associated with my parents is going to come looking for all this stuff. I might have made a wrong move by bringing all the stuff from the Florida house here. For all I know, we could be in danger, Angie. There must be some kind of network involved."

"If it turns out that your parents were the good guys, then we shouldn't be in danger," Angie whispered.

"True. But we have to be prepared to find out that maybe they weren't the good guys. Then we **are** in danger. Those people will want all this stuff. Wouldn't it be great if we could box it all up and put it on the front porch with a sign that says COME AND GET IT?"

"Yeah, I can see that happening. What are we going to do with all that stuff you have packed up in your father's truck?"

"I don't know, Angie. What do you think we should do with it?"

"I saw this movie once where these

people hid everything in a washing machine, then just put dirty clothes on top of it and filled it with water. The stuff they were hiding was in sealed plastic bags."

"Did they get caught?"

"Well, yeah, at the end of the movie. Someone turned on the washer, and it wouldn't go through the cycle or something."

"Scratch the washing machine. Let's go downstairs, build a fire, and make something to eat. I always think better when I have a full stomach. A few glasses of wine won't hurt either one of us."

Lucy took the chair rail down to the first floor, while Angie bounded down the stairs and out to the kitchen. Lucy headed for the family room, where she threw some logs on the grate and pressed the gas starter. She blinked when the gas flame shot upward. The birch log caught immediately as the flames did a wild dance. She threw in some pinecones from a basket on the hearth that she had gathered weeks before. She sniffed at the aromatic scent of pine that assailed her nostrils. Satisfied with the fire, she limped out to the kitchen, where Angie stopped banging pots and uncorked a bottle of wine. She poured sparingly.

"What's for dinner?"

"That's a stupid question, Lucy. All you have is frozen food. I have some hamburgers here. We can do some baked potatoes and some frozen vegetables. Do you ever eat fresh stuff?"

"On the day I go to the store, I do."

"Why don't you hire a cook or a housekeeper or something?"

"Now it's my turn to say what a stupid question that is. Because . . . growing up, I had to live with that. It was a different cook every few months. I didn't like it then, and I don't like it now. If I can't do it myself, then it simply doesn't get done. I kind of like cooking and cleaning. It's not hard to clean a bathroom and kitchen and change the sheets on my bed. Why do I need someone to do that for me?"

"To free you up to do other things, I guess. It wasn't a criticism. It was a suggestion."

"I know. I never had that . . . that family thing in my life. I'm trying to make it on my own here. Does that make sense?" Lucy asked anxiously.

"Yes. Yes, it does. How do you want your burger?"

"Medium rare. Wow! Listen to that wind out there. Typical Halloween weather. Halloween is tomorrow, isn't it? I kind of lost track of time here."

"Day after tomorrow. Have some more wine."

Lucy held out her glass. "I like it when it gets dark early, don't you? What I mean is, I like it as long as I'm inside and cozy warm. I really need to talk to a shrink, and I'm going to as soon as we get things squared away. I made that decision when I was down in Florida."

"Sounds like a good idea," Angie said as she peered at her friend over the rim of her glass. Lucy noticed that Angie had yet to actually drink the wine in her glass.

"I can't believe my parents are dead. I also can't believe they are still in the truck in the garage, wrapped up in bubble wrap. I should have brought them into the house as soon as we got here. I didn't do that. It's not bothering me that they're out there in the truck. Why is that, Angie? And don't forget, I almost forgot to pick them up from the mortuary. What does that say about me? What kind of shitty daughter am I?"

Angie shrugged and finally took a sip of the wine in her glass.

"That's it? You don't have anything to say?" Lucy all but screeched.

Angie set her wineglass down on the table. "You are not a shitty daughter. You are a good, kind, wonderful person and the best friend in the whole world. We spent hundreds of hours talking about this when we were roommates in college. If you feel the need to place blame, then the blame goes to your parents, not you. Never you, Lucy. Some parents just don't know how to show love. Some parents who have careers never figure out how to juggle a family and the career, and sometimes they mistakenly choose the career, thinking that once they become successful, they can go back and reclaim all they let slip away with their children. In your case, that didn't happen, and you were forced to go on basically alone, knowing only that you had parents somewhere in the background. We both know that putting a roof over your head, feeding you, giving you money and a car, and whatever else money can buy doesn't make up for being a good parent. You had to suck that up, so from where I'm sitting right now, you are golden, and it was your parents who were shitty. More wine?" Angie asked breathlessly.

Lucy held out her wineglass, tears rolling down her cheeks. "What would I do without you, Angie?"

"Ah, you'd muddle through. Listen, what do you say we dump these burgers and head out for some sushi?"

"Oh, God, I thought you'd never ask," Lucy said, wiping her eyes on the sleeve of her sweatshirt.

In the blink of an eye, both young women had their jackets on and their purses on their shoulders. Angie ran into the family room to turn off the gas starter and close the glass doors of the fireplace before they made their way to the garage.

"I'm driving. You had too much wine. Not that you could drive, anyway." Angie tried not to look at the packed Range Rover as Lucy slid into the passenger seat of the yellow Saturn.

Lucy caught Angie's furtive look. She

clenched her teeth so tight, she thought her jaw would crack. "I don't know who they are, but they aren't my parents. I don't know how I know this, but I'm positive that they aren't my mother and father. We do not need to discuss this again, Angie, okay?"

"Okay."

# Chapter Eleven

Lucy managed to slide out of the bright yellow Saturn on her own. She danced around on her good foot until the garage door slid into place. "Whew, it's windy out there! I just love this kind of weather. Did you see that harvest moon? Autumn has always been my favorite time of year. Don't you just love the smell of burning leaves? It's against the law, but people still do it. Dinner was good, though, and we don't have a mess to clean up."

"You can stop babbling now, Lucy," Angie said as she dumped her purse and car keys on the kitchen table. "We're in the house, not the garage."

"Am I that obvious?" Lucy asked as she flopped down on a kitchen chair.

"Yeah, you are, and don't go reading my mind."

"You're thinking how tired you are, and I'm sorry, Angie. You've had a full day, with all the driving and then this stress piled on top of it. Let's lock up and go to bed."

"It's only eight thirty!"

"So? Your eyes are drooping, and so are mine. Tomorrow is another day. A full day, so let's both get a good night's sleep. There are no answers right now, and we both need clear heads to deal with . . . with whatever all of this is. Okay?"

Angie brushed at her dark hair, then yanked it back and tied it in a ponytail. "Sounds good to me. I can change your dressing upstairs since I left everything up there. Another day or so, and I think you can just put a sock on your foot. Maybe even wear a slipper."

"I can't wait to get back to normal," Lucy said as she checked the back door and the door leading to the garage. "Okay, we're good here. One more time, Angie, thank you so much for . . . for being my friend and for just being you."

Angie wrapped her arm around Lucy's shoulders as they made their way to the foyer and the staircase that led to the second floor. "That's what friends do for each other. Sometimes friendships are deeper and more meaningful than family ties. It shouldn't be that way, but sometimes it is. Remember that old saying, 'You can pick your friends, but you can't pick your family'?"

Lucy laughed, but it was a tired, weary laugh.

Forty minutes later, Angie was sound asleep, and Lucy was propped up in bed, but she was still wide awake. Her mind whirled and twirled, and she knew she wouldn't sleep, at least not for a while. She reached over to her night table for the pad and pen she kept in the drawer. She flipped the yellow sheets of previous lists. She had to be the all-time queen of lists. She started to scribble. Before she knew it, she had a page full of things she needed to do, calls to make, e-mails to send, decisions to make. She scribbled some more. Phone calls were a pain in the neck.

E-mails, she decided, were the way to go. That way, she wouldn't get put on hold, have to call back, or wait for a return call. Yep, e-mails would do it. E-mails also meant "Don't bother me, and I won't bother you. Time is money."

It occurred to Lucy that she hadn't checked her messages since their return from the restaurant. Not that they were gone that long, but in two hours, someone could have called at the end of the business day. She checked her voice mail to hear a robotic voice announce that she had three new voice mails. She pressed ONE and listened to PSE&G say they would read her meter tomorrow between ten and two. The second voice mail was from Atkins Gutters, reminding her it was time to have her gutters cleaned and for her to call back with a time and a date. She added Atkins Gutters to her list, then pressed ONE again to hear her third message. Ooooh. Luke Kingston calling to tell her he had put all the paperwork he promised in the mail. He went on to say he hoped her foot was healing and that he was always available if she needed any help concerning the house in Palm Royal. He signed off with his cell phone number and wished her a wonderful evening.

Aha. Suddenly it was, indeed, a wonderful evening. She looked down at the number she'd scrawled on her list, and before she could think twice, she pressed in the numbers. She almost disconnected the call when she saw the time on the digital clock on her night table. Was 9:50 P.M. too late to be returning a call? She was just about to end the call when she heard Luke Kingston's voice. She felt a shiver of delight. She announced herself, then asked if this was too late to be calling.

The voice was breezy, confident sounding. "Actually, your timing is perfect, Miss Brighton. I was just finishing up a bunch of paperwork. It's been a long day. I appreciate your returning my call. I think I told you I dropped off the same information at the Schwager firm that I sent on to you.

"So, how's the weather in New Jersey? When we lived up north, I loved this time of year. So did my parents. I miss it."

Lucy scrunched deeper into her nest of pillows. "Today it's been really windy. I'm sure the rest of the leaves will come down in the next day or so. There's a harvest moon, though. Autumn is my favorite time of year."

"Windy, huh? Kite-flying weather?"

Suddenly, Lucy felt stupid. "What?"

The voice on the other end of the phone chuckled. Lucy loved the masculine sound. "You know, wind, flying a kite in the wind. Didn't you ever fly a kite?"

"Ah . . . no, I never did. Is it fun?"

"Oh, yeah. My sister, Marie, was the best kite flyer I ever met. Her string never got tangled. Mine always did. My mom was always convinced she was going to go skyward and never be found again. My mom was a worrier. To be honest, I loved it but was never half as good at it as Marie was, but yes, it was fun. My sister was fearless." Lucy heard the chuckle again.

Lucy smiled. "Does that mean you aren't fearless?"

"I learned my lesson when we went sled riding one time, and I hit a tree and broke an arm and an ankle. Marie hopped off in time and just rolled away in the snow. Stupid me stayed on the sled. I think it's a girl thing. Were you like that?"

"Actually, no. I . . . ah . . . no, I never went sled riding."

"Skiing?"

"No."

"Rollerblading, roller-skating? Did you ever do a zip line?"

"Sorry, no. What's a zip line?"

"This might sound stupid, but did you live in a bubble? What did you do with your friends when you were a kid?"

What did she do? Lucy suddenly felt embarrassed. "I guess I more or less did live in a bubble. I didn't do much. I went to boarding school at the age of ten, and it was all about learning, and there was no playing. I read and sketched. I guess I was never really a kid," Lucy said, sadness ringing in her voice.

"I'm sorry, I shouldn't . . . I didn't mean . . ."

"No, that's all right. I love hearing about other people's childhoods. Someday, I plan to do all those things. You didn't tell me what a zip line is."

"Well, for starters, parents frown on zip lines, or at least mine did. It was Marie's idea to begin with. You tie a nylon cable between two trees. You know, on a slant. One is up high, and the anchor is down low. And then you slide down it. It is a really breathless experience. Of course, I fell and broke a leg. Marie wore this shiny tiara and her outfit from her dancing class. She, of course, aced it. So did all the other kids. When I got out of the hospital, my father whacked my behind so hard, I couldn't sit down for a week. Marie wasn't allowed to watch television for a whole month. We never did that again."

Lucy laughed. "Your sister sounds very interesting."

"Trust me, she is very interesting. You wouldn't believe how she watches over her own kids now. I tease her constantly that her kids are going to give her a run for her money the way she did Mom and Dad."

"Are you a good uncle? Do you spoil her children?"

"As much as I can. They live in Seattle. Did your aunts and uncles spoil you? Is that why you're asking?"

"I don't have any aunts or uncles, so that means no cousins, either. And before you can ask, I didn't have friends the way I think you and your sister did. Until I went off to college, I never had a best friend. Now I do."

Luke didn't mean to say it. The words

just somehow tumbled out of his mouth. "That's sad, unbelievable, actually."

"Yes, I know. I survived, though."

"Look, Miss Brighton, I'm sorry. I didn't mean to . . . I hope I didn't upset you."

"I think you can call me Lucy. You didn't upset me, Mr. Kingston. Sometimes I just wish I could have . . . you know, one day been a kid to see what it was like. But, hey, I'm all grown up now, the CEO of a publicly traded corporation, so the past is prologue, as they say. The flip side to all of that is, I can still enjoy other people's experiences. That's a good thing."

"Stop calling me Mr. Kingston. Mr. Kingston is my father. I'm just plain old Luke."

"Okay, Luke. Well, I guess I kept you on the phone long enough. I have to call Adel and Buddy to let them know we arrived safe and sound. To be honest, until just this moment, I forgot. That's so unlike me. I'm becoming scatterbrained of late."

Luke didn't want her to hang up. He was enjoying the conversation. "Don't be so hard on yourself, Lucy. After all, you were struck by lightning. That's enough to make anyone scatterbrained. I don't mean that you're scatterbrained. Oh, hell, you know what I mean. But I am sorry if my childhood tales made you sad."

"Not at all. I'll call you when the package arrives."

"Okay. Have a nice evening, and if you happen to look out your window at that harvest moon, tell it I miss being there. Is that stupid or what?"

"No, and I will be sure to do that. It was nice talking to you, Luke."

"You too. I mean that. You know, you have beautiful eyes. My mom had green eyes."

"Really?"

"Yep, and they weren't contacts, either. My dad loved my mom's eyes, said they were greener than emeralds. They were, too. The eyes are the mirror of one's soul. You know that, right?"

Lucy could feel her neck grow warm. "Yes, I did know that. Thanks for the compliment."

"That is your real eye color, right? You don't wear contacts, do you?"

Lucy laughed. "No, I don't wear contacts. I do wear glasses when I sketch, though. Shell-rimmed."

It was Luke's turn to laugh. "Good night, Lucy Brighton."

"Good night, Luke Kingston."

Lucy flopped back into her nest of pillows, a smile on her face. Things were looking up. Really looking up. As in seriously looking up. Then she laughed out loud. The sudden giddiness she was experiencing stayed in her voice when she called Adel and Buddy to tell them that she had arrived home safely and her foot was feeling 100 percent better. She signed off by saying she would call them tomorrow and they could talk more.

Lucy hung up the phone, slid her notepad and pen onto the night table, and turned off the light. She was going to sleep like a baby this night. She was sure of it. So sure, she smiled as she tucked herself against the pillow, her thoughts on the tall guy with the unruly dark hair who had had a wonderful childhood and who had just shared it with her. Her last conscious thought before slipping into dreamland was that she would dream about the tall, good-looking Luke Kingston.

\* \* \*

Luke Kingston looked down at his watch. Noon already! He'd been up since five, grabbed a bagel and a coffee on the way to the site from the furnished efficiency apartment he rented on a short-term lease near the construction site. He suddenly realized how hungry he was. A quick pizza last night had been his dinner, along with three Bud Lights. The truth was, he'd been way too excited to think about food after talking to Lucy Brighton. Way too excited. Come to think of it, he was still excited as his brain tried to backtrack to every word said during the conversation. She'd flirted with him. And he with her. Did it mean anything? He sure as hell hoped so. He could hardly wait for her to call him when the real-estate packet reached her doorstep.

Luke reached for his car keys, which were lying on the counter. His intention was to drive two miles down the road to a diner so he could get some real food, like meat loaf, mashed potatoes, and gravy. A sandwich from the roach coach, which was due any minute, just wouldn't cut it today. He looked around for his sunglasses but couldn't find them. He must have left them in the truck. Probably on the visor. He checked to be sure his wallet was in his hip pocket and left the trailer. Satisfied that he had everything he needed, he waved to his foreman and headed toward his truck.

That was when he saw them. He blinked and took a second look. Cops? Building inspectors? No, not building inspectors. Those guys always wore short-sleeve shirts, khakis, and were thick around the middle. They were up to speed on everything, and no inspections were scheduled. Cops? Cops didn't wear the kind of suits these guys were decked out in. The cops here were friendly, not ominous looking like the twins headed in his direction. If they were cops, his foreman would have handled it. Feds? Possibly. This was, after all, Miami.

Dark suits, pristine white shirts, subdued ties, aviator glasses. Tall, muscular, the kind of guys you knew could hold their own in any situation. He didn't hire illegals—everyone working for him had papers.

Luke reached into his truck for his sunglasses. Ray-Bans. He put them on as he planted his feet a little more firmly on the sandy soil and waited. Now they were even; no one could see anyone else's eyes.

"Mr. Kingston?"

"That's me, unless you want my father."

The guy on the left opened his suit jacket and removed a slim wallet. It also allowed Luke to see the shoulder holster he was wearing. He flipped open the slim wallet and gave Luke time to peruse it. "Special Agent Leo Spalding, Federal Bureau of Investigation. This is my partner, Special Agent Tom Jackson." Special Agent Tom Jackson flipped open his own slim wallet. Luke took his time checking both.

"What can I do for you?"

"Talk to us," Spalding said.

"About what?"

"Palm Royal. Phase One. This is Phase Two, is it not?"

"Yes, this is Phase Two. What do you want to know?"

"We're interested in a particular property back in Palm Royal."

Luke decided to play dumb. "You mean you want to buy one of the properties? If that's the case, there are none for sale, and you have to go through our realty division, and that's back in Palm Royal."

Jackson rocked back on his heels a bit. "We're not interested in buying. We're interested in seeing a particular house. We thought you could help us."

Luke pretended confusion. "Why would you think that? Talk to the owner."

"Well, you see, there's a problem with that, Mr. Kingston. The owners are dead. We thought you might be able to help us out here."

**Oh shit!** "Talk to the heirs. Or their lawyers. I don't see how I can help you. What am I missing here?"

It was Spalding's turn to speak. They must have a plan, Luke thought. **First one speaks, and then the other speaks. Frick and Frack.**

"Your company has a policy that if one of your properties goes on the market, your firm handles it. In other words, no outside Realtors, correct?"

"That's true. So what? We don't have any properties listed for sale."

Frick and Frack seemed genuinely surprised at that statement. Jackson took his turn. "We'd like to inspect the Brighton house, the one you won an award for building."

An army of ants crawled around Luke's stomach. **Shit, shit, shit.** "The house is in probate. Actually, I just dropped off a batch of paperwork yesterday to the law firm handling the probate. You'll have to go through them, not me."

"What's the name of the firm?"

Luke pretended to think again as he removed his baseball cap and scratched his head. "Let me think. Strange spelling. Yeah, yeah, it's Schwager, Schwager, and Schwager. They're in town. Why didn't you just call me instead of driving all the way down here?"

"We're based in Miami," Jackson said. "Simpler to come here first."

"Simpler for what? Why would the FBI be interested in an empty house? I feel I have a right to know. My father, my sister, and I are responsible for that gated community. If you know something we should know, I'd appreciate it if you'd tell me what it is. I can tell you right off the bat, no one in the community knew the Brightons, and that was by their choice. Mr. Brighton was the renowned heart surgeon, and his wife was also a doctor of some note. They did not mingle with the other owners. From what I understand, the Brightons were rarely in residence. If they were there ten days out of a year, it was a lot. If you care to check with the neighbors, I'm sure they'll tell you the same thing. So, you understand my . . . curiosity at this visit."

Luke could see Spalding's back stiffen. **He thinks I'm a pushover. Big mistake, buddy.**

"We understand your curiosity. So, what you're saying is you won't give us a tour of the Brighton home. Is that correct?"

"That's exactly what I'm saying. I abide by the law. Unless you have a warrant, I don't see you getting into that house. Where do you get off even thinking that I would break the law or have the keys to the Brighton house? On top of that, you're talking to the wrong person. You need to speak with the law firm that is handling the Brighton probate or the heirs. From here on in, if you want to pursue this matter further, contact my attorney. His name is Joshua Fielding, and he's on Sumpter Avenue in Palm Royal. Now, if you'll excuse me, gentlemen, I'm already late for another appointment."

His brain buzzing like a beehive, Luke

climbed into his truck, waited until Frick and Frack moved out of his way, then backed up and left the construction site. On his way to what he had hoped would be his meat loaf and mashed potato lunch, he called his father, explained what he was doing, and told him he was taking the next flight to New Jersey. He then tried to call Lucy Brighton, but the call went to voice mail, so he left a message. He hoped his voice didn't convey how upset he was. His third call was to the airline, where he was told he could get a straight-through flight to Newark at two thirty. That would give him just enough time to get to his rental apartment, pack a bag, then drive like a bat out of hell to the airport. With no delays, he could be in Jersey in a little under three hours. He was sure he could make it happen.

Every nerve in his body was telling him that something was seriously wrong. Like really, seriously wrong. His gut was telling him that whatever it was, Lucy Brighton of the green eyes was in it up to her neck. What he wasn't sure of was if it was willingly or unwillingly.

# Chapter Twelve

Lucy walked into the kitchen, stunned at what she was seeing and smelling. Angie laughed at her expression.

"I was up at the crack of dawn, showered, and in the supermarket at seven thirty. Eleven hours of sleep was just what I needed. So, sit down, and I will serve you this delectable breakfast."

"Yes, ma'am. In the supermarket at seven thirty, huh?"

"Yep, and you'd be surprised how many people were already shopping, but I whizzed in and out. How'd you sleep?"

"I didn't," Lucy said, shaking out her

napkin. "I was up all night with my lists and composing e-mails to send out. I just set the mail timer, and they'll all go out at nine this morning. Frees me up to do other stuff."

Angie scooped fluffy scrambled eggs onto Lucy's plate. "And by **other stuff,** you mean what?"

"Have you seen those commercials on TV for storage units that are so big you can store your car in them?"

Fork poised in midair, Angie stared across the table. "Yeah. Are you thinking what I'm thinking?"

"I think so. It's one way to get all that stuff outta here until we can figure out what to do with it. It makes me way too nervous to keep it here."

"Won't that make us accessories to something or other?"

"Probably. Do you have a better idea?"

"No, I don't."

"Well, think about this, Angie. The stuff upstairs has been there since my parents left to go to Florida. Five long years. There's no reason for us to think anyone will come looking for it right away."

"There's a teeny tiny blip in that theory,

Lucy. Your parents died. That was a game changer right there. Someone somewhere knows about those two safes. We need to start seriously thinking about talking to the authorities. And the sooner the better. And don't forget, you keep saying that the people who lived in the house aren't or weren't your parents."

"I thought of something last night, and I opened the safe after you went to bed. All those passports were blank. By blank I mean they didn't have pictures in them. The credit cards had names on them, as did the driver's licenses. No pictures on the driver's licenses. That tells me there is some forger out there who at some point enters the picture and, no pun intended, affixes somehow, some way, pictures of whoever is going to be needing those identities. Did I say that right?"

"You're way above my pay grade here, Lucy, but I understand what you're saying. It all smacks of spy stuff. This is so James Bond, it is creepy. I mean it. We need to talk to someone."

"Who? The FBI? The local cops? I sent off an e-mail to the real-estate broker and asked him if he would get in touch with the estate people in Freehold and ask them if we could move in now and pay the estate a month's rent until the closing. I think we need to get out of here, and the sooner we do that, the better. I can call a packing company, and if they have people available, we could be out of here by tomorrow. What do you think?"

"I don't know what to think. You're scared, aren't you?"

"Damn straight I'm scared," Lucy said in a strangled voice.

Angie nibbled on a piece of crisp bacon. "All the more reason for us to go to someone. My vote would be the FBI."

"Isn't the FBI crime and all things related to crime? Maybe the CIA. They're international and can't operate on U.S. soil. I think that's how it works. All that stuff in the safe, the passports and such, is from other countries. The CIA and the FBI are not warm and fuzzy partners. I think they're in competition with each other. At least that's what I remember reading at some point. Maybe I saw it on the news," Lucy said fretfully. "I'm sorry I'm scaring you, Angie."

At that moment, the old-fashioned phone hanging on the wall in the kitchen rang.

Both women jumped. Angie reached for it and handed the receiver to Lucy.

"Lucy Brighton," she said briskly. She listened and mouthed the words, "It's the real-estate broker." She listened some more. Finally, she said, "That's wonderful. I'll stop by for the key tomorrow, then. I'll bring a check for the month's rent with me to tide us over till the closing. I'd appreciate it if you could get a cleaning crew in there today or in the morning. We'll be there at some point tomorrow afternoon. Again, I appreciate your going out of your way for me."

The moment Lucy hung up, the phone rang again. She listened and said, "Now is a good time. There isn't all that much, mostly office equipment. Is it at all possible for you to transport my belongings to Freehold tomorrow, late morning? You can? Yes, I understand there will be a moving charge. Fine, fine. I'll see you in an hour."

"We're in business, Angie. God, I cannot wait to get out of here. Listen, you check to see about the storage unit. I have to call the probate lawyer to give him my new address, and Dr. Lyons to report on my foot. I still haven't gotten a bill from them. I hesitate to leave a forwarding address, so that means I have a lot of calls to make or e-mails to send. You can call FedEx, ask for Toby, and give him the news. By the way, what did he deliver yesterday?"

Angie beamed. "Okay. It was a box. It's still on the dining-room table. Be sure to tell the doctor all the blackened skin has sloughed off your foot. Ask him if we use the greasy ointment or the one that absorbs, or do we stick with the honey?"

Lucy nodded. It would be such a relief to take the heavy bandage and the rolling wheel off her foot and actually wear a sock and a slipper. **The gods must be smiling on me.**

Twenty minutes later, the two women compared notes. "Mr. Schwager thanked me and said probate moves slow, but all the wheels are in motion. He said he would file the necessary papers with the insurance companies. I explained about the car, and he said to fax him the title and he'd take care of that, too. Dr. Lyons said he was pleased at my progress and that the honey worked much more quickly than he thought possible and to go ahead and keep using it as long as I didn't mind my foot being sticky, which I don't. A cotton sock and a slipper is okay. What do you have?"

Angie cleared her throat. There was a devilish gleam in her eye when she said, "A date for Saturday night. You know, a date, a he's-going-to-knock-on-the-door kind of date. And he said he knows exactly where we're moving and I should tell you it was a good choice on your part. I'm talking about Toby here. Ooooh, I am so excited. There's a storage unit on Route One in Woodbridge. They have two available for vehicles and only four units for personal items. It's ninety dollars a month for the personal one and three hundred dollars for the vehicle one. I reserved them both in my mother's maiden name. I'm getting pretty good at this spy stuff."

"Good thinking, Angie. I never would have thought of that. We'll need to pay cash. That means we have to stop at an ATM before we get there. I don't keep that kind of cash lying around."

"Lucy . . . ah . . . what about the stuff upstairs? You can't fit any more in your father's Rover. Your car and mine are too small. Well, they aren't really, but where and how are we going to pack it all up?" A look of horror crossed her features. "You aren't planning on leaving it here, are you? Two trips aren't good. It will call attention to us. We have to do it all at once."

"It's the artillery that we need to worry about transporting. I'm sure I have boxes in the studio. The packing company will have boxes. We'll just wrap it all up in towels and sheets, like I did in Florida, then seal up the boxes and label them. We can pack up the papers and the . . . other stuff separately. I think it will be better to have everything in one location, as opposed to scattering it around. Do you agree? You know, once it's out of our hair, and we aren't worrying about it, we can make a decent decision about what to do and who to call. I think, or at least I hope, that will work."

"Sounds like a plan. If you're okay with it, then I'm okay with it," Angie said, though there was an edge in her voice.

"We really don't have too many options here, Angie."

"I hate to ask you this, but what about

those . . . urns and the people in them?
Are you going to put them in storage or
leave them here in the house? This is so
grisly."

"They're going into storage until we find
out who they are. At some point, we can
always put them in a mausoleum. They
are **not** my parents. If they were my parents, I would feel something. I didn't feel
anything from day one, and that hasn't
changed. I'm telling you, Angie, those . . .
ashes are not my parents' ashes," Lucy
replied, a note of hysteria creeping into her
voice.

"Okay. Calm down. What do we do first?"

"Well, as soon as you fix my foot and I
get a slipper on, we're going out to the studio to stack up my personal files. That way,
all we have to do is box them up when the
packers get here. Then we can leave them
to do their work while you and I go to the
storage place. First, though, we have to
get the boxes for . . . for the artillery."

"Okay, let's do it!"

It was eleven thirty on the dot when
Angie ripped off the last strip of packing
tape and stuck it on a cardboard carton in

the studio. "That does it, I think. The packers can load up their van and transport
everything tomorrow. Be sure they sign off
on it."

"Yes, Mother," Lucy drawled. "I cannot
tell you how good my foot feels. I don't think
I'll have a bit of trouble driving. The slipper
has a thick sole. I'm good, and do not even
think about trying to talk me out of it."

"Stop reading my mind, Lucy."

"Then stop thinking such negative
thoughts," Lucy snapped. "Bring the boxes."

"I have them. Can we take this roll of
tape?"

"Why not? I'm paying for it."

The two young women worked like bea-
vers as they emptied out the safe and
wrapped up the guns and ammunition in
towels and bed linens and loaded them
into four different boxes. Angie taped the
boxes, and Lucy used a black grease pencil to label them PALE BLUE BED LINENS. The
second box was labeled WINTER BLANKETS,
and the third, SUMMER CLOTHES.

"They aren't too heavy for you to carry
out to the chair rail, are they?" Lucy asked.

"I can carry them. Are you sure we didn't
forget anything?"

"I'm sure. The safe is closed. And I have the umbrella wires in my purse. I think we're good to go, Angie. When we get back, all we have left to do is pack up our clothes and we'll be ready to go in the morning. Oh, and empty out the fridge and freezer."

"Are you taking your Crock-Pots?"

Lucy had to think about that for a moment. "Absolutely, I'm taking them."

Angie laughed. "Now, that's the Lucy I know and love. I'll pack them up."

It was exactly 12:20 when Lucy climbed behind the wheel of her father's Range Rover. Angie was driving the packed-to-the-roof Saturn.

"Phone's ringing!" Angie shouted. "Do you want me to get it?"

"They'll call back if it's important. Or they'll call my cell phone." **Well, no, they won't, actually,** Lucy thought, **because I left it on the kitchen counter.** She told herself it wasn't a problem as she backed the Rover out of the garage. Butterflies skittered around inside her stomach. This was really happening. She was breaking the law. She just knew it. **Too late now.**

Sometimes, you just had to do what you had to do.

The three-mile drive to the storage center on Route 1 took all of fifteen minutes. Angie pulled in first. She hopped out of the car and went into a dusty, cluttered office, where a man sat reading a newspaper with a magnifying glass. He looked up. That was when Angie saw the milky white eyes and knew the man had cataracts. His voice was sweet and gentle when he asked how he could help her.

"I called a little while ago to reserve a car-storage unit and a personal unit."

The man laid aside his newspaper and slid a clipboard across the counter. "Just fill it out, and I'll give you the keys."

"I'm paying for two months on both units, and I'm paying in cash. My brother and I just moved here and haven't had time to open a bank account. Is that all right?"

"Right as rain, little lady. Cash is always good. Where are you from?"

"Memphis, Tennessee. By the way, my name is Brenda Tolliver. My brother's name is Justin. I'm putting his name on the contract, so we'll need two keys. Is that okay?"

"Right as rain, little lady. Soon as you turn over your money, I'll turn over the keys. I'm supposed to tell you that you can access your units twenty-four/seven. This is my son's business, but he's in Iraq, guarding the embassy." The old gentleman pronounced it I-rack. "My daughter-in-law and I are running it till he gets back. The children only have half a day of school today, and she went to pick them up. I'll leave the paperwork for her, as my eyes aren't what they used to be."

"Can you see to count the money?" Angie asked anxiously as she handed over the wad of bills Lucy had gotten from four ATM machines.

"With this magnifying glass, I can see just fine, little lady. I do thank you for your business," he said, shoving the bills into a drawer. "Here are two keys. If you lose them and need new ones, there is a twenty-five-dollar charge for the replacements. Drive straight back, and you'll find the car units at the end. Yours is J-5. Your personal unit is B-19. They're right across from each other. Nice to make your acquaintance, Ms. Tolliver."

"Likewise," Angie said, beelining for the door. Outside, she motioned for Lucy to follow her, which she did.

Both women moved like lightning then and were back on the road in fifteen minutes. It wasn't till they were on the highway that Angie explained about the old man's bad eyesight and the daughter-in-law who had gone to pick up her kids from school.

"We aced it, Lucy. I listed our address as Memphis, Tennessee, and said it was me and my brother renting the units. In case anyone comes looking. He didn't have a problem with me paying cash, and as you suggested, we paid in advance for the second month. I even tried to disguise my handwriting, you know, writing backhand."

"Ah, you're starting to think like a criminal. I think I've corrupted you, Angie. Sorry about that, but I think we can both rest a little easier now. There's a really good Chinese restaurant right down the road. You want to stop for some lunch? They have a great buffet, with some of everything. They even have that Mongolian barbecue stuff. You ever had any of that?"

"Lead me to it. And, yes, I've had Mongolian barbecue," Angie quipped.

"Then turn right at the light and take the first left. It's called Pagoda."

Three pots of tea and two trips to the buffet table later, including enough Mongolian barbecue to fill up a small yurt, both Angie and Lucy professed to be stuffed. So they waddled out of the restaurant to the bright yellow Saturn and headed home.

"I feel like I need a nap," Lucy grumbled. "I can't remember when I ate that much. Probably never is when. At least we won't have to worry about cooking dinner. A fried-egg sandwich will do it for me, I'm thinking."

"Me too. Looks like rain, Lucy. Look at those dark clouds. Sure is windy. Nice night for a fire and a good movie, along with a bottle of fine wine. Or maybe some beer. If we don't finish it, we either have to throw it away or take it with us. I'm just saying." Angie giggled as she made a left-hand turn.

"I vote that we finish it. I hate wasting anything. I also do not like transporting liquor or beer or anything alcoholic in a car."

"But guns and ammunition don't count?"

"God, yes, they count. There are no words to tell you how glad I am we got rid of that stuff, at least for the time being."

"Let me ask you a question, Lucy. Do you have any kind of feeling that time is of the essence here? You know what I mean. I figure you must feel like that, because I have never in my life moved so fast to do something. Think about it, Lucy. Bam, bam, bam, it all got done, and we're moving to Freehold tomorrow. That has to be some kind of record."

Lucy nodded. "It's just a little over a week. I kind of think whoever is responsible for all this had to maybe fall back and regroup and try to decide what to do. So, yes, time is of the essence, and we are probably getting out in the nick of time. I hope I'm wrong, but I don't think I am."

"Okay, we're home," Angie said. She pressed the remote Lucy had given her, and the garage door slid open. The space where the Range Rover had been parked looked immense. She parked in the same spot and got out of the car. Lucy joined her at the door, then entered the kitchen, but not until the garage door had slid down and was locked securely.

"Check the phone, Lucy. Someone called as we were leaving. It might be important."

Lucy sniffed. She'd already touched all the important points she was willing to deal with that day. It was probably some paper supplier, but she pressed the code that would allow her to get her voice mails.

Angie was buzzing around the kitchen, doing her best to empty out the fridge, yet watching Lucy's reaction to the voice mail she was hearing. She watched her friend's face drain of all color. "What?" she almost screamed.

Lucy hung up the old-fashioned phone and stared at her friend. "That was Luke Kingston. He said . . . what he said was . . . He said two agents from the FBI came to his construction site in Miami at noon today, just as he was leaving to go to lunch. They wanted to know if he had a key to the house in Palm Royal. He sounded really upset. Last night, when I talked to him— okay, flirted with him—his voice was totally different. It was almost like he thought I was . . . involved in something concerning that house. Crap, Angie, now what are we going to do? It's just a matter of time before they send someone here. I think there's an FBI office in Newark. Do you think we should go to a hotel?"

Angie dumped a stalk of celery in the trash can, followed by two soggy-looking weeks-old tomatoes. She looked up at Lucy and said, "Let's pack up our clothes and head out. I really don't care where we go as long as we are anywhere but here when the FBI or whoever shows up."

# Chapter Thirteen

The packing the girls had intended to do never got under way, because they decided first to have a glass of wine to toast their decision to clear out and head for what they considered safer accommodations. One glass of wine led to two glasses of wine, then three glasses, until the bottle Angie had opened the night before was empty. With only one bottle left, both women decided not to carry it with them, and they didn't want to throw it away.

"Waste not, want not," Lucy chirped as Angie uncorked the bottle and poured generously. "We're sloshed, Angie. We aren't going anywhere today, and we haven't packed our stuff, either. This is just soooo decadent, isn't it?" Lucy chirped again.

"I'm loving it," Angie said, raising her glass to clink it against the one in Lucy's hand. "Tomorrow is another day."

"Yes, it is. In the morning we will both have king-size hangovers, but who cares?"

"Certainly not me," Angie said as she kicked her shoes across the kitchen. "What should we talk about? We need to talk about something besides . . . besides . . . you know what."

"Do you want to talk about Toby or that hottie that called me from Florida? Oooh, he has such a sexy voice. And he was so easy on the eyes. He said he was a wuss and that his sister, Marie, was a daredevil. He said she wore a tiara and a tutu when she went down the zip line. I didn't even know what a zip line was. He had to explain it to me. He broke a lot of bones when he was a kid. He used to fly kites and go sled riding and all that stuff. Things I missed out on. Did you do those things, Angie?"

"Nope. We lived on a farm, and all we did was work." Angie finished the wine in her glass and poured more. "Drink up, Lucy. I'm ahead of you here."

"Fill 'er up, friend." Lucy downed the entire glass in one long swallow. "Okay, now we're even."

"Your eyes are crossed," Angie sing-songed.

"Ha-ha! So are yours."

"This will finish off the wine," Angie said, trying as hard as she could to peer into the wine bottle. "But the good news is there are four bottles of beer left, which we either have to drink or throw out."

"You know my feeling about wasting stuff. I say we drink it."

"You are the boss. By the way, when we officially get down to work, do I call you boss or do I just call you Lucy?"

"You can call me whatever you want, because you are my best friend in the whole world. You are my only friend. You're better than a sister. Sisters always fight and are jealous of each other. That's what the slick magazines say," Lucy said, then hiccuped.

Angie got up and teetered over to the refrigerator. She pulled out two bottles of

Bud Light and removed the tops. "One glorious hangover coming up."

Just as Angie started to say something else, the doorbell rang, sounding its three loud musical notes. Lucy's eyebrows shot up to her hairline. Angie, holding the two bottles of beer, flapped her arms wildly at the sound and almost dropped the Bud Lights.

"Who do you think it is?" Lucy hissed. "I never get company at this time of day. I never get company, period."

"We should have kept one of those damn guns. I'll see who it is, but I'm taking this with me," Angie said, putting down the bottles of beer and removing a wicked carving knife from the butcher-block container.

"Tell them . . . tell them . . . the mistress of the house is not receiving guests today," Lucy said as she struggled to get up from the chair. Angie pushed her back down as the doorbell's musical notes sounded again.

Angie sniffed as she waved the wicked-looking knife around. "Persistent, aren't they? If I have to stab them, we can drag them inside, and no one will know."

"We'll know," Lucy bleated.

"Yes, but we're leaving, and the house will be locked up."

"That's drunken logic," Lucy said as she tried once more to get up. Angie pushed her back down for the second time. "I will handle this!"

Lucy shrugged and leaned back in her chair. She had faith that her friend would do just that.

A moment later, she heard Angie call out, "It's that wuss you were telling me about, the one with the broken bones. Should I let him in?"

Lucy's hands immediately went to her hair to smooth it down. She realized she wasn't wearing makeup or perfume. Damn! This time she managed to make it to her feet and weave her way to the foyer. "You didn't stab him, did you?" she asked as she tried to focus on the good-looking man standing in the doorway.

"Not yet. Well, should I invite him in or not?"

Before Lucy could respond, Luke Kingston said, "Invitation or not, I'm not setting foot inside until you get rid of that knife."

"Well, Lucy said you were a wuss. Remember this. There are two of us and one of you."

"I'll remember that. The knife please."

Angie dutifully handed it over.

Lucy decided it was time for her to say something. She fumbled for words that wouldn't offend. "What are you doing here, Mr. . . . I mean, Luke? I'm sorry we can't offer you any refreshments. We . . . we drank them all. You said you were a wuss. I was just repeating what you said to my friend."

"There are two bottles of beer left," Angie said brightly.

Luke tried his best not to laugh. "Coffee would be good. It's cold out there," he said, jerking his head sideways.

"We can make a fire if you're cold. We can, can't we, Angie? What is he doing here?"

"No, we can't make a fire. I think we have some coffee."

"Ladies, show me the kitchen."

"You can't take charge like this. This is my house. What are you doing here? How many times did I ask you that?" Lucy asked belligerently.

"Two times. Just in case you're counting.

I'm going to make some coffee for you ladies. I came here to talk to you because . . .
because . . . Oh, it doesn't really matter
why, since there's no point in my trying to
talk to you when you are . . ."

"Drunk?" Angie said helpfully.

"I was going to say indisposed, but yes,
**drunk** also works. So, where is the coffee?"

Lucy tried to clear her fuzzy brain. Luke
Kingston was standing right here in her
kitchen, and she was drunk as a skunk.
**Such an impression I'm making,** she
thought sourly. She blinked. "You came all
the way here to make coffee and to talk to
me . . . us? About what?" That sounded
not too terribly drunk. She struggled to focus more clearly.

**Oh, hell, they both look guilty. But,
guilty of what? Maybe this was a mistake. No, it wasn't a mistake. You feel a
connection to this young woman. Sober her up and see what shakes out.**

Lucy took a deep breath. "Just because
we're . . . in . . . inebriated doesn't mean
we're guilty of something. Sobering me up
is your game plan. Aha, I'm right. See, Angie, he wants us to sober up so he can . . .
so you can what, Mr. Kingston?"

"Talk to you about something very important. Show me where the coffee is," Luke said curtly, "and stop reading my mind."

"Why should I?" Lucy said stiffly. "This is my house, and I can do whatever I want to do. Isn't that right, Angie?"

"That is absolutely right, spot-on, Lucy."

"It's impossible to talk to a drunk and doubly impossible to talk to two drunks," Luke said as he measured coffee into the wire basket.

"I heard that," Angie snorted.

"So did I," Lucy growled. "We aren't stupid. Tell us what you have to say."

"Good. Fine. Okay, then, the FBI came to see me today. About your house in Palm Royal. The house I built for your parents. They wanted a key to get into the house. Since I don't have a key, I couldn't give it to them. Even if I had a key, I would not have given it to them. They're going to get a warrant. We're talking the FBI, ladies. I told you all that in the message I left for you. Don't you pay attention to what you hear?"

Luke had seen his share of drunks during his lifetime. Until that moment, though, that very minute, he'd never seen two drunks sober up in a nanosecond. It had to be his mention of the FBI. "You can say something now, ladies."

Lucy's tone was several degrees beyond defensive when she said, "So let them look at the house, but I would think they'd need a warrant or something. There's nothing but furniture in the house."

"I can attest to that," Angie said smartly.

Luke just looked disgusted. "What did you take out of the house, and where is whatever you took out? FBI agents aren't stupid. They know something. Otherwise, they wouldn't be wasting their manpower. They were wearing guns, and they made sure I saw the shoulder holsters. Tell me what's going on and let me help you."

"We took . . . I took my parents' clothes. There wasn't anything in the house. They barely lived there. You were inside. Did you see even one personal memento or picture? No, you did not, because there were none. The place gave me the creeps. That's why I couldn't wait to leave."

"That's true," Angie said, backing up Lucy's story.

Luke poured coffee. **They're lying. One**

**lies, and the other backs her up. What the hell am I doing here?** "Drink!" he said, handing over cups of coffee.

"Why would I lie about my parents' clothes? I have no idea what the hell you're doing here," Lucy said tightly.

Luke let his eyes roll around in his head. **Damn, she really can read minds.** "I'm here because . . . because I felt . . . feel a connection to you, Lucy Brighton. I know that sounds corny, but my mother had green eyes just like yours. I wanted to get to know you better. Goddamn it, I want to help you. You are so out of your league here if the FBI is involved. Where are the things you brought back with you?"

**Ah, caught like a rat in a trap.** "What? You want to see my parents' clothes! Why? I understand the part about wanting to know me and feeling a connection to me, but my parents have nothing to do with what either you or I feel or don't feel. Isn't that right, Angie?"

"That is absolutely correct," Angie responded, right on cue.

"You stashed the stuff somewhere, right? You can't produce it, right? Is that what you're going to tell the FBI when they come knocking on your door? Do you know the penalty for lying to the FBI? The FBI can hold you for seventy-two hours without letting you call a lawyer. Then they can charge you with obstructing justice."

Luke had not the slightest idea if what he'd just said was true or not, but it sounded good. Evidently, the girls thought so, too, because both of them looked like they were going to start bawling any second.

"Talk to me!" he roared.

Angie started to wring her hands.

Lucy narrowed her eyes. "What kind of connection do you feel toward me?"

Luke threw his hands high in the air. "It's hard to explain. I just felt like I wanted to get to know you better. I liked your eyes. I think they're incredible. I guess I saw something in your eyes that just made me want to know you better. I tried flirting with you, but if you recall, you had just come home from the hospital, and I was the last person you wanted to see or talk to, or at least that was the impression you gave me. But, having said that, you did invite me in and let me look around the house I had built. I appreciated that. I also appreciated that you were in pain and still trying to be nice to me. I tried to think of ways to get to see you again, to talk to you. That's why I put that packet together, then called you. I was devastated when I went by the house and Adel told me you had already left the day before. And, by the way, Adel said she felt we were meant for each other. Then today, when the agents from the FBI came to the site in Miami, I had this awful feeling you were in some kind of trouble. So, here I am."

"Ooooh, that's so sweet. Isn't that sweet, Lucy?" Angie said, dabbing at her eyes.

"There's sweet, and then there's sweet," Lucy said flatly. "You just automatically assumed I did something wrong, and that's why the FBI came to see you. Didn't you for even one minute think maybe it was a mistake?"

"No, actually, I didn't, because my gut told me something was wrong. I didn't think it was you as much as I thought maybe your parents did something. Did I forget to mention that I also thought when I met you that you had the saddest eyes I had ever seen? Beautiful but sad. Look, I didn't know your parents. I heard rumors about how aloof they were, how they were never there, and, of course, about your father's refusing to treat Carl Palmer on the golf course. It was logical, I thought at the time, that you were either into something or covering something up. I still believe that. Whatever it is, those agents are going to find out. So, please, talk to me and let me help you before it gets out of hand."

Lucy drained the coffee in her cup. She no longer felt the least bit drunk. She looked over at Angie, who nodded ever so slightly.

"The people who lived in that house in Palm Royal and who died in that car crash were not my parents. I can't prove it, but my heart and my gut tell me they are not my biological parents. You're right. It isn't me. It was them. You might as well get comfortable, because it's a long story."

"I have all the time in the world. Are we going to need more coffee?"

"I'll make it," Angie volunteered. She busied herself getting out cups, spoons, powdered creamer, and sugar packets from one of the cabinets.

Luke settled himself at the table and folded his hands as he prepared to listen to whatever was going to be divulged. He tried to make his mind blank so as not to distract the beautiful young woman with the green eyes.

Lucy took a deep breath. "This is going to sound, for want of a better word, unbelievable, but I can't help that. Just let me get it all out, and don't say anything until I'm done." Another deep breath and she was like a runaway train as she started to talk.

From time to time Angie interjected with the words "It's true. Everything she's telling you is true." And, periodically, she would pour coffee, which no one drank.

"And there you have it," Lucy said forty-five minutes later. "If we hadn't decided not to waste the wine, we would have left, and you would still be standing on the porch, knocking on my front door. We didn't want to stay alone in this house another night, especially after the message you left on the phone. You can talk now, Luke. Do you have any questions?" Lucy asked anxiously.

"We can prove everything. We can take you to the storage unit. We didn't even unload Lucy's father's SUV. We just drove it into the pod, locked it up, and left." Angie related the story about the false name and the story she'd given the old man at the storage facility. "We could go there if you want to. I said I had a brother. So, what do you think?"

Luke's mind raced. He'd heard some stories in his life, but this one took the cake. All he had to do was look at the two women to know they were both scared out of their wits. "I don't know what to think. But I do believe you."

Lucy bent down to scratch at her foot.

"Stop that right now," Angie said. "You're going to get an infection."

Lucy shook her head. "What do you think we should do? Maybe we shouldn't have told you. We barely know you, and now you're involved in . . . whatever this is."

"Well, off the top of my head, I'd say you need to talk to someone. The fact that the FBI has made the first move kind of makes me think you should talk to them. Then again, I'm just not sure. It's a given that they will get a warrant to search the house in Palm Royal. Are you sure you cleared everything out?"

"I didn't leave so much as a thread behind. Unless they know that safe is there, the house will give up nothing. Seeing is believing, so let's go upstairs, and I'll show you the safe in this house. It's identical. You can make up your mind after you see it."

Angie led the way to the second floor, while Lucy took the chair rail.

"Where are the wires, Lucy?"

"In my purse on the bed. Turn on the lights, and let's get to it."

Inside the walk-in closet, Lucy turned to Luke. "Since you are seeing this closet for the first time, do you see any signs, any indications that there's a safe in this closet?"

Luke dropped to his knees and peered at everything, the floor, the molding, the walls. "No. This is an exact replica of the closet in Palm Royal. Your mother was insistent as to how much room she wanted in the closet. She even had a drawing to scale with the measurements. We had to make the master bath a little smaller to accommodate the square footage in the closet because she was so insistent. We did not install a safe. That had to have been done after they moved in."

The umbrella wires in hand, Lucy turned

to Luke and met his gaze. He had nice eyes, she thought. They were a soft gray, the color of the mourning doves who perched on her windowsill in the morning. She blinked. Gray eyes. With his curly dark hair, she would have thought he'd have dark eyes, smoldering eyes. Instead, his eyes looked kind and gentle.

"Okay, watch this," Lucy said, fiddling with the wires in her hand. She pressed the button, and Luke's jaw dropped as the floor started to slide open. He dropped again to his haunches and stared at the yawning opening.

"My hat's off to whoever installed this. It's a work of art. On his best day, my father couldn't have done this, and I know I sure as hell couldn't. This is true craftsmanship. I don't think I've ever seen a safe like this."

"That makes two of us," Lucy said quietly. "The one in Palm Royal is just like this one. A true duplicate." She pressed the digits on the keypads, then opened the doors to the three compartments.

"This safe had to be made to order. That means there are no serial numbers to identify the manufacturer. I'm also thinking this is foreign made."

"Considering the contents we told you about in both safes, do you think my parents were spies? I'm talking about my real parents. Not the people living in the house in Palm Royal."

Luke felt sick to his stomach. "I don't know, Lucy. I don't want to tar someone with a brush like that, but I would have to say it is definitely a possibility. We need to figure this out."

"We need to get out of here is what we need to do," Angie said.

"I don't think anything is going to happen tonight. Tomorrow is time enough to follow through on your plan to relocate. You do realize you can't hide from the FBI, don't you? What's that saying? 'You can run, but you can't hide'?"

Lucy sat back and leaned against the wall. She stared into the open safe. "My mistake was taking everything out of the safe in Palm Royal. I packed it up and moved it. I should have left everything just the way it was. The same thing goes for this safe. If I had left it alone, I wouldn't be going through this mess right now. If I hadn't panicked and moved everything and had gone to either the police or the FBI, I would have more credibility. Right now I have none. No one is going to believe me."

Angie slid down on the floor and wrapped her arms around Lucy's shoulders. "We could put everything back. We can go to the storage unit and get the car and drive it back to Florida. After we put everything back in this safe."

"That won't work, Angie. I destroyed the umbrella. I just have the wires. They'll know someone, meaning me, figured it all out when the umbrella isn't in the closet in Palm Royal. Why didn't I just leave it there?"

"Because you thought . . . you were going to find the same thing here, and you did. Minus the umbrella. This is so above my pay grade," Angie said morosely.

Both women looked up at Luke, who was towering over them. "I don't have a magic bullet, ladies, if that's what you're thinking. We need to put our heads together and come up with a plan."

"What kind of plan?" Lucy asked, her eyes full of hope.

"That's what we have to work out. We'll go downstairs and have a round table. We'll talk till we can't talk anymore. Something is bound to jump out at us. And we'll go from there. I'm staying here tonight. I'm not letting you two out of my sight."

Lucy almost swooned with relief. "That's . . . that's kind of you, Luke."

They were halfway down the stairs when Luke stopped and literally shouted, "I think I have an idea. Two of my closest friends live in New York. Jack has an older brother who works for some hush-hush branch of the government. I don't know what he does, and I don't think Jack knows, either. Maybe we could enlist his help or at least ask him to point us in the right direction. But if we do that, that means someone else knows about this . . . problem. Do we want to risk that? No, we don't. Forget I said anything. Jack can't keep a secret to save his soul. That's probably why his brother would never tell him anything."

Both women looked like he'd just rained on their personal parade.

"Don't worry. We'll come up with something," he assured them. "After all, there are three of us. Let's have some more coffee and run some ideas up the flagpole."

It was almost midnight when Lucy's eyes started to droop. Angie called a halt to their discussions. "We're beating a dead horse here. The bottom line is this . . . and, you two, tell me if you agree. Tomorrow morning we are moving lock, stock, and barrel to Freehold. When we get there, we are going to call the FBI office in Newark and ask to speak with an agent. We'll pick the time and the place. Perth Amboy sounds like a middle-of-the-road place. We'll tell him our story and go on from there."

"That's a plan," Luke said.

Angie laughed, but there was no mirth in the sound. "It should be. It's your plan. I was just summarizing it for us. So, do we all agree?"

"It works for me," Lucy said.

"Me too," Luke said.

"You two are forgetting something," Lucy said, a devilish glint in her eye.

"What?" Luke and Angie said at the same moment.

"I'll be able to know what the agent is thinking. Unless my mysterious power evaporates, and I do have to say that it is not as strong as it was. Dr. Lyons was right. My brain short-circuited, and it's mending itself little by little."

Luke grinned. "Well, that definitely gives us a leg up. If you girls don't mind, I need to call my dad and my foreman to tell them I'm staying on here for a few days."

"Go ahead. Angie and I will make a fire with what's left of the wood, and we'll spread some blankets and pillows down. We are not sleeping on the second floor tonight."

"Okay, that works," Luke said, fishing in his pocket for his cell phone.

Lucy and Angie left the room, their steps a little more jaunty than they had been earlier in the day.

"I'd say that guy is a keeper, Lucy," Angie whispered. "You like him, don't you? He sure seems to like you. You can see it in his eyes. And by the way, he really does have nice eyes."

Lucy nodded. "I like the way he stepped right in and offered to help us. He didn't judge us, either. The best part is, he believed us. But he's now involved."

"I think he's the kind of guy who can

handle anything. And what a body on that man!" Angie whispered as she clicked the switch on the gas starter. Flames raced up the chimney.

"Shhh, he might hear you," Lucy cautioned. Lucy's eyes twinkled. "And that would be a bad thing . . . ?"

Angie grinned. "Guess not. You know what, Lucy?"

"No, what?"

"I'm feeling a lot better about things now that Luke is here. How about you?"

"Absolutely. Definitely. You know it."

This time Angie laughed out loud. "Why don't you tell me how you really feel?"

"I thought I just did."

The women doubled over laughing.

"What's so funny?" Luke asked from the doorway.

"You really don't want to know," Angie said.

"Yeah, I do. No secrets here, okay?"

"Well, in that case . . ."

# Chapter Fourteen

Lucy lay quietly, wrapped in blankets and listening to Angie's soft, even breathing. The glowing numerals on her watch said it was 2:10, and she had yet to fall asleep. Across the room, where Luke Kingston was sleeping, all remained quiet. For some reason, she thought he would be a lusty snorer. Was there such a word as **snorer**? she wondered. She squeezed her eyes shut, trying to force sleep. It didn't help. It must be all the coffee she'd consumed. As far as excuses went, that was about the lamest she could come up with. In the past, coffee had never kept her awake.

What was keeping her awake was fear and concern about how she was going to deal with what she was facing.

Lucy looked at the orange-red embers in the fireplace. In another hour there would be nothing but smoldering black ashes, and then the room would be freezing cold, unless she got up and adjusted the thermostat. She squeezed her eyes shut again. Maybe, instead of thinking about the mess she was in, she should think about the white knight named Luke Kingston, who had shown up at her front door. She felt the same connection to him that he said he felt to her. **How strange is that?**

What was really strange was that he hadn't cut and run when she'd told him about her present predicament. He'd jumped right in and offered to help. Most people would have thrown up their hands and run like hell. Not Luke. She liked him. Not just a little bit, but a lot. Kissing him, she knew, would be an experience to end all experiences. And then . . .

Lucy squirmed in her cocoon of blankets. Thoughts of Luke and the possibilities that loomed out there would keep her awake forever if she continued. **Damn, I might as well get up and make a cup of tea. More caffeine.** Then she could take some of the big lawn bags and go upstairs to get a head start on packing up her stuff so she didn't have to do it in the morning. That was exactly what she should do. She moved then, quietly, and got up. She tip-toed, or tried to, across the room and out to the kitchen.

Lucy was taking the first sip of tea when she looked across the room to see Luke standing in the doorway. She wanted to smile, to say something witty, but the words wouldn't come.

"Couldn't sleep, huh?"

"I tried, but sleep wouldn't come. I tried every sleep trick I've ever heard of, but nothing worked. I'm too wired. Guess you couldn't sleep, either."

**If I could get you out of my mind, I might have had a shot at sleep. All I wanted to do was get up and crawl under the blankets with you.**

"TMI, Luke," Lucy said, setting her cup down on the table. "There's one tea bag left. Do you want me to make you a cup of tea?"

"You're right, too much information. Damn, I keep forgetting about you and your . . . special abilities. Well, would you have let me crawl under the covers with you?"

A devil perched itself on Lucy's shoulders. "Well, yeah. The fire died down, and I was cold. Nothing warms up a person like another person's body heat. No problem now, though. I turned the heat up."

The same little devil that was perched on Lucy's shoulders danced his way over to Luke's shoulder. He chuckled. "I don't much care for tea. So, here we are," he said.

**Well, that was brilliant for a one-liner.**

Lucy laughed. "On a scale from one to ten, I'd give it a three."

"You know, Lucy, it's really hard to keep my mind blank. And yet I never considered myself much of a thinker. Can we call a truce here, where you stop reading my mind?"

"That's your end. What do I get on my end?"

"My undying support."

"Okay. It's a deal."

"You're lying, aren't you? You can't turn it off, can you?"

"Yes and no."

"Like I said, here we are. What should we do?"

"Talk, I guess. Why don't you tell me more about you and your sister and how you got into the construction business. I like hearing about people's childhood. Like I told you, my own was far from normal. Tell me about your best memories, and this will go a long way toward . . . you know . . . our friendship."

They talked then like two very old dear friends until the sun came up.

Lucy's eyes were misty when she said, "Do you have any idea how lucky you are to have so many wonderful memories?"

Luke leaned across the table. "I do know, Lucy. Every day of my life I thank God for being so good to me. I'm just sorry you had such a . . . I don't know what word to use to describe yours."

"**Shitty** will do it."

Luke laughed. "When you have kids, you'll be able to revisit childhood with your own kids. It will be all the more precious to you."

"Kids? I just assumed I would have only Izzy, Bizzy, and Lizzy. I never let my thinking get beyond those cartoon characters."

"See, that's where you're wrong. My sister told me that those characters are so real to her kids, so imaginative, that she just assumed the person who created them, meaning you, was transferring her own childhood antics to Izzy, Bizzy, and Lizzy."

"Your sister is right. I do have a vivid imagination. I guess you could say they were my hungry dreams and wishes that never came true."

"Did you ever make a wish, like on the North Star, or when you blew out your birthday candles?"

Lucy made a strangled noise in her throat. "All the time, but they never came true."

**I'm going to make it my business to make all those wishes come true, come hell or high water. As soon as I find out what those wishes were.**

Lucy wisely remained silent as she stared out the kitchen window.

"Are you going to tell me what your wishes were?"

"I wished for a dog who would be allowed to sleep with me. A golden retriever.

I wished for a special friend who I could tell my secrets to. I wished for my parents to love me so much, they couldn't bear to send me off to boarding school. I wished for a big red wagon so I could put my dog in it and pull it around. I wished someone would teach me how to swim. The list is kind of endless. It doesn't matter. Not a single one of my wishes ever came true. Don't feel sorry for me, okay? If you do, I'll just feel worse."

"Okay." Luke sighed. "If you tell me where the nearest diner is, I'll go and get us some breakfast. And then we can get this show on the road."

"Go out to the end of my street, and make a right, then a left. Stay on Grove till you come to James Street. Stay on that and you'll see the Parsonage Diner. You can get Angie and me fried-egg sandwiches with bacon and a smidgen of ketchup. Get some coffee and real cream. And whatever you want, of course. They'll pack it in a heat bag, so it will still be warm when you get back. The food is really good. For diner food."

Luke was at the door when he turned

around. "I think I can truthfully say, this was the best all-nighter I ever pulled. I like you, Lucy Brighton. Your turn, Lucy Brighton."

"I like you, too, Luke Kingston. A lot, Luke Kingston."

The minute the door closed behind Luke, Angie burst into the kitchen. "Wow! All I can say, Lucy, is wow! That guy is so hooked on you. I mean hooked."

"You were listening!"

Hands on her hips, Angie looked indignant. "Of course I was listening. How did I know he wasn't . . . What if he had some kind of ulterior motive? I wanted to be ready to jump in and save you. I'm your friend."

"Well, now, don't you feel silly?"

"Not one little bit, my friend. I enjoyed the whole conversation. I'm thinking this guy might just be the one for you, Lucy."

Lucy laughed. A joyous sound. "I think you might be right."

Angie walked over to the kitchen door to look at the temperature gauge hanging underneath the hurricane lamp. "Oooh, it's forty-four degrees. How's your foot?"

"Really itchy. I was able to fix it myself when I got up. I can't believe how quickly it healed. Some spots are still very tender, but I'm out of the woods, and I'm almost finished with the pills. I know, I know. Don't say it. I am so lucky, and I know it. By next week I should be able to wear a tennis shoe if I don't lace it up."

"Lucy, are you taking all your things? Or are you going to leave some stuff here?"

"Well, believe it or not, I don't have all that much. I pretty much live in jeans and shirts. My fashionable wear is all in two garment bags. I plan to just dump everything in some lawn bags. Shoes and boots in one, winter jackets and sweaters in another. Three bags plus the garment bags, and I'm good to go. What about you?"

"My stuff is still in my car. I never unpacked when I got here, because you weren't here, and I don't know . . . I just didn't feel like unpacking. And then I called and found out about you and headed for Florida. Fifteen minutes, and I'm with you."

Lucy grinned. "When was the last time you slept in your clothes?"

"I don't think I ever did. We should do it more often. Look! We're ready!"

Luke took that moment to blow through the door. "It's cold out there, ladies, so be sure to dress warmly. Breakfast is served!" he said, opening the heated silver bags and setting out three fried-egg sandwiches.

"Oh, God! This is so good. You should try Lucy's fried-egg sandwiches, Luke. They're even better than these are, and these are good."

Conversation consisted of Luke's telling the girls about his father's cooking obsession after his stroke and how he tried to replicate his wife's recipes. "Sometimes, he is spot-on, but I never admit that to him, and neither does Adel. We always tell him something is missing or he almost has it but not quite. I don't want him to give up and sit in front of the television. He lives to cook. I think he feeds half of Palm Royal."

"That is so sweet," Angie said. "Does he bake, too?"

"Sort of. He has tried for two years to bake a better angel food cake than Adel. And, according to Adel, he actually succeeded, but she wouldn't tell him. She just keeps saying he doesn't get the vanilla right or he beats the egg whites too long. One thing about my dad is that he doesn't give up. I'd love to tell him about all of this, but I can't take the chance he won't say something to someone. Sometimes he forgets. He'd know exactly what to do."

"When he isn't cooking, what does he do?" Lucy asked.

"He plays poker one night a week with Bud, Judge Wylie, who is a widower, too, and lives two doors away, a couple of the neighbors, and a stock boy from Publix, who, according to my dad, is the biggest cardsharp he's ever seen. He walks twice a day. There are two widows he favors with his company from time to time. He goes into the office at least twice a week to tell everyone what to do. He spends quite a bit of his evening time on the Internet with my sister and the kids. We keep him busy. When my mother died, he went completely to pieces. They weren't husband and wife—well, they were—but they were one entity. That's how my sister and I thought of them. Actually, anyone who knew them thought the same thing. It was a hard couple of years till he came out of his cocoon and joined the world again."

"I hope I get to meet him someday," Lucy said. "He sounds just the way a father should be."

Angie, sensing a possible Lucy shut-down, interjected forcefully, "I think it's time for all of us to get on the stick and get out of here. I, for one, am ready. I folded everything up in the family room. The fire is out, and I closed the glass doors. Refresh my memory, Lucy. Are we leaving your parents' winter clothes in the closet? Or are we packing them?"

"My gut says leave them. Luke, disconnect the fridge and all the TVs. It will take me only fifteen minutes to toss my stuff in the bags. Don't forget my Crock-Pots. I'm taking all three of them. They're right there on the kitchen counter."

"You have three Crock-Pots?" Luke asked in amazement.

"She's the Crock-Pot queen!" Angie laughed.

"Now, that's funny. My guys call me the Crock-Pot king. That's how I cook when I'm on-site. You got any good recipes?" He twinkled.

"Nah. I just toss everything in the pot and hope for the best."

"Yeah, me, too." Luke continued to laugh.

Angie jabbed Lucy in the ribs. "Who knew! You guys have sooo much in common. Guess you're really meant for each other. I bet you could somehow work that into IBL."

"Where's that FedEx box? Don't let me forget it."

"What is it?" Angie asked.

"The prototype of Dizzie, the duck. I'm adding a new character to my trio."

"Oh, Lucy, that's great!" Angie said, clapping her hands.

"I'm excited about it, and so is Henry. He said the sales department told him that advance orders of everything have tripled, and once the advertising gets under way, they expect everything to go through the roof."

"Okay, then, let's get to it," Lucy said, looking around her bedroom. She quickly straightened out the covers on the bed and started dumping her clothes into the plastic bags. "See," she said, "I was right. Fifteen minutes on the dot."

"Did you check your night tables?" Angie called from the doorway.

"Good thinking. I forgot."

"What did you forget?" Luke asked from the doorway as he picked up one of the plastic bags.

"My drawers in my night table. Oh, my gosh, I would have forgotten this," Lucy said as she reached into a drawer and pulled out a little box. "It's my first tooth. The tooth fairy left me a silver dollar. I re-member how shiny it was. Look!"

Angie and Luke crowded closer to look into the little box. "You lost two teeth at the same time?" Luke asked.

"No, no. The little tiny one is mine. The other one is my mother's first baby tooth. She gave it to me." Lucy bit down on her lower lip as her eyes started to burn.

"Are you sure it's hers?"

"Why wouldn't I be sure? I remember her giving it to me the morning after I lost my tooth. We laughed at how funny I looked. She told me to wait, and she went out of my room. And when she came back, she had her baby tooth and a picture of her smiling with her missing tooth. She told me to sit still, smile, and she took my picture. I remember that clear as a bell."

"Where's the picture?" Angie asked.

"I don't know. She never showed it to me, or if she did, I forgot. Why are you two looking at me like that?"

"If that's your mother's tooth, then it has

her DNA. You said the cremated ashes in the storage unit might have teeth in them. You could, I would think, take those ashes to be tested, and if there is a tooth or even a remnant of a tooth, it will prove that the people who died in the crash are or are not your parents," said Angie.

Lucy nodded. She closed the little box and stuffed it in the pocket of her sweatpants. "I never thought of that," she said sadly, her eyes still burning.

Ten minutes later, the three of them were a caravan and were headed to the Garden State Parkway, with Lucy in the lead, Angie in her car, and Luke bringing up the rear in his rental car.

Forty-five minutes later, Lucy listened carefully to the robotic voice of her GPS and made a right turn down a gravel road, which she followed for a mile and a half. She wanted to tell the robotic voice this was the middle of nowhere, but she didn't. When she finally pulled up to the long circular driveway in front of a farmhouse that looked like it was built from tree trunks, she saw a huge van that said they were the MONMOUTH COUNTY NUMBER ONE CLEANING

SERVICE. Seven people were busy loading all manner of cleaning equipment into the van. A lady who said her name was Myrt walked over and held out her hand.

"We're done. We've been here since five this morning. I'd appreciate it if you'd do an inspection before we leave. I'd hate having to come back in case we missed something."

"I'll do it!" Angie said, running into the house. Ten minutes later, she was back, beaming from ear to ear. "Looks fine to me. What about the bunkhouse?"

"Around the back and down the embankment. A thousand feet or so," Myrt said.

Angie dashed off again and returned, huffing and puffing, little circles of steam jetting out of her mouth. "Just as good as the house."

"How do I pay you?" Lucy asked.

"You don't, hon. We have an account with the realty company. We do all their work. We just bill them. If you need us, just call. We left a card on the kitchen counter. We have a sideline in case you're interested. We decorate houses for Christmas. All with fresh evergreens. Like I said, if you need us, call. Thanks for the business."

The trio watched the big white van disappear down the driveway.

"Oh, Lucy, wait till you see the inside of this farmhouse. You are going to absolutely love it. And that bunkhouse, wow! We are going to have so much room to work, we will have to shout to each other to be heard. It all smells new and clean, and it is gorgeous. The furniture is just great. You didn't say anything about its being furnished. You won't have to buy a thing. It's warm and cozy, and wait till you see the fireplaces. There are six of them! And . . . it looks like a ton of wood piled into the cutout next to the fireplace."

"Then, let's check it out!" Lucy said, excitement ringing in her voice.

All Luke could hear were oohs and aahs as the girls went from room to room. He did a little oohing and aahing himself as he inspected the farmhouse. He liked the open rooms, loved the old beams. And Angie was right: the fireplaces were crafted by someone who knew what he was doing. He wasn't sure, but he thought a person could roast a whole steer in the fireplace in the family room. He just itched to build a fire. He decided to scratch his itch and got to it. By the time the girls came down the steps, he had a fire blazing.

"Is there a landline here?" Angie asked.

"In the kitchen, and it's on. The number is on the wall, next to the phone. Whoever it was that lived here was not high tech. There is a satellite dish on the roof, though, so I guess you get cable on that TV," Luke said.

"The beds are all made up," Lucy said, amazement ringing in her voice. "This is just beyond perfect. I love it all."

"How many acres come with this place?" Luke asked.

"Fifty-five," Lucy said smartly, "and don't ask me what I'm going to do with all that land, because I don't have a clue."

"Now what?" Luke asked.

"Now we unpack. One of us needs to go to the grocery store," Lucy said.

"The way you're looking at me indicates I'm the one to go. Do you want to make a list, or should I just pick up stuff as I go up and down the aisles?" Luke asked.

"Whatever works for you," Angie said, giggling. "Lucy and I will start bringing our stuff in."

"And then what?" Luke asked again.

"And then we call the FBI after we have lunch sitting at our new kitchen table with the food you are going to buy at the grocery store."

"So, that's the plan?"

"Yep," Lucy and Angie said in unison.

When the door closed behind Luke, Angie turned to Lucy and said, "You know, I really do like that guy. I bet he comes back with one of everything in the store."

Lucy laughed. "That's a sucker bet. By the way, did you call Toby, like I asked you, to bring our mail down at the end of the week?"

"I did, and he said no problem. He said he's on your street every day, delivering something or other to that software guy who lives across the street from you. We talked a bit, and I'm really looking forward to our date on Saturday. Hey, if Luke is still here, and we aren't in jail, we could double-date. What do you think? This way, none of us will feel the stress of a first date."

"That works for me. But what makes you think Luke is still going to be here?"

"Trust me when I tell you that guy is going to be here until you boot him out or some crisis in Florida needs his attention."

Lucy smiled as she headed for the stairs with one of the trash bags.

It took the girls exactly one hour to unpack their belongings and settle into their rooms.

"This," Lucy said, waving her arms about, "is what a bedroom should look like. In my opinion. Hard rock maple, braided rugs on pine floors, a four-poster with a wedding-ring quilt that even I recognize as hand quilted. Don't you love those organdy tieback curtains on the windows? The fireplace is great. The bathrooms aren't all that modern, but that's okay. How's your room, Angie?"

"Just like this one, but the quilt on the bed is a different color. It's perfect, Lucy."

"Now, if we can just keep it like this, I will be one happy camper."

"Lucy, just don't think negative thoughts. We are going to come out of this just fine. It's going to be the getting there that will pose the problem, but we'll definitely prevail."

"I love your optimism, my friend. I am so glad you are here with me. You know, I just had an idea. You know those fifty-five acres? We could build you a house of your own, and you will be just down the road from me and will be my neighbor for when you and Toby tie the knot."

"What did you say?"

"C'mon, you heard me. I know in my gut you two are a perfect match. The house will be my wedding present to you."

"If you weren't my best friend, I'd push you down these steps right now." Angie laughed. "I suppose it could happen. Do you think our kids will have red hair? I'm not sure how I feel about redheaded kids."

Lucy laughed and couldn't stop. "When they're your own redheaded kids, you will love them as much as you will love their red-haired father. Trust me."

In the kitchen both girls looked around.

"Hey, this is a Wolf stove. These appliances are top of the line. This breakfast nook is simply out of this world. I don't know all that much about handcrafted furniture, but I think the table and chairs are handmade. And the table in the nook looks like it was made from old oak trees. Look how wide the planks are. I bet Luke will know, since he's a builder," said Angie.

"Did I hear my name mentioned?" Luke asked as he walked into the kitchen, carrying two huge grocery bags. "I have eight more in the car."

Angie and Lucy rushed out to the driveway and started to haul the bags out of the car assembly-line style. Luke grabbed them and sprinted for the door, then returned for another armful.

"You bought one of everything, didn't you?" Angie asked.

"Pretty much. I bought ham, turkey, and cheese subs, and I stopped to get Dunkin' Donuts coffee. Bought five bags. I know how you gals love coffee, and I didn't want you to run out."

Working together, they had the groceries all put away within twenty minutes, and coffee was dripping into the pot.

They ate off paper plates that Luke had bought, bright red ones to go with the kitchen decor.

"Eat slowly," Lucy said. "Because the minute we're done, we have to call the FBI."

"Not so fast," Luke said. "My dad called me while I was shopping, but I had left the phone in the car. His message said to call him as soon as I got the message. He said he played poker last night, and Jonah Wylie told him something that made his blood run cold. Jonah Wylie is the judge I told you my dad plays poker with. I can't be sure of this, but if I had to take a guess, I'd say those two FBI agents who paid me a visit at the construction site went up to Palm Royal and tried to get a warrant for your house. From the tone of my father's voice, it didn't sound to me like Wylie caved in to them, FBI or not."

"Is that bad or good?" Lucy asked in a shaky voice.

"I don't know. That's why I waited till I got here to tell you, so we'd all be together when I called Pop."

"Okay, call him," Lucy said in the same shaky voice.

# Chapter Fifteen

Luke thought he could feel the anxiety from the two women, which seemed to be swirling about the room, as he stared down at the phone in his hand. He took a deep breath and pressed the number one on his speed dial. He hoped his father was having a good day and wasn't too upset with whatever news he had to deliver.

Father and son made small talk as the girls listened. They both understood that Luke was trying to be calm and not rush his father, but when the conversation didn't turn to the judge, Luke prodded his father.

"So, Pop, what was it you wanted to tell me about Judge Wylie?"

"Oh, we were playing poker last night, and Jonah lost his shirt, which made him cranky. Even my double chocolate fudge cake didn't help, and you know how he loves my double chocolate fudge cake."

"And . . . ," Luke said, trying to get his father back on track.

"First, he asked me if the Brighton house was for sale. I explained about the daughter and how she got struck by lightning. Then Bud went on and on about what a lovely girl she was and how he and Adel took care of her. Bud is the one who said she packed up everything and went back to New Jersey. We both explained how the house couldn't be sold by an outside broker and that the daughter didn't know what she was going to do with the property. Jonah knows that we don't allow outside brokers. He didn't know anything about the Brightons' daughter, though, until we told him.

"That's when Jonah got real cranky and lost the hand he was playing and threw the cards down on the table. He said two

FBI agents came to him to ask for a warrant. He said they were out of the Miami bureau. That ticked him off right there— agents stomping on his turf, as he put it. He said they didn't have probable cause for a warrant, and he denied it."

"Then what happened?"

"Then Jonah got really ticked off. He'd lost three dollars by that point. He was fuming. You know how he hates losing. After Jonah left, Bud said that he thought smoke was going to come out of Jonah's ears."

"Yeah, Pop, but then what happened?"

"Jonah said the two agents were like wet one-legged roosters as they fussed and fumed at him. He said he sent them packing. He did ask me what kind of security locks were on the doors at the house. I told him the best money could buy. That's it, son. Are you worried about the girl's house, Luke? Do you want me to hire some security? I can, you know."

Luke looked at the girls to see what their reaction was. They just stared at him, both shrugging their shoulders.

"No. Just tell Adel and Bud to keep their eyes open. And maybe the neighbors across the street. Try not to make a big deal out of it, Pop. If you hear anything else, call me."

"How long are you planning on staying up there, son?"

Luke looked at the girls and smiled. "As long as it takes me to help out here." He smiled again when he saw Lucy's look of relief and Angie's closed fist shoot in the air. Ah, it was nice to be loved and wanted. Very, very nice indeed. He slid the cell phone back into his pocket and stared across the table. "What's our next move?"

"Is that normal for Miami FBI agents to go all the way to Palm Royal? I would think agents in a field office in that area would be the ones to ask for a warrant. Or is it one of those turf things you see in the movies, where different agencies don't co-operate with each other?" Lucy asked.

"I don't have a clue, Lucy. This is all as new to me as it is to you. The bottom line here is that someone wants in that house, and Judge Wylie denied them access. Where it goes from there, I have no idea. I'm thinking the next move will be that either someone from Florida will come here or someone from here will seek you out.

It's just a matter of time before they find you. They have resources we can only dream about."

Lucy whirled around. "Angie, call Toby and tell him that if anyone spots him on the street and tries to question him, he knows nothing. I'm sure he will cooperate. Tell him that whatever he does, he shouldn't give out this address."

"I'm on it," Angie said, delighted that she had a reason to call the redheaded FedEx driver.

"Now you've involved a fourth person, Lucy," Luke said.

"I know. Five if you count your dad, and seven if you count Adel and Bud. Although Adel and Bud might suspect something is going on, they don't know for sure."

"Unless Pop tells them. He's not into secrets and such. He thinks everything is open for discussion. He didn't used to be that way but after . . . What I'm trying to say here is, we can't count on Pop to keep quiet."

"So now what? Do we call the FBI or wait for them to find me? I'm also thinking Newark would be the office I would call if I were still at home. There must be one closer, here in Monmouth County. I'm thinking Red Bank. Maybe even Asbury Park. I don't know if Asbury Park is in Monmouth or Ocean County. We're now in Monmouth County. Where I lived before is Middlesex County. Help me out here, Luke," Lucy said fretfully. "What do you think we should do?" Lucy looked over at Angie, who was babbling a mile a minute to Toby, a huge smile on her face.

"Honest to good God, Lucy, I don't know. It's one of those 'damned if you do, damned if you don't' kind of things. The fact that you found the safes and moved the contents both in Florida and here in New Jersey could raise eyebrows. Those agents looked sharp to me, so they'll probably automatically think you're guilty or somehow involved. The fact that they're openly sniffing around means they think they're onto something. If you call them, you can defend yourself by saying you panicked and didn't know what to do. And there is the fact that you got struck by lightning and were hospitalized, and therefore, you weren't thinking clearly." Luke threw his hands high in the air just as Angie finished her call to Toby.

"He said okay, no problem. What did I miss? You two look like you lost your last friend."

Luke repeated what he'd just said to Lucy for Angie's benefit.

"Well, if my vote counts, I say call the local office closest to here. Ask them to come here. You can use your foot as an excuse as to why you aren't traveling. Think of it as a preemptive strike of sorts. We'll just bandage you up before they get here. I say **they** because I assume agents travel in pairs."

"I'm going to call for the simple reason that I cannot, I will not, live like this." Lucy got up, and in her haste to get to the portable phone on the kitchen counter, she stumbled and hit her foot on a claw-foot of the round table. Her yelp of pain was so loud, Luke later said she could be heard all the way out to the highway.

Lucy's face drained of all color, and her eyes rolled back in her head. Luke caught her just as she was about to crumple to the floor.

"Oh, God, this can't be good. Quick, carry her into the family room. There's a recliner. Put her in it, and raise the foot-rest," Angie instructed.

Tears rolled down Lucy's cheeks from the pain she said was shooting up her leg.

"I'm going to call Adel."

Angie's voice could be heard clearly by both Luke and Lucy in the family room. It was short of hysterical as she related what had happened.

Luke wiped the tears off Lucy's face with his shirttail. "Just hang on, Lucy. We'll have you fixed up in no time."

Luke bent over to remove the soft slipper on Lucy's foot, and to his horror, it seemed as if the foot had ballooned out to twice its size. Heat? Cold? He couldn't think.

"Crushed ice! Or frozen peas. We don't have any frozen peas. Elevate her foot!" Angie roared from the kitchen. Luke could hear the ice maker in the refrigerator engage.

Angie dumped the contents from the ice maker into a plastic grocery bag, then wrapped the bag in a soft dish towel. She had it wrapped around Lucy's foot in a nanosecond. "I'll get you one of the pain pills. Where's your purse?"

"On the counter," Lucy gasped.

"I know this says 'Take one,' but I'm go-ing to give you two. The worst thing that can happen is you fall asleep. Luke and I will watch over you. Is the pain lessening?"

"It's not shooting up my leg now, but it's settled into the deepest part of where the burn was. God, this hurts."

"Adel is calling Dr. Lyons. She said she'll call us back."

"Thank God for Adel and her forty years of nursing experience," Luke said gruffly as he watched Lucy swallow the two little white pills Angie had handed her.

Angie looked down at Lucy's foot and gasped. It was twice the size of her right foot. "I didn't know it was that swollen. Should I call Adel back?"

"No, wait for her to return your call. I think she'll figure it out on her own. Lucy jammed her foot. That's the bottom line. When I played football in high school, it happened all the time, but mostly with the guys' hands. Coach made them work through it. He used to say, 'Ah, stop being a baby. You just stove your fingers.' Mean-ing you jammed them straight on against a hard object. How's it feel now, Lucy?"

"Cold and numb. The pills are starting to work. We should call the FBI now, before I fall asleep."

"Screw the FBI," Luke said indignantly. "Your foot is more important."

"Maybe so, but I want to do it and get it over with. Can you get me the phone, Angie?"

"Can you wait till Adel calls back? I don't know if this phone has call-waiting or not. She should be calling any minute now."

"I can call on my cell or your cell or Luke's cell. Crap, no, I can't. No sense giving them any more information than they need. Okay, we'll wait till Adel calls, but then I'm calling. Luke, do me a favor and see if there's a field office in Red Bank or Asbury Park and copy down the number."

The words were no sooner out of Lucy's mouth than the phone rang. Angie listened and kept nodding. "Okay, I did that. And I did give her two pills. I just heard that term from Luke a minute ago. Yes, it means she jammed her foot head-on. I forgot to tell you, it's swollen to twice the size of her right foot. **Stove.** It doesn't matter if it's an old-fashioned term or not. I understand it. Okay, twenty minutes on and twenty minutes off. Frozen peas . . . Yes, I got that, too. I'll send Luke out to the store. Thanks, Adel. Of course I'll call you. I will be sure to give Lucy a hug from you and Buddy."

Lucy was asleep before Angie could hang up the phone. "Ice is to be twenty minutes on and twenty minutes off until the swelling goes down. She said Dr. Lyons said she should be good in twenty-four hours. He said she might have some discomfort and some minor swelling, but that's normal. Oh, and she is to stay off her foot for twenty-four hours. I'm sure that's going to go over like a lead balloon when Lucy hears it."

"That's it? That's all she said?" Luke asked gruffly.

"Of course that's all she said. Why are you still standing here? You're supposed to go to the store for the bags of frozen peas. Get two bags, so we can alternate. Stop looking like that. Lucy is going to be fine. Go already!"

Luke beat feet and was back in exactly thirty minutes. He was breathless, and his eyes were glazed, which made Angie smile. Lucy slept peacefully in the recliner.

\* \* \*

"Now what?"

Hands on her hips, Angie glared at the anxiety-driven man standing in front of her. "Do you think I'm an authority on everything? Now would be a good time to build up the fire so this room stays warm. Check out all that food you bought and prepare or start to prepare some dinner for us."

"Okay, okay. What are you going to do?"

"Me? I'm going to sit here and watch the soaps."

"Is that another way of saying I'm in your hair, in the way?"

Angie tried her best not to laugh. "Kind of. Sort of. Yeah."

"You are so cruel!" Luke walked over to the fireplace and sat down on the hearth. "I think I'm in love with Lucy," he said in a dazed voice.

"Ya think, Luke? Wow! Big revelation there, big guy," Angie said as she turned on the television.

Luke threw some logs on the already blazing fire. Sparks shot upward as the flames danced and shot in every direction. "Are you always such a wiseass?"

Angie grinned. "The answer is no, I am not always a wiseass. Well, hardly ever. I was just jerking your chain. Let's be clear on something right now. Lucy and I are survivors of a sort. If I think or get the feeling that you're going to hurt my friend, I will personally slice off your balls and jam them up your ass without a second thought. How's that for clear?"

"Crystal," Luke said, turning his head so he wouldn't laugh out loud.

"So, what's for dinner?" Angie asked sweetly.

Luke made a mental note never to cross the young woman sitting in the recliner next to Lucy's chair. "How does grilled chicken, Tater Tots, and a spinach salad with my own special dressing sound? The dressing is pretty much vinegar and sesame oil with a little ginger."

"Sounds good, except I don't eat chicken."

Luke sucked in his breath. "Okay, how does grilled shrimp, Tater Tots, and a spinach salad with my own special dressing sound?"

"Go for it. Shhh, this is getting good now," Angie said, pointing to two people with clenched fists preparing to square off on the wide-screen TV.

Luke threw his hands in the air and sat

down at the kitchen table, a cup of coffee in front of him. He needed to think. For some reason, he always did his best thinking at the kitchen table, with a cup of coffee in hand. His thoughts took him to the magnificent house he'd built for the Brightons and the misery it was now causing. Now he understood why Lucy had said she might take a wrecking ball to it. He felt the same way.

His cell phone found its way to his hand, and he called Bud, who picked up on the second ring. He identified himself and asked for a favor.

"Sure. What can I do for you? I checked on your dad a little while ago, and he's fine."

"No, Bud, it's not Pop. I want you to call Zeke and have him install top-of-the-line security locks on the Brighton house. That's an upgrade from the ones we installed when we built the house. They cost a small fortune. Just have them put it on the Kingston account. Can you do that for me?"

"Well, sure, son. But why do you want me to call Zeke? First of all, God alone knows where he is, so I'd probably waste hours trying to find him. I can do it. Just tell me what you want, and I'll get right on it. Luke, what the hell is going on with that house?"

"If I knew, I'd tell you, but the fact of the matter is that I just don't know. Go to Denby's. We have an account there. Get what you need, and do it as quick as you can. One other thing. Do you know anyone who could dust the inside of the house for fingerprints?"

"I know a guy, Lionel Atmore, who is in this line of work. I'll give him a call."

"Thanks, Bud. Call me when it's all done, okay?"

"Look, Luke, I'm not trying to be nosy here, but does this have anything to do with Jonah and what he said at the poker game last night? You mixed up with the FBI somehow?"

"Not me, Bud. It's Lucy, and through no fault of her own. It was her parents' house. When I get this figured out, you'll be the first to know. Don't say anything to Pop, okay?"

"Gotcha. Okay, I'm on my way. I should have it all done before dark. I'll call you."

Luke shoved the cell phone back in his pocket. He looked up to see Angie standing in the doorway.

"I heard. You're worried, aren't you?" Angie asked as she poured the last of the coffee into a cup. She sat down and stared across the table at Luke.

"I am. I just cannot wrap my brain around any of this. What's your feeling on the people who lived in the house? Do you think they were Lucy's parents or not?"

"I'm inclined to believe Lucy," Angie said quietly. "She's their daughter. That didn't sound right. You know what I mean. She said she didn't feel anything. Lucy is very intuitive. She has strong feelings about everything, and she's usually right. She can get emotional like the rest of us, but she can sift through the crap, if you know what I mean. Look at how she figured out the combination that finally opened the safe. If she says they aren't her parents, then they aren't her parents. End of story."

"No, it's not the end of the story. If they weren't her parents, then who the hell were they? And why were they masquerading as Helene and Fritz Brighton?"

"If I knew that, we wouldn't be sitting here having this discussion now. Would we, Luke?"

"I think I know how we might be able to

figure out who they were. They must have left fingerprints in the house. If we can find someone who knows how to dust for prints, we might be able to find out. The problem is, I don't know anyone like that. From what I've read and seen in movies and on TV, there is this gigantic database that can be accessed. And guess where it is?"

"Where?"

"The FBI. That's where."

"Let's go on the Internet and see what we can find out. Someone out there will know how to dust for fingerprints. We can find out, and Bud said he knew someone who could do it in Palm Royal. Then we can go back and check the house we just moved out of. I'm on it! I'm on it!" Angie said. "I just have to find my laptop."

"Lucy's okay?"

"Yes, she's sleeping soundly. Two more hours, and the pills will wear off. I checked the swelling, and it's started to go down a little." Angie looked at her watch. "Time to put the frozen peas on again."

"I'll do it. You do the Internet thing."

"So it's shrimp and those crummy pota-toes and salad for dinner?"

"I'm revising my menu. What was I thinking with Tater Tots? I'm going to make shrimp scampi. And salad, of course. I might whip up something for dessert," Luke quipped as he opened the freezer section of the refrigerator.

Angie lounged in the doorway. "Just out of curiosity, where did you learn to cook?" Luke thought it sounded like the most serious question on earth.

"From my mother. She made sure Marie—that's my sister—and I both knew how to cook, how to wash clothes, clean a house, and do the marketing. When I was in college, I was the only one who had white T-shirts and underwear, because I knew you didn't wash your whites with blue jeans or red shirts. One of my friends went through four years of wearing pink socks and pink underwear. I also had the fluffiest towels, because I knew you had to put fabric softener into the last rinse. Because I knew how to cook, I aced free food for the last three years, when I shared a house with five other guys. They paid for the food, and I cooked it."

"Bet that looks good on a résumé," Angie said, a big grin on her face.

"Now you are being a wiseass."

"Ha-ha."

Luke sprinted into the family room and checked on Lucy. She was still sleeping, but he knew she was going to have a stiff neck when she woke up. He didn't disturb her, though, other than to brush her hair back and stroke her cheek. She didn't so much as twitch. He nestled the frozen peas around her ankle. Angie was right—it did look like some of the initial swelling was receding. Satisfied that all was as well as could be expected with the new love of his life, he added another log to the fire before he returned to the kitchen. No sense in Angie telling him he was like a lovesick teenager, even if he was acting and feeling like one.

Back in the kitchen, Luke cleaned two pounds of shrimp and returned them to the fridge. He did his prep work for the salad. Remembering his promise to whip up something for dessert, he pulled a frozen coconut cream pie, one of his favorites, from the freezer and set it on the counter to thaw. That would have to constitute whipping something up.

Now all he had to do was wait. Unfortunately, waiting had never been one of his passions in life. In fact, he downright sucked at waiting and had the scars to prove it. He realized he was way too wired to stay there in the farmhouse, so he put on his jacket and decided to go for a fifteen-minute run. When he got outside, he was stunned to see that it had begun to snow very lightly. Flurries. He made a mental note to check on the weather report when he got back inside. What could be better than being snowbound with the woman he was falling in love with? Silly, silly, silly.

# Chapter Sixteen

Zaretsky and Associates was located in a one-story building on a busy street in a suburb of Fort Myers. It was not clear from the sign outside exactly what sort of business was carried on inside. Once one entered the building, one encountered a very long corridor leading to a room at the very end. From the outside, at first glance, that room could have passed for a storage room. There was no nameplate on the door to designate what it was used for. What there was, was an eyeball scanner on the left side of the massive door, which pretty much said no admittance unless your eye-ball scan was on record.

Inside the room, it was a different story. There were no windows, but the room was filled with brilliant fluorescent lighting. The room was also soundproof. The carpet was deep and lush. The table, which could seat eighteen, was solid mahogany and highly polished. The chairs were covered in buttery-soft beige leather. They were the kind of chairs in which a person could easily fall asleep. But no one ever fell asleep in the chairs, for the simple reason the people sitting on them couldn't relax. There wasn't so much as a piece of paper or a paper clip to be seen. Everything in the room was as high tech as the government could make it. Although there was a sideboard covered with delectable pastries and a variety of drinks, not a single one of those seated around the table would eat or drink.

Entrance to the room was by invitation only. Those who had the good fortune, or in this case, the misfortune, to be invited into the room referred to it as the chicken coop.

Four agents, whose official jobs were handlers, sat quietly as they waited for their host to appear. They were on time. Their host was not. Each was thinking the man's lateness was not a good sign. And they were right.

Their host roared into the room like a lion, justifying the fact that, among his staff, he was referred to as a lion. He was tall, six-foot-four in his bare feet. He had a mane of snow-white hair that hung to his shoulders. It was full and lush. He was deeply tanned, with incredible blue eyes, and his teeth were strong, even, and pearl white. It was impossible to tell the man's age. He could have been sixty, or he could have been forty. The man exuded power and confidence in his custom five-thousand-dollar suit, designer tie, and handcrafted shoes. He wore an expensive Rolex and a three-carat diamond in his right ear. It was rumored among the staff that he had a fleet of cars, a yacht, and his own Gulfstream. He came from old money—so old, it was moldy. His current job for the government paid him one dollar a year. To date, he had collected a total of twenty-two dollars for his years of service. And he always cashed the check when it was issued on December 30 and bought a roll of antacid Tums with his yearly salary.

The man went by the name of Julian Metcalf, but only a fool would think it was the name on his birth certificate. Just as the names the guests in the room went by were aliases.

Metcalf's voice was deep and melodious when he said, "Talk to me, ladies and gentlemen. Time is money, and our government is running so far in the red that you need to make every word count." He pointed to the man on his right, who went by the name Ken Blevins. "You're up, Blevins."

Ken Blevins spoke. His voice sounded confident when he said, "The assets checked in at 4:02, as usual. There were no problems. I recorded the conversation per instructions, as I have done every day at the same time for the last five years. Nothing happened that day prior to the check-in call. I did my two drive-bys at ten A.M. and again at three A.M. Both covered in my report. I signed off, and Charlene Davis came on duty."

"Charlene?"

"I did my two drive-bys, one at ten P.M. and the second at five A.M. Everything was normal. We didn't know anything was wrong until the daughter showed up late that morning. The assets did not indicate they were expecting the daughter to visit at any time prior to the check-in calls. We just assumed it was a spur-of-the-moment visit. I called Ken and informed him and tried to figure out why she was there. That's how we found out the assets had been killed in a head-on car crash late the day before. The daughter met with the detective assigned to the case on her arrival, then went to the mortuary. She returned to the assets' house, and that's all the information we have on her arrival. There was no way to get into the house, so we just waited it out. I called Don Henderson in New Jersey, and he verified that Lucy Brighton had left the house, gone to the airport, and flown to Florida that same morning."

"Don?"

Don Henderson looked across at their host. "I checked with the airline. Lucy Brighton booked her flight the night before on the Internet. She flew in first class, rented a car at the airport, and that's all I know about her trip. I confirmed with Charlene. Then I called Ellie, and we met up, entered the house, and checked everything, just as we have done numerous times before when Ms. Brighton would leave the premises. We perceived everything to be normal.

"Once we apprised Ken and Charlene about what we had seen, we faded into the background and waited to see what would shake out. When they told us the assets had been killed in a car crash, we made out our report and waited for further orders, and here we are. I should add that two days later, a young woman named Angela Powell showed up at the house, her car packed to the rafters, as though she were moving in. She was there overnight. Then she booked a flight to Florida, leaving her car and belongings behind. Everything in the house at that point was intact and normal. That's the end of my report," Henderson said.

Julian Metcalf stood up and swung his head from left to right, his mane of white hair swirling about so that he looked like an avenging lion on the prowl. "There is nothing normal about this at all. Ken?"

"There was no way to get into the enclave, sir. The Kingstons have security that rivals the White House, and the residents pay for it. Our visitor's passes, compliments of the assets, were rescinded at the time of the assets' death, so we were not able to enter the community. At least we assume they were rescinded, because when we tried to go through, we were denied, and the guards confiscated our passes. The guards are not rent-a-cops or the kind you find at Walmart. These guys pack heat and aren't afraid to show it. They're all ex-paramilitary. They make more in salary a year than some bankers. Not to mention their medical benefits are off the charts. And they get bonuses at the end of the year. The rich know how to live," Ken Blevins said. "Short of a warrant, no one gets into that enclave."

"Ms. Brighton, from what we could gather, packed up her parents' belongings in the father's SUV. She was going to drive it back to New Jersey. Unfortunately, she was struck by lightning in the driveway on the day she was scheduled to leave. A UPS driver on the road at the time and two neighbors, the Longhursts, saw it happen and called 9-1-1, and Ms. Brighton was taken to the hospital. Ken and I at that point thought, and **thought** is the operative word here, that we could enter the house, citing an emergency, but in the end we had to back away and, as he said, our passes had been rescinded. The neighbors are on watch, as well as the Longhursts. It was simply too risky to try anything else. We found out all of this on the news and from the local paper," Davis said.

The four handlers waited for Metcalf to respond to the information they had provided.

When he did, he asked, "Where do we currently stand?" There was so much ice in the man's voice that the four handlers inwardly winced.

"The house in Palm Royal is now empty, but we have to assume that the neighbors are still on watch. Angela Powell arrived the day after Lucy Brighton got out of the hospital, and they packed up and left. The neighbors, Adel and Bud Longhurst, are front and center in all of this. It appears they've taken over the care of Ms. Brighton. Powell drove the father's car all the way to New Jersey. They stopped overnight, but that's all we know," Henderson said. "Ken and I put it together. Via Skype."

"Yesterday, we're told, two FBI agents from the Miami office visited the Kingston building site in Miami. In less than two hours, Luke Kingston, Jr., was on a flight to New Jersey," Davis said. "As you know, sir, the locals do not like sharing information. We were lucky we got what we did."

"We also know that Luke Kingston went straight to the Brighton house. Today they departed the premises, locked it up tight, and are now in a farmhouse in Freehold. We did an Internet search, and it looks like Lucy Brighton bought the fifty-five-acre farm and has moved in. She took everything from her studio. A packing firm came in and packed up everything and took it away. Don and I were about to check the house when we got the call to come here instead."

Julian Metcalf stood. He took a moment to shrug his broad shoulders and shoot his cuffs. He looked at Henderson and Ellie

Carter and said, "Take the next shuttle back and give me a report on the house the minute you check it out." He looked over at Ken and Charlene. "You two go with Don and Ellie and stake out the Freehold place. Since there is no electronic security at either the main house or the farmhouse, you shouldn't have any problems. If you run into a problem, squelch it by whatever means necessary. If you need help, request it. I'll send a new team of agents to Palm Royal. There are many ways to secure a warrant, and I know them all."

Metcalf leaned across the table and, in a normal-sounding voice, said, "I want this wrapped up as soon as possible, with little to no blowback. The reassignment schedule is due in two weeks, and there are four openings in Egypt and Caracas."

The door opened and closed. The four agents looked at one another without saying a word. Metcalf's warning was all too clear. "Screw this up, and you're on the first plane to Caracas or Egypt." The four handlers knew everything in the room was recorded, so they wisely remained silent, but their eyes and expressions spoke volumes.

Outside, in the brisk October air, the four agents/handlers clustered around their respective rental cars.

Ken Blevins, senior in the group, said, "We'll talk on the plane."

# Chapter Seventeen

The clock on the range said the time was 6:15 when Luke entered the house from his run. The phone was ringing, but no one picked it up, so it went to voice mail. Lucy woke just as Angie locked the door behind Luke to keep out the snow that was spiraling behind him.

"It's snowing!" Luke said as he ran his fingers through his damp, curly hair. He hung his jacket on a hook by the back door, then shook his whole body like some big shaggy sheepdog. "It's not just flurries now. It's actually snowing."

"Well, we certainly have enough food to

weather a blizzard. When I parked in the garage, I saw a snowblower. Guess who gets to try it out first! In case you're interested, I'm hungry, and Lucy just woke up. And it's time for the frozen peas," Angie said, opening the freezer.

Luke snatched the frozen vegetables out of Angie's hand and sprinted to the family room. Lucy was indeed awake and squirming in the chair.

"How does it feel now?" Luke asked, his expression one of concern.

Lucy tried to smile. "It aches, but the pain is mostly gone, so that's a good thing. Even I can see that some of the swelling has gone down. How long did I sleep?"

"A few hours. I just went for a run, and it's snowing out now. I was going to start on dinner. I hope you're hungry. Do you need another pain pill?"

"I am hungry, but no hurry. I don't want any more pain pills. I'll just take some Advil. I don't like taking drugs unless I absolutely have to. Who called?"

"I let it go to voice mail," Angie said. "Luke came in, and I just couldn't get to the phone. I'll check it now, while Chef Luke starts our dinner." She winked at Lucy, who grinned from ear to ear.

Lucy looked up at Luke, the grin still on her face. It was all Luke needed to rush to the kitchen to prepare his new love's dinner.

With Luke out of earshot, Angie said, "Yep, I think you got that guy wrapped up."

Lucy just smiled as she snuggled into the deep recliner, her thoughts skittering all over the place. She watched and listened to Angie as she went through the process of checking the voice mail. At least she now knew the phone had voice mail. The smile left her face as she saw Angie's eyes pop wide, then saw how she clenched her teeth.

"What?" The one word exploded from Lucy's mouth so loudly, Luke ran in from the kitchen.

"That . . . that was Toby. He said he was running late on his deliveries and just hit your street, and he said there was a man and a woman going into your house! He said he was standing on the stoop of the software guy, waiting for him to open the door, and he saw them clear as a bell.

He said they were driving a blue PT Cruiser. He said he turned his truck around and started back up the street to pretend he had a delivery on your side of the street. He wanted to see if any lights went on in the house. None did, but he said he thought he saw what looked like a flashlight's beam on the second floor. He wants us to call him back to tell him if he should call the police. What should we do, Lucy?"

Lucy looked up at Luke. "What should we do, Luke?"

"Tell him to call the police," Luke said. "By the time they get there, the intruders will probably be gone. Then tell Toby to get out of there."

Angie's hands were shaking so badly, she had two false starts before her call went through. When Toby picked up, she blurted out Luke's decision.

"When you didn't call me right back, I went ahead and called the police. They're on the way, and the people are still in the house. I hope I did the right thing."

"You did, Toby. You did. But you need to get out of there or else move farther away, where you can watch what's going on. Keep this line open, and I'll stay on the phone."

"He called the police. They're on the way. You heard my side of the conversation."

"Tell him to get the license plate off the Cruiser," Luke ordered.

Angie relayed Luke's message. "He says he already did that. He said he even gave it to the cops when he called it in."

"This is rush hour. By the time the cops get there, whoever is in my house will be gone. I just know it, and just my luck," Lucy said.

"Maybe not," Luke said soothingly. His forced tone did nothing to calm Lucy's already frayed nerves.

"Dammit! Toby said they're coming out of the house, and there is no sign of the cops. He said he can't hear a siren, either. He said they aren't carrying anything, so they didn't steal anything. Okay, they're in the car, and they're moving. He wants to know if you want him to ram his truck into their car. He said he'll probably get fired if he does that, but he's willing to do it."

"No, for God's sake, no!" Lucy bellowed. "We can't involve him any more than he is already."

"Toby wants to know if he should follow them."

"No!" Luke shouted. "Just tell him to get the hell out of there."

Angie relayed the message. "Okay, he's leaving and will call us back. He's going to park around the corner and wait to see what happens. He said he's going to take a package out of the back and walk down the street."

"No, no, no! Tell him not to do that. Did he call in anonymously, or did he give his name?" Luke asked.

"Anonymously at first. Both, actually. He said he got scared and gave up his name so they would take him seriously. Okay, he's leaving. He's driving by the house now, and the cops are walking around with flashlights. There are two of them. One is heading for the back. He's out of sight now. That's it," Angie said, breaking the connection.

"If Toby is right, and they . . . whoever they are . . . headed to the second floor, we know they know I know about the safe and probably removed everything. How long before they find their way here?" Lucy asked.

"Since you didn't tell anyone in the neighborhood you were relocating, how can they possibly know you're here?" Luke asked as he smacked one balled fist against the other.

"Doesn't the FBI have carte blanche in things like this? They can tap into your phone records, follow your credit-card purchases. We stopped for gas and charged it. They have eyes and sources everywhere," Angie said. "Let's face it. We wouldn't even be thinking in terms of the FBI if you hadn't told us they showed up at your construction site. Now they probably know you're here. Where does all of this leave us?" Angie asked, fear ringing in her voice.

"I knew I should have called them before you gave me those pills. Hand me the phone, Angie. I'm going to do it right now."

"Shouldn't we discuss this a little more?" Luke asked.

"I think we've discussed it a little too much already. We're past the stage of discussing." Lucy reached for the phone in Angie's hand.

"What's the number, Luke, the one for the Red Bank office? You looked it up earlier." Luke repeated it to her, and without a moment's hesitation, Lucy pressed in the digits that would connect her to the Red Bank field office of the FBI.

When an operator came on the line, Lucy identified herself and asked for an agent to come to the farm as soon as possible on a matter of the utmost importance. She listened a moment and said, "No, I do not care to discuss this matter on the phone. If you don't want to hear what I have to say, then you can read all about it in the **New York Times** tomorrow or the day after tomorrow, depending on how quickly they can get a reporter here, and I'll be sure to mention how helpful you people at the FBI are. I am sure that they will be very anxious to obtain an interview with the founder and CEO of IBL. Yes, that IBL. You realize, of course, that you are public servants, and that I and my fellow citizens pay your salaries? Of course you do. I'm hanging up now."

"Wow! That was good, Lucy."

"Yeah, except for the threat," Luke drawled.

"You mean the **Times?** That wasn't a threat. That was a statement of fact. They have been trying to get an interview with me for the past six months. How's dinner coming?"

"Oh, it's coming," Luke drawled again. "Fifteen minutes, and we'll be chowing down on the best shrimp scampi you've ever eaten."

Angie looked down at the watch on her wrist. "But you're still standing here."

"Yes, I am. The frozen peas have two more minutes to go. Double duty is how I look at it. So, make that seventeen minutes till dinner. It would be nice if you'd set the table."

"I can't. I'm waiting for Toby to report in." Angie laughed. "Go ahead. I'll take the bag off and take Lucy to the lavatory. Get cracking so we can eat. With our luck, that FBI team will show up just as we sit down to eat."

Dinner was every bit as good as Luke said it would be. They were just getting ready to start on the dessert Luke had whipped up when Lucy instructed Angie to go around the house and turn every light on.

"Even all the outside lights. In case the

agents can't find us in the dark, since we are two miles off the highway. You did say it was snowing out, didn't you, Luke?"

"Yes, it's coming down pretty hard now, and the ground and bushes are covered," Luke said, peering out the kitchen window. He sliced the pie and served everyone.

Angie poured coffee. "We're lit up like a Christmas tree. I think they'll be able to see all the lights a mile away."

It was just shy of nine o'clock when the front doorbell chimed to life. Both women looked at Luke and said, "Showtime!"

Luke hurried to the front door to answer it while Lucy and Angie remained in the kitchen. The women looked at one another as they strained to hear any conversation coming from the front of the house. They could hear conversation but couldn't make out what was being said.

Luke entered the kitchen a minute later, followed by two men wearing heavy outerwear. They looked angry and sullen. No doubt, Lucy thought, they had been pulled out of a nice, warm, comfortable office. She didn't care.

Luke took the initiative and introduced everyone. "I checked their credentials, Lucy.

They're who they say they are. Have a seat, gentlemen. Coffee?" To his surprise, both men accepted the offer of coffee. Angie moved over to the counter to get it.

"This is my story. These are my friends. First off, they have nothing to do with any of this. They're here trying to help me. Aren't you going to write this down?" Lucy asked.

Special Agent Brad Gerrison patted his pocket. "It's recording."

"Well, in that case, here we go." Lucy spoke quickly and concisely for a full forty-five minutes. She barely stopped the whole time to take a deep breath, but she did watch both agents carefully, trying to figure out if they believed what she was telling them. When she finally wound down to what had just transpired via Toby's phone call, she said, "And here we are."

Special Agent Jim Restin leaned his elbows on the kitchen table and stared directly into Lucy's eyes. She didn't blink. "So, what you're saying is, the people who died in the Florida car crash are not your parents, but people masquerading as your parents. Is that correct?"

"Yes, that is correct. Right this moment,

I can't prove it, but I think that in a day or so, I can. As odd as this may sound, I have my real mother's baby tooth, and it will have her DNA on it, and it can be compared to that of the woman who died in the car crash. Even though the couple was cremated, I was told that often there are tooth fragments in the deceaseds' ashes." As an afterthought, she added, "They're in a safe place."

"And you say you secured the contents of both safes."

"Oh, yeah, and we covered our asses on that, too, Special Agent Gerrison. We sent off a letter to two different lawyers to hold for us in case anything goes awry," Luke lied with a straight face.

"Are you telling me your agents in Florida didn't tell you about all of this?" Angie asked, suspicion ringing in her voice.

"No, ma'am, they did not. This is the first Agent Restin and I are hearing about this."

"Are you going to call the local police in Edison about the break-in at my house? They were given the license-plate number of the car."

"We will check on it all, ma'am. Let's go over some background again. Is there anything else that makes you think the people you say were masquerading as your parents are not your parents?" asked Agent Gerrison.

"Like I told you, my father is a renowned heart surgeon. You can Google him and see for yourself. There is no way on this earth my father would not have treated a man suffering from a heart attack, the way those people said he did. Think about it. The reason the man posing as my father didn't offer to help was that he's not a damn doctor. Even an idiot can figure that out. Plus, those people did not mingle. In fact, from all accounts, they barely lived there. The one time I went to visit them, I knew that something was off, wrong somehow. They couldn't wait to get rid of me. I was only there for eleven hours, and I slept for six of them. And yes, they more or less looked like my parents, but cosmetic surgery can work miracles. They are not my parents. Were not my parents," Lucy said adamantly.

Agent Restin blanched at the intensity in Lucy's voice. "If the people in Florida weren't your parents, where are your real parents? Do you suspect something? Or do you know something that will help us locate them?"

"If I did know, do you think we'd all be sitting here having this conversation? I don't think so. I don't know. This is just my opinion, but I think my parents are/were spies of some kind. My father had the perfect cover. He traveled all over the world, operating on people. My mother went with him most of the time because she's a doctor, too. I think the house in Florida and the one I lived in in Edison were what spy novels call safe houses. When you see the safes built into the floor in both houses, and we show you the contents, I think you'll come to the same conclusion. Why else would there be a box of false documents and all that money? Don't forget all that artillery, either."

Luke weighed in. "You're the FBI. Can't you find them?"

"No crime has been committed," Agent Gerrison said, looking over at his partner.

"That we know of," Angie said forcefully.

"It's not illegal to have fake passports and driver's licenses that are locked up. It's when they're used that it becomes a crime," Restin said.

"And the guns!" Lucy asked.

"They were locked up, too. For all we know, your parents . . . the people living in the house had permits to keep them. Maybe they belong to someone else, and they were just storing them," Gerrison said.

Luke thought that neither man believed a word they were saying.

"I might buy that if it was just the one house. But two houses with identical safes that were custom made, both opening with the same combination, kind of knocks your opinion out the window, wouldn't you say? Not to mention that the contents in both safes were almost identical," Luke all but snarled.

"Why did someone break into Lucy's house a little while ago, and why did your agents in Florida try to get a search warrant for Lucy's house there?" Angie blustered, her eyes wild. "We're not stupid here, so don't go thinking we are."

"I don't think either Agent Restin or myself indicated in any way that we thought any of you are stupid. What you're telling us is bizarre. Neither of us said we don't believe you. There's nothing we can do tonight. We're going to go back to the office, and we'll be back first thing in the morning, and you can take us to where you've secured all the things you told us about. Will that work for you?" Gerrison asked.

"I'm not sure. I think I am going to want to talk to my attorney before I turn anything over to you. I think I speak for Angie and Luke, too. None of us are anxious to have this melodrama continue with us as the bad guys."

"Understandable," Agent Restin said. "Let's agree to talk tomorrow morning at eleven. That way, Agent Gerrison and I can work through the night, trying to pin down some of this. Are the three of you okay with that?"

Angie and Lucy looked over at Luke, who nodded slightly to show he agreed.

"Then we'll say good night, and we'll be back in the morning."

"I'll show you out," Luke said as he reached for the agents' down jackets, which were hanging next to his own on the clothes rack by the back door.

"Drive carefully," Luke said in his most neutral voice. The moment the two agents were outside the door, he slammed it shut and ran back to the kitchen.

"It's snowing like hell out there. Cross your fingers those guys make it safely back to their office. All things considered, they took it better than I expected. Let's face it, it is a bizarre story. My gut says they believed every word we said. Now, Lucy, was that a threat about calling your lawyer or not?"

"I'm smart enough to know you never agree or sign anything without your lawyer okaying it. And how are we going to get him here tomorrow by eleven o'clock? Especially if the weather is bad. The flip side to that is, what if he says, 'Do not take the agents to the storage unit, and do not turn anything over'? Then what do we do? We're back to square one. And worse yet, we're swinging in the wind. My house has been violated. Sooner or later, they're going to find us. Whoever **they** are."

"I think this calls for a drink," Angie said. "I know you bought wine, Luke. Where did you put it?"

"In the cabinet on your right."

"And tomorrow is another day," Lucy said wearily.

# Chapter Eighteen

Luke swept Lucy up in his arms and carried her into the family room, where the fire was blazing and the room was cozy warm. He was amazed at how light she felt in his arms, how right she felt, like she belonged there. He hated to settle her in the recliner. His heart was beating triphammer fast. He was in love. There was no doubt about it.

"My first day in my new house, and I haven't had time to enjoy it," Lucy grumbled, just to have something to say because she wasn't quite understanding what she was feeling where Luke Kingston was concerned. Was it possible she was falling in love? She'd never been in love. Yes, she'd had so-so relationships, but nothing that even came close to what she was feeling at that moment.

"I meant to ask you, Lucy," Luke said gruffly. "How is it this place is furnished so nicely and you got to move in so quickly?"

Lucy was glad of the reprieve. "When I first took the virtual tour months ago and expressed interest, the Realtor said the estate of the man who lived here wanted to sell it, so they renovated it and furnished it, thinking that would help sell it quickly. Then, when the lawyers did the title search, they came across some irregularities, and they had to take it off the market. Since I was the first one to make an offer back then, they contacted me when all the legalities were settled. I paid extra for the furnishings, and I'm paying rent for this first month, but the house won't be officially mine for thirty days. It was win-win for me and the estate. They wanted a quick sale, and I wanted out of that house in Edison. The main thing that caught my eye about this farm was the bunkhouse. It just seemed so perfect for a studio."

Angie had made a nest of pillows by the fireplace. She looked over at Lucy and Luke and decided that three was a crowd. "If you guys don't mind, I think I'm going to go up to bed."

Lucy and Luke nodded as Angie got up and headed for the second floor.

"I've been thinking about something, Lucy. I know we touched on this earlier, but I think we should talk about it some more. I know you and Angie both think that your parents were spies. And you know what? Maybe they were, but for the good guys. For the United States. Right now I refuse to believe that the parents who produced you could ever do anything wrong. That didn't come out quite right, but you know what I mean. Any mother who gives her daughter her own baby tooth had to have loved you deeply. You told me about that memory of your father playing train with you. That's love. Why would they go off the rails and turn into spies? You said everything changed when you were ten. That was when they sent you off to boarding school. Maybe that's when your parents were approached to . . . to spy by our own government."

"God, Luke, you have no idea how badly I want to believe that."

"I want you to believe it, because I believe it. The thing is, which agency would they spy for? Homeland Security didn't exist back then. That leaves the CIA in Langley, Virginia. The CIA is foreign. The FBI is domestic. And yet all contact seems to be coming from the FBI. That's what isn't making sense to me. You know what else, Lucy? It didn't make sense to Gerrison and Restin, either. I could tell."

Lucy nodded in agreement just as Luke's cell phone rang.

"Bud! Talk to me."

"The new locks are on. I even put a new security panel on the garage door. The guy I told you about, Lionel Atmore, spent three hours dusting the whole house for prints. I was there the whole time, so don't worry about his being alone in the house. I don't know where he got it, but he had something called a mobile print reader, and it takes a digital thumbprint. First, though, he had to lift the prints and do some stuff to them. He said cops use it at homicide scenes. He got Lucy's print, Angie's print, your print, along with four other prints. I didn't add my and Adel's prints, but if you do, that means he recovered nine sets of prints total. Two of which are the Brightons' or belong to the people posing as the Brightons. He has some kind of in with someone who works for the DMV. We have four sets of prints with names. I'm going to upload them and send them off to you."

"Who do the prints belong to, Bud?"

"I don't know who they are, Luke. They're just names to me. All I know is they are registered with the Department of Motor Vehicles. Is there anything else you need me to do? Adel wants to know how Lucy is. What's going on, son?"

Luke gave him the short version but managed to cover everything. Bud was speechless. "I'll call you tomorrow, after we speak with the agents again. Lucy can't decide if she wants to call her lawyer or not. Listen, Bud, thanks for everything. Give my love to Adel."

Luke looked over at Lucy, who was sound asleep in the chair. How beautiful she looked, how peaceful in sleep. He hoped she wasn't dreaming about this mess. He got up and added some logs to the fire. He stared into the flames for a long time as his thoughts ricocheted all over the place. He let loose with a mighty sigh and walked out to the kitchen, where he finished off the pie, which was still sitting on the counter. Then he popped a Bud Light and sat down at the table.

Luke looked at the kitchen clock. It was almost midnight. He called his foreman, knowing full well that Jim Denver never went to bed before one in the morning.

"Jim, listen, I want you to do something for me. Pull the blueprints for the studio we built for that wannabe Jackson Pollock artist in Boca. I want you to file for all the building permits, hire a new crew, and have them build that exact structure behind my house in Palm Royal. No, I'm not planning on becoming an artist," he snapped before he severed the connection.

Was he jumping the gun? Putting the cart before the horse? What if Lucy didn't want to marry him and live in Florida during the winter months? He told himself that if he could make the move painless, she would agree if she loved him. Then, when they went back north during the summer months, he could build something there. Win-win! He didn't want to think about the possibility that Lucy might say no to a marriage proposal.

**God, I haven't even kissed her yet. They need to lock me up and throw away the key.**

As he swigged his beer, Luke's mind raced. Where was all of this going? What would be the outcome? There were so many what-ifs, he was getting dizzy. Then again, maybe the wine he'd had before, together with the beer, was giving him a buzz.

Luke realized he wasn't the least bit sleepy, so he made his way back to the family room, where he checked on Lucy, then poked at the fire. **Well, that took all of three minutes,** he said to himself. **Maybe I should walk around and check out this old farmhouse.**

At first glance, he'd realized they just didn't build houses like this anymore. This place had character, and its flaws just made it perfect in his eyes. He eyed the open beams with the wooden pegs used for nails. He came to the conclusion that a tornado couldn't destroy the place. Everything was solid. He loved it and applauded Lucy's good taste in buying it.

As he walked around, Luke turned off the lights one by one. The fire in the room gave off plenty of light, as did the television, which was set on mute. He was in the kitchen. He could see the swirling snow underneath the light fixture. He turned it off, and the kitchen went totally black. That was when he saw through the kitchen window the pinpoint of light off in the distance. The farmhouse was much too far from the highway for a car light to shine this way. He hadn't seen any lights on the barn at the back of the house. No, this pinprick of light was on the road that led to the house. He quickly checked the stout Dutch door, which Lucy had said she loved the moment she saw it. Iron hardware, top-of-the-line security locks. No one was getting in through this door. He ran back to the front door and checked it. Just as stout, the same iron hardware and security locks. No one was getting in this door, either. He ran back to the kitchen to check the door that led into the garage. The previous owner obviously believed in safety and security. Always a big feature when one was trying to sell a house. He sighed so loudly, he scared himself.

Luke inched closer to the door leading to the laundry room, which gave him a partial view out the kitchen window. By stretching his neck almost off his shoulders, he was able to see that the pinprick of light he'd seen earlier was now more like a large dot of light. Someone must be slogging through the snow on foot. Did one light mean one person? Well, if it was an LED light, then yeah, that would be enough light for a small army. His stomach crunched into a knot.

Luke thought about the weapons they'd hidden in the storage unit. They should have kept one, just in case. **Yeah, right,** he told himself. **If the girls had done that, I probably would shoot myself in the foot.** Nonetheless, he needed a weapon. What was available? A butcher knife? The poker from the fireplace. One good swing could do some serious harm. A knife, now, that was iffy. He'd have to be in just the right position to make that work. The only experience he had with a knife the size of the one on the kitchen counter was last year, when he'd carved the turkey at Thanksgiving.

Luke debated then. Should he go up-stairs and wake Angie? It wasn't that he was a coward, because he wasn't. He knew he'd die trying to protect the two women, but he didn't want them to be asleep and not know what was going on. He'd let Lucy sleep, but Angie needed to be aware of what was going on. He checked the dot of light, and it seemed that it was in the same position as it had been in a few minutes ago.

Luke sprinted down the hall and up the staircase. He poked his head in every room until he spotted Angie under a mound of covers. He ran over and shook her shoulder. "Shhh, it's just me, Luke. Some-one is outside with a flashlight. Lucy's sleeping," he hissed in Angie's ear.

Startled, Angie gasped. She had been about to scream until she heard Luke's voice. She swung her legs over the side of the bed, wide awake already. Dim light from the bathroom night-light filtered into the bedroom. Luke blinked as he consid-ered Angie's getup. She was wearing flan-nel pajamas and heavy socks. He watched as she pawed around the bed for her fuzzy robe. She slid her feet into slippers that looked like snow boots. "What? Didn't you ever see pajamas before?"

"That's a lot of clothes to be wearing to bed with all those covers you have piled on the bed. Don't you sweat?"

"No, I don't sweat, and I like to be warm. What? You think Lucy doesn't go to sleep wearing the same thing? You think she wears chiffon and lace? It's cold out. It's snowing. It's probably thirty degrees outside and sixty in this bedroom. Why are we having this conversation, Luke? Furthermore, I wouldn't need all these clothes if there was a man in my bed to keep me warm. I see you have the poker. Where's my weapon?"

"You get the butcher knife. I checked the house from top to bottom. Trust me, no one is getting in here. This is . . . this is just in case."

"If no one is getting in here, just in case of what? The intruder is going to come down through the chimney?"

They were at the bottom of the steps and tiptoeing out to the laundry room.

"Take a look and tell me what you think."

Luke had to grab hold of the back of Angie's robe so she could lean farther out to look through the window to where he had seen the light.

"You're right," she whispered. "That's an LED flashlight. I have one in my car in case I break down at night. The light is amazingly bright. It's hard to tell how close or far away they are. The beam seems to be small, so they could be closer than we think. What should we do, Luke?"

"Wait and see what they do. I debated calling the police, but I didn't. I wasn't being macho or anything like that. I kept thinking about Lucy saying too many people are involved in all of this. There's no way anyone is getting into this house. That I can guarantee."

"From your lips to God's ears," Angie whispered.

Luke could sense Angie trembling, so he brought her up to date on Bud's endeavors. "The thing is, the names Helene and Fritz Brighton did not come up on the DMV data list. We have names. That's all. I'll turn them over to Gerrison and Restin when they get here in the morning, if Lucy okays it."

"That has to mean Lucy is right. The people living in the house weren't her parents."

"Yeah. Who the hell were they? Isn't the end of October too early to have this much snow?"

"Yes and no. Last year we got a storm the first week in November that practically crippled the northern part of the state. Florida is looking better and better as the days go on."

"Tell me about it. Whoever it is out there isn't making very good time. Or else the snow is knee deep," Luke said.

"So, when they get here, what? Are they going to knock on the door? Are they stupid enough to think we'll open it at this time of night in the middle of a snowstorm? Have they seen too many of those **Halloween** movies? Give me a break!" Angie scoffed.

"Well, if you really want to go for a stretch, try this on. They could bomb the house, set fire to it, and throw tear gas through a window."

"You really had to say that, didn't you?"

"You asked. That's what they do in those

thriller movies. The good guys always make it out safe and sound at the last second," Luke said testily.

"Luke, just between you and me, where do you really think Lucy's parents are? Do you think they're dead?"

"If they were alive, don't you think they would have gotten in touch with their only daughter? What kind of parents would go through all this crap and have it come down on their child's head? Who the hell needs or wants parents like that? I don't know, Angie. We can speculate until the cows come home, and we won't know unless someone tells us."

Angie looked up in the dim light of the laundry room to see the anguish marked on Luke's face. "I'm going to check on Lucy."

"Juke down and stay away from the windows."

"Okay."

Julian Metcalf looked as confident, poised, and pristine as he had earlier in the day. He bent down so the reader at the side of the door could scan his eyeball. He hated these late-night meetings. He should be sitting in his favorite reading chair with his pipe and a snifter of hundred-year-old brandy, but he was here, and he was freezing. The trip from his residence in Georgetown to here at CIA headquarters in Langley, Virginia, following the flight back from Fort Myers had been a nightmare, what with the snow and sleet that were icing the road. He knew he would end up bunking there for the night. Just the thought irritated the hell out of him.

It pleased him to see the three men seated at the table, waiting for him. His immediate superior, the assistant director of the FBI, and the head of the Florida office of the FBI.

"Has the snow let up?" Metcalf's superior asked.

"No, and it's getting worse. Can we get to it? It's late."

A pudgy little man with owl-like eyes, who was the assistant director of the FBI, spoke. "Might I remind you, Mr. Metcalf, that you came to us to pull your chestnuts out of the fire. We cooperated all the way down the line in the spirit of interagency commitment. This has turned into a cluster fuck the likes of which I've never seen.

Your people, Blevins and Davis, were spotted entering the Brighton house in Edison. The local police have the license-plate number on the car they were driving. There was a witness, whom the police refuse to name. They came out of the house empty-handed, so that tells me the contents of the safe you told us about at our first meeting are gone. Meaning the Brighton woman has figured it out and stashed it somewhere. Am I right so far, Mr. Metcalf?"

Metcalf clenched his teeth. He hated this little toad of a man. "Yes, sir, that is correct. Henderson called me and said it was dry. Everything is gone. However, we know where the Brighton woman went. Blevins and Davis are on the way to Freehold as we speak. In fact, they should have gotten there well over an hour ago."

Metcalf's superior spoke. "Call them off."

"What? Why?"

"Because earlier this evening, some clown ran a DMV check on the fingerprints found in the house in Palm Royal. The guy's name is Lionel Atmore. He fancies himself as a part-time detective and computer hacker. And he sometimes works as a security guard at a local Walmart. He did it on the request of someone named Bud Longhurst, who lives directly behind the Brighton house in Palm Royal. We picked Atmore up and sweated him till we got what we wanted. He said this Bud person was doing it for Luke Kingston, Jr., who, by the way, is with the Brighton woman in Freehold. They now know that the people living in the house in Palm Royal were not the girl's parents.

"Assistant Director Brewster is spot-on. This is a real cluster fuck. The woman somehow found the safe and cleaned it out. That's the only reason she would drive that big SUV from Florida to New Jersey. She had a first-class return ticket to fly home. And even if she didn't, as the founder and CEO of IBL, the cost of an airplane ticket is nothing to her. Hell, she could have chartered a Learjet on her own. Are you following me here? We need to fall back and regroup. Call them off. Now."

While the other three men watched, Metcalf pulled out his cell phone and fired off a text message, telling Blevins and Davis to abort their mission. Metcalf longed for one of his Tums, but he'd left them in his car.

"It's logical, then, to assume that since she found the safe and figured out how to open it, she took everything, then did the same thing when she returned to New Jersey. The young lady is not stupid, gentlemen. Plus, she now knows that the ringers in the house were not her parents," Metcalf's superior said.

"It might interest you to know that the Brighton woman called the Red Bank, New Jersey, field office earlier this evening and literally demanded that someone go to her farmhouse and talk to her," said Brewster. "She threatened to go to the **New York Times** with her story if they refused. I do not know if she was bluffing or not, but as the CEO of IBL, there is no chance the **Times** would not jump at the chance to interview her about anything she wanted to talk about. Can you imagine the headline in the **Times?** FBI REFUSES TO INVESTIGATE POSSIBLE TERRORIST ACTIVITY. WORLD-FAMOUS HEART SURGEON GOES MISSING: DAUGHTER ALLEGES CIA CONNECTION."

Brewster went on. "Two of our best agents, Agents Gerrison and Restin, met and talked with her and her two friends, Angela Powell and Luke Kingston. She told them about the safes and offered to show them the contents later. But she flat-out refused to tell them where she stashed the contents of both safes. She said she wanted to talk to her lawyer, and the Kingston guy indicated that they'd sent letters to other lawyers outlining everything. My agents have spent the last few hours trying to figure a way out of this so you crackers at the CIA don't give the FBI a black eye or a bad name. Since this is your puppy, we're signing off right now."

"Hold on, Brewster. You can't do that. Where's your spirit of interagency cooperation?" Julian Metcalf demanded. "The CIA has saved your sorry asses more than once. Turnabout is fair play."

Brewster grimaced. "Where are the real Helene and Fritz Brighton? Do they know about the deaths of the imposters? Do they have any idea their daughter is now involved in any of this?"

Julian Metcalf chewed on the inside of his lip. "They're safe. They're half a world away, but like everyone else in the world, they have Internet access, and they use that to stay in touch with this world. They found out earlier today about the auto crash and the two deaths. And the answer is yes, they know that their daughter has become involved. Fritz told me that his wife collapsed when they heard the news. They want out from under."

"Like I said, a real cluster fuck," Brewster intoned.

# Chapter Nineteen

Lucy stirred and moved slightly, stretching her neck one way, then the other. She was definitely going to have to stand under a hot shower to work the kinks out. She looked down at her ankle and was stunned to see that it was its normal size. And there was no pain to be felt. "Thank you, God," she whispered.

Lucy looked over at the other recliner and saw Luke sprawled half on the chair and half on the floor. A smile tugged at the corners of her mouth. He certainly was good-looking, not that looks counted, because he was also a kind, warm, gentle person, and without a doubt, she felt . . . what? That she wanted him in her life, and not on a temporary basis. What would it be like to kiss him? To feel him take her in his arms and make the world go away? Damn nice, she was sure of it.

She realized she needed to tell him how she felt, to tell him how thankful she was that he had taken the time to come here and help her and Angie. Wiggling and squirming, Lucy got up and tested her weight by planting her injured foot on the floor. She winced, but it was okay. She moved gingerly then over to the chair where Luke was sprawled. She dropped down to her knees and brushed the dark curls from his forehead. "I know you can't hear me, but I just wanted to say thank you again and to tell you that I . . . that I . . ."

"Love me?" Luke whispered, his eyes popping open.

"I've never been in love before, so I'm . . . I'm . . . Yes, I think so. Isn't the guy supposed to tell the girl first?"

Luke smiled. "I did, but you were sleeping and couldn't hear me. I'm kind of gutless that way. I was afraid you'd tell me to pack up and hit the road."

"Is that what you thought?"

"Uh-huh. So it's okay to stay?"

"As long as you want," Lucy whispered.

Luke moved.

Lucy moved.

Just when their lips met, Angie barreled into the family room, then barreled back out. "Guess no one cares that the coffee is ready," she muttered, a devilish smile on her face. Her clenched fist shot high in the air. She offered up a little prayer that Lucy would find the happiness she so rightly deserved.

Back in the family room, Lucy nuzzled her nose against Luke's cheek. "Hmm, that was sweet."

**Sweet?** "Well, I was just warming up," Luke said, his voice charged with emotion. **Damn, I can barely get my tongue to work.**

"What happens when you get to the warming-up stage?" Lucy asked, rubbing noses. She loved the way his breathing changed. **Or is it my breathing?**

"Well, then I work on the next stage. That's the simmering stage, and from there, I go on to the sizzling stage," Luke said in a strangled voice he didn't recognize as his own.

"And then . . . ?"

"What? You want a picture?"

"Uh-huh," Lucy drawled as her tongue found its way into his ear.

"Stop that!"

"Why?" Lucy teased.

"Because I'm not like a fine-tuned motor on a car. Well, I am, but I can't go from sweet to simmer to sizzle in a nanosecond. I need to . . . ah, work at it. There's a protocol. . . . Will you stop that! Oh, myyyyy God!"

"My fine-tuned engine is revving at the speed of light. What are you going to do about it?" Lucy hissed into Luke's wet ear.

Luke was a hair away from showing the fine-tuned engine that was revving at the speed of light and leaning over him what he was going to do when Angie bellowed from the kitchen, "Phone's ringing. Must be those agents! I'll get it! I'll get it!"

As he rose from his chair, Luke snarled, "Oh shit!"

Lucy growled, "Oh crap!" She followed that statement up with, "And you haven't even kissed me yet!"

Angie whirled around to see Lucy and Luke standing in the doorway. They both looked guilty as sin, in her opinion. Both of them glared at her. Flustered at the expressions on their faces, all she could say was, "Agent Gerrison would like to speak with you, Lucy."

Lucy made her way across the kitchen and mouthed the words, "Your timing sucks, Angie!"

"So . . . how did you sleep, Luke?"

"Like a log, except when you and I were checking out the LED light I saw outside last night while Lucy was sleeping. Whoever was out there came pretty close to the house and then left rather abruptly."

"That's sweet. What I mean is that you slept so well. You know, a new house and all. And you were sleeping in a chair. I'm glad. What I mean is, I'm glad you slept well considering the circumstances. I think I'll just . . . What I'm going to do is . . . head on upstairs and take a shower. I'm sure you won't miss me. Coffee's ready."

"Sweet! Sweet! Don't you girls know any other word?"

Angie turned, flipped Luke the bird, and

said, "**Sweet** is a girlie word. It means a whole host of things to us. We're girls, and we're sweet. I rest my case. Just out of curiosity, why is your ear so red?"

"Just you never mind why my ear is so red," Luke said, blushing like a schoolgirl.

"A man with a secret!" Angie wiggled her eyebrows, then giggled. "Oh, how sweet it is!"

Luke massaged his ear, a wicked grin on his face, as he walked over to the coffeepot. Any hopes of picking up where he'd left off in the family room were dashed when Lucy slammed the phone down and whirled around.

"Why is your face so red, Luke?"

"I've . . . ah . . . been rubbing it. Guess I ground my face into the material on the chair I was sleeping in. What did Gerrison say?"

Lucy poured herself a cup of coffee. "You're not going to believe this, but he said the assistant director of the FBI got orders from the director himself, who told him to order his men to stand down. What does that mean, stand down?"

"It means cease and desist. I take that

to mean the FBI is not interested in you, the two safes, or the contents of those two safes. I guess that means you can do whatever you want with them. Meaning the contents. Hell, Lucy, I don't know. I'm as new at this as you are. Did he say anything else?"

"Oh, yeah. He said someone named Julian Metcalf would be coming here to see me. Today, weather permitting. Just so you don't think I'm anyone's pushover, I told Agent Gerrison to tell Mr. Metcalf to call to make an appointment, and if I was available, I would see him. If not, oh, well! He didn't like that, and I hung up."

Luke huffed and puffed. "Well, I could have told him you're no pushover." He burst out laughing at the expression on Lucy's face. "By the way, how's your foot?"

"Actually, Luke, my foot is feeling much better. Thank you for asking, and thank you for being honest about recognizing that I'm not a pushover. Angie makes good coffee, doesn't she?"

"I wouldn't know. I haven't had any yet."

"Well, there's the pot, and there are the cups hanging off those little pegs. See, I'm no pushover. Get your own coffee."

Luke turned and grinned from ear to ear. "It's still snowing out there."

"I see that. I estimate maybe eight inches or so by the time it stops. I really liked nibbling on your ear. I got all tingly and . . . Oh, it was so sweet. I never had anyone stick their tongue in my ear. Tell me, how does it feel?"

Luke stopped in the middle of the kitchen and stared down at Lucy, who was looking up at him with adoring eyes. "Why don't I just let you feel it for yourself."

"Feel what? What happened?" Angie said from the doorway.

"The cold weather," Luke said, blushing all over again.

Lucy's dancing devil proceeded to do his jig on Lucy's shoulder. "Actually, Angie, I was just telling Luke no one has ever stuck his tongue in my ear, and I asked him how it felt. And the reason I asked him that was that before you interrupted us, I was experimenting with his ear. Your timing just out and out sucks."

"I'm going to take a shower," Luke said, beelining for the doorway that would lead him up the back staircase to the second floor.

"Do you want me to go out and play in the snow so you two can get it on or something?" Angie asked as she did her best not to laugh out loud. "How about from now on I wear a whistle around my neck and blow it before I enter a room? Will that work for you guys?"

"God, no. I was just teasing. He's sweet, isn't he?"

"Downright delectable," Angie replied, laughing. "Tell me. What did Agent Gerrison have to say?"

"On orders from the director via the assistant director of the FBI, Gerrison and his partner, Restin, have been ordered to stand down. That means—"

"I know what **stand down** means, Lucy. Did he say why?"

"Nope. But someone named Julian Metcalf is going to be paying us a visit, depending on the weather. I told him to relay the message to Mr. Metcalf to call and make an appointment. What do you make of this, Angie? What's for breakfast?"

"How about French toast and bacon? I guess it means you're in the clear as far as the FBI is concerned. But whom does Mr. Metcalf represent? And who was it who broke into your house in Edison? Were they FBI? Stands to reason they were since the two guys Luke had visit him said they were with the FBI. Now, suddenly, all of them are standing down. Doesn't make sense to me unless whoever this Metcalf guy represents supersedes the FBI. I don't know how any of that works, you know, the chain of command from all those alphabet agencies."

"Let's think about it a minute. There's Homeland Security. There's the CIA, and there's the NSA. If we put them all in a bag and shake it up, I think they'll come out the same. And yet one of them enlisted the aid of the FBI. What's up with that?"

"Maybe when it looked like you weren't going to kick up a fuss, they thought it would work. I would imagine that after you called the FBI, they had to fall back and regroup. First, you're in Florida for the funeral. Then you get hit by lightning. Enter more people on your side, then I come along, Luke comes along, and then suddenly we're all back here and finding the exact same thing you found in Florida. Too many people are now involved. We know of six agents. The two in Florida who went to see Luke. The two who broke into your house, even though we aren't really sure which agency they belong to. Then the two who came here last night. Although to be perfectly clear on this, we do not know for sure that the two who broke into your house yesterday were FBI. Still, four agents on a case like this is a bit much. Six agents would be more than a bit much, wouldn't you say? And they didn't sweat us, either. That in itself is suspicious. It is to me, at least. If you believe what you read, the FBI can take you in and hold you for seventy-two hours without giving you a lawyer. They didn't do that to us. Why?"

"I don't know why for sure, but I doubt very much that even the FBI would detain the CEO of a publicly traded company unless they were prepared to file serious criminal charges, like for insider trading or stock manipulation. And yes, I agree, it is a bit much. I suppose we can speculate till the end of time, and we won't be any closer to an answer until someone gives us one. In the meantime, we just have to wait it out."

"I'm not good at waiting, Lucy. I think I'm worse at it than you are."

Lucy shrugged. "What I want to know . . . no, what I need to know is who the hell I had cremated down in Florida. Those people must have families. I can't keep their remains. I would never throw them away, but I need to know who they are. I keep asking myself over and over why I did that. Why was I in such a hurry to turn my parents—because at that time I thought they were my parents—into ashes? No one ever told . . . I didn't know. . . . I just wish I hadn't done that." Tears rolled down Lucy's cheeks. Angie reached for a paper towel and handed it over.

"Don't take it so hard, Lucy. You did what you felt was right at the time. There was no way for you to know. Like you said, your parents never told you what their intentions were, and there was no will to be found at the time. No one is ever going to blame you for this."

"I just want this to be over so I can get on with my life. I want to start the new year fresh by creating Dizzie for IBL. That's my life, and I don't want to screw all of that up. And now Luke is in the picture. I have to start thinking about that. Right now I should be happier than a pig in a mud slide. But

I'm not, because all of this is hanging over my head."

Angie ran out of words. She patted her friend on the shoulder to let Lucy know she was there for her no matter what, and she knew that Lucy understood. And with Luke in the picture, they had it covered. If ever there was a trifecta, this was it.

"Who in the damn hell is Julian Metcalf?" Lucy snarled.

Julian Metcalf hated it when he could smell his own sweat. The temperature in the room was a chilling sixty-eight degrees, and he was still sweating. And he really hated rubbing his hands over a day's stubble on his cheeks. He looked up at Clarence Carpenter and winced at what he was seeing in his superior's eyes. "I can't believe what I'm hearing, Chuck," he said, using the man's nickname, something he did only when they were together in a private room or on the golf course. "That weasel chickened out!" he said, referring to Assistant Director Nolan Brewster of the FBI.

"On orders from the director himself. If you remember correctly, time was of the essence, and you agreed with me, Julian. Besides, Nolan Brewster owed me, and I wanted to collect. I didn't think the director himself would intercede. Who the hell knew the assets were going to get killed? We all did what we did on the fly. Now we have to fix it. So much for interagency cooperation."

"I don't see how, Chuck. Look, Helene and Fritz Brighton are two of the best agents ever to come out of Langley. They were so natural, it was almost sinful. We didn't even have to build them a cover. It was so damn perfect, it was scary, and it worked all these years. Then one drunk teenager comes along, and bam, it's all shot to hell. No one, and I stress no one, could have seen that coming."

"Not to mention the daughter," Carpenter said morosely. "They want out. They said they were breached. We were not able to convince them that the deaths were accidental. They won't buy it. They are 100 percent convinced their cover is blown. They don't feel safe anymore, and they want to see their daughter. They know too much. The two of them **are** safe, aren't they, Julian?"

"Of course they're safe. As long as they don't do anything stupid. If you're looking for a guarantee that they won't do something stupid, I can't give it to you."

"What? Suddenly they want to be parents again? Twenty-two years after they walk away from their daughter, they're suddenly feeling parental love? I think it's more likely they're scared. And all of a sudden, with the death of the substitute parents, they're looking at their own mortality," Carpenter said, an ominous ring in his voice. "Did you . . ."

"Of course I did. I have two teams guarding them twenty-four/seven. They aren't going anywhere, no matter how much noise they make. Worst-case scenario, we move them again," Metcalf said as he rubbed at the stubble on his chin. It itched like hell.

"They're beyond clever. They'll figure something out if they want out bad enough. Maybe it wouldn't be such a bad idea to arrange a meeting between the daughter and her parents."

"All calls on their sat phones are monitored, as well as the Internet. I'm not sure that's a good idea, Chuck, but I won't discount it, either. I'm going to try to make it home to get cleaned up, and if the shuttles are leaving D.C., I'll make my way to New Jersey and have a heart-to-heart with Ms. Lucy Brighton, CEO and general pain in the ass. Unless you want to play it differently."

Clarence Carpenter shook his head. "Keep me in the loop."

# Chapter Twenty

Julian Metcalf barely resembled his usual dapper self as he paced his spacious house in Georgetown. Oh, he was freshly showered, shaved, and coiffed, but instead of his designer duds, he was wearing fleece sweats and stout snow boots. The only concession to the designer wear he was known for would be the top-of-the-line ski jacket he'd don when his driver arrived to take him to the airport.

Frustrated with the commercial airline ticketing, he'd commandeered an agency jet, which would take him all the way to Freehold. No sense paying for the fuel for his own Gulfstream when this was agency business. For the life of him, he couldn't remember where it planned to set down and how he was to get out to Lucy Brighton's new farmhouse. He took a second to wonder if he was losing it.

**No, I am not losing it. What I am is goddamn cranky at the way things are playing out.** He needed to put a lid on things, and he needed to do it quickly.

Metcalf looked down at the cell in his hand to see a text that said his driver was three minutes away. Just time enough to put on the designer jacket, secure his three cell phones in his zip pockets, and make his way down the icy front steps of his Georgetown home. He thought about Agents Blevins and Davis then. He'd learned a whole new language when the agents tore into him by saying they were less than a hundred feet from the farmhouse when they were ordered to halt the operation. He winced when he thought about the early morning call he'd gotten saying Davis was in the hospital with frostbite. What was it Blevins had blustered? Oh, yeah. "Just give me the name of the asshole who ordered this caper so I can rip him a new one." Metcalf had surprised himself when he manned up and admitted he was the asshole. That hadn't stopped Blevins, though. His rant went on for another five minutes before he hung up.

Metcalf let his mind wander to the last phone call he'd gotten from Helene Brighton. She'd been crying and whining about how he could have allowed this to happen and demanding to know what he was going to do about it. He had set her straight and had asked to speak to Fritz. The same Fritz Brighton he hated with a passion. Superior agent or not, he still hated him. Almost as much as he hated Helene Brighton, Fritz's bitch of a wife. How, he had always wondered, could the two of them be such outstanding agents, such qualified doctors, yet be such ugly people on the inside? Forget parenthood.

Never having been married, never having had children, he didn't understand how the two of them could have created a child like Lucy Brighton. From everything he'd heard, from all the reports he'd seen over the years, from his own personal hands-on contact, which he'd filtered through to her parents, Lucy Brighton was top-notch, a first-rate human being, as well as a highly talented artist and businesswoman. And now she was in a heap of trouble and demanding answers. Answers she had every right to.

Metcalf thought about the dossier he had on Lucy Brighton, which he'd skimmed with his early morning coffee. There wasn't one negative thing in the report. She was a stand-up person, with a flawless moral compass. She'd single-handedly built a company she could be proud of. She was kind, loyal to friends, generous, and hard-working. Who could fault someone like that? Yes, she deserved the truth. He had to wonder how she would handle it, though.

A black car covered in snow slid to the curb. Metcalf waved to the driver to let him know not to get out. He opened the door and slid in, grateful for the warmth. Their destination? Andrews Air Force Base, where his plane waited.

The breakfast that Angie was supposed to make never materialized, with Luke and Lucy both saying they weren't hungry.

Lunch or brunch would be good later. They were all too tense as they waited for what was to come.

"I don't get it. Whoever it was out there in the snow last night with that LED flashlight was within a hundred feet of us. And then they turned tail and went back the way they came. That has to mean something," Luke said, his arms flapping in his own breeze.

"Maybe whoever it was, was staking us out. For all we know, they could be hiding out there somewhere," Angie said.

"Then they're dead, frozen to whatever tree they were hiding behind. It's thirty degrees out there, and if you look out the front window, the tracks they made have been filled in. Gerrison's phone call pretty much confirmed to me that whoever it was got called off. Now this new person is coming to visit," Luke said.

"What's that noise?" Lucy asked, running to the front window. "Oh, look. It's a snowplow. Wonder how that happened. Oh, I bet the Realtor called someone to plow the road. It is a mile and a half long. Luke, will you check it out?"

Luke already had his jacket on and was

opening the door when the driver of the snowplow waved to him. Lucy heard him bellow, "Jackson Realty sent me. You're clear all the way to the highway. The snow is tapering off. I'll be back around three to give it another shot."

"Thanks," Luke bellowed in return. "How are the main roads?"

"Pretty clear, sanded and salted. If you go out, be careful."

"Yeah, thanks."

Back in the house, Luke shrugged out of his jacket. "At least we aren't stranded."

"You mean in case we have to make a quick getaway?" Angie asked in a jittery voice.

"Yeah, something like that," Luke mumbled. "It's really cold out there. I think I'll build up the fire. We can have lunch in front of the fire when you two are ready."

When Luke was out of the room and out of earshot, Lucy looked over at Angie. "I think he's worried. I don't think he's a worrier by nature, and that bothers me."

Angie nodded as she opened the refrigerator. "Are you worried, Lucy?"

"No. I'm scared. There's a difference. What about you?"

"I'm with you. The bright spot, if you can consider it a bright spot, is that we weren't hauled away last night by those two agents. I think it was because we said we sent out letters to lawyers and threatened to go to the media. And I suppose it doesn't hurt that it would be pretty difficult to make the CEO of IBL just disappear. Given how many people know something about what is going down, I doubt that even the FBI could handle the hullabaloo when the shit hit the fan. What's going on now is probably what those people call damage control."

"I think you're right, Angie. We need to get back on track here. Did you happen to see where we put that box with the Dizzie duck prototype?"

"I carried it in. I remember that. I think it's on top of the dryer in the laundry room. Why?"

"I'm trying to shift my thought processes into work mode so I don't go off the deep end where all this other stuff is concerned. And I like to think about things before I commit them to paper. I need to figure out how Dizzie will interact with Izzy, Bizzy, and Lizzy. You know, what a duck is capable of that will come across as believable. We have three boys, Izzy, Bizzy, and Lizzy, and since Dizzie is a girl duck and Lizzy is a boy parrot, that's going to take some ingenuity on my part, doncha think?"

"Here you go," Angie said, handing the FedEx box to Lucy, who pulled the packing strip and withdrew a bubble-wrapped stuffed duck.

Lucy took one look at the duck and burst out laughing. "Oh, this is so perfect, I can't tell you. She captured Dizzie to a T."

Angie smiled at the white duck with a crooked beak. "Why does she have a green and red feather on her wings? By the way, I've been meaning to ask you. Isn't Lizzy a girl's name?"

"It is if you spell it Lizzie, but I spell it Lizzy, so that makes it a boy. I wonder why no one ever asked me that before. Anyway, Dizzie got in a fight with another duck, and Izzy, Bizzy, and Lizzy saved her. She was wounded, and Lizzy gave her two of his feathers. Ducks are monogamous. Did you know that? They have only one mate for their entire life. Up till now, Dizzie has not had a partner. I'm thinking Lizzy wants to apply for the position, not understanding he's a parrot and Dizzie is a duck. He thinks that because he gave her two of his feathers, she now belongs to him."

Angie flopped down on a chair at the kitchen table. She cradled the stuffed duck in her arms. "Lucy, that is so perfect, I don't have the words to tell you. That is going to take off like a rocket. What is Henry saying?"

"He loves it. Said orders will go through the roof. We are going to go into production January 2nd. Dizzie will be made in the good old US of A, just the way Izzy, Bizzy, and Lizzy are. Just so you know, Angie, come the first of the year, we will be working around the clock until mid-June to get all of this up and running. Are you sure you're up to it, compadre?"

"Oh, yeah. I can't wait. My pencil is just itching to get started. This sure beats working for that slave driver at that advertising agency I used to push a pencil for."

Standing outside the kitchen doorway that led to the family room, Luke unashamedly eavesdropped. Working around the clock till mid-June. Where would that leave him in the scheme of things? He had houses to build, a commitment to buyers who had signed on the dotted line. Lucy had a duck to prepare for market. What was that old saying, something about the best-laid plans of mice and men? In his life, he'd never heard such excitement from anyone as he was hearing from Lucy as she talked about her cartoon characters, who, if he didn't know better, sounded like her children. And perhaps, in some way, they were the playmates and siblings she had never had. It was her answer to make up for all those lost years. How in the hell could he ever quibble with something like that?

Luke sucked in his breath, knowing that he would have to fold his tent and steal off into the night. He might not be the sharpest tool in the shed, but even he knew he couldn't compete with Izzy, Bizzy, Lizzy, and Dizzie. He felt sick to his stomach at the realization. Damn, he'd had such wonderful plans. Truly, truly wonderful plans. **That's what you get for putting the cart before the horse,** he chided himself.

"Yoo-hoo, Luke! Where are you? Quick. Come out to the kitchen. I want to introduce you to Dizzie Duck," Lucy called.

Luke plastered what he hoped was a

silly smile on his face and bopped into the kitchen. He hoped he sounded sincere when he agreed with both women that yes, indeed, Dizzie was a charmer. He kept the smile on his face until he thought his face was going to crack wide open.

Lucy appeared oblivious to Luke's discomfort, but Angie sensed his turmoil and wondered what, if anything, she could do. How much had he heard? Surely, the part about working round the clock till mid-June. Even if she offered to take on the bulk of the heavy lifting so Lucy could spend quality time with Luke, Lucy wouldn't buy into it. She was hands-on for every phase of her creations. She would just assume Luke would wait in the wings for her. Angie wasn't so sure about that.

The phone on the counter shrilled to life. The trio looked at one another.

Lucy came out of her duck trance, reached for it, and said, "Hello. . . . Yes, this is Lucy Brighton. . . . Yes, I was told you would be calling me. As a matter of fact, I am at home because of the weather. Yes, I can see you at three o'clock."

Lucy broke the connection and dusted her hands dramatically. "Mr. Julian Metcalf will be favoring us with his company at three o'clock, ladies and gentlemen."

"Is he coming alone?" Luke asked, just to have something to say. His brain was still swirling around Lucy's working round the clock till mid-June. He looked over at Angie and hated what he was seeing in her eyes.

"He didn't say," Lucy said, stroking the duck's feathers, which felt like silk.

Angie bolted up from the table. "Why don't you two adjourn to the family room and take Dizzie with you, while I make us some lunch? How does soup and sandwiches sound? Or maybe I could whip up some baked Alaska and that dark brown stuff on a shingle?" Angie said, knowing full well neither Luke nor Lucy was paying attention to a word she said.

"Fine," Lucy said, sensing something going on that she didn't understand.

Luke muttered something about toasting something or other as he followed Lucy out of the kitchen.

Angie sat down at the table and poured herself a cup of coffee. She needed to think. Just when things were looking up for her friend in the romance department, she was going to shoot herself in the foot. The words "You never appreciate what you have until you lose it" rang in her ears. How could she convince Lucy that love should come first? How? Maybe she just needed to mind her own business and stay out of Lucy's personal life.

Angie sat at the table for a long time. Her coffee turned cold. She drummed her fingers on the tabletop, her eyes on the glass window in the back door and on the snow, which appeared to be tapering off. Off and on she thought about her promise to make lunch. How long could it take to slap some ham and mustard on two slices of bread and heat up some canned soup? Ten minutes? She wished she knew what was going on in the family room. If she was nosy and sneaky, she could stoop low enough to go to the door and listen.

She nixed that idea almost immediately. She went back to trying to figure out a way to have a dialogue with Lucy that wouldn't seem like she was interfering in something that was none of her business.

Even if she had stooped low enough to eavesdrop, Angie wouldn't have been able to hear what was going on, because Lucy and Luke were across the room, sitting cross-legged in front of the fireplace.

"So . . . ," Luke said.

Lucy smiled. "So . . . what?"

"Listen, Lucy, I'm not the kind of guy who suffers in silence, and I am suffering here. I'm not going to pretend I didn't hear what you and Angie were saying in the kitchen when you opened the box with the duck in it. I had myself convinced you and I . . . What I mean is, I hoped that you and I had something going on here. Speaking for myself, I want you to know I'm falling in love with you. I thought . . . hoped . . . you were feeling the same way, and then, oops, suddenly I'm competing with a stuffed duck named Dizzie, who has a red and a green feather. I don't know how to compete against a duck. Are you going to help me out here before I say something really, really stupid?"

"What are you trying to say here, Luke? Whatever it is, I'm not getting it."

Luke continued to flap his arms, his eyes wild. "I heard what you said to Angie about working round the clock till mid-June.

Working round the clock doesn't leave any room for a . . . social life or me. You live here. I live in Florida. There, I said it!"

Lucy leaned forward. "Luke, welcome to the high-tech world. There are telephones, e-mails, Skype, and there are airlines that fly between here and Florida. Not to mention long weekends and holidays. Why do you think I hired Angie? Even I knew I was burning the candle at both ends. Back when Dizzie was just a crazy thought, I had plans to make Angie a big part of IBL. I knew then I had to have a life outside of the company and its cartoon characters. By June the new series will be launched, and IBL can hire people to help us out with the details. But first, we have to get it off the ground. Can't you cut me some slack here?"

"So what you're saying is you want us to be . . . together, and we'll both have to work at making it happen. It is happening. Every time I think about leaving here and going back home, it makes me nuts. I want to be with you."

"That is sooo sweet, Luke. I want the same thing, and we'll get it. You need to believe that. You have houses to build and houses to finish. We both have commitments. We can't start a life reneging on those commitments. And we need to save our money to put our kids through college. Do you have any idea how much college costs these days? If the last couple of years have taught me anything, it's that I cannot rely on the stock value of my interest in IBL, which is very substantial even with this recession, to let me coast through life."

Whoa. There was that word **sweet** again. This lady was so far ahead of him, he was dizzy trying to keep up. Luke cleared his throat. "Kids means marriage."

"Well, yeah. I'm not planning on living in sin. How would that look to all their fans if the mother of Izzy, Bizzy, Lizzy, and Dizzie lived in sin? Look at me, Luke! Did you really think I'd put my business before you? Wait, let me rephrase that. Do you think I can't operate a business successfully and carry on a relationship? Shame on you if that's what you thought."

Right that second, Luke didn't know what the hell he thought.

Lucy leaned forward. "And you still haven't kissed me, yet here we are, talking about the future and kids, college, and make-believe animals. I bet if I stuck my tongue in your mouth and took a deep breath, I could suck your tonsils right out of your throat."

**What the hell!** "Go ahead. You just try it!" Luke blustered as he wondered if he should tell Lucy he had had his tonsils taken out when he was ten years old. **Nah. Let her find out the hard way.**

Angie chose that moment to bound into the room, then stopped in her tracks as she bellowed, "You guys ready for lunch?"

"Kill her right now! If you don't, I will," Lucy snarled.

Luke rolled over and over on the floor, holding his sides.

In spite of herself, Lucy burst out laughing. "I guess your tonsils are safe. For now."

"Promises! Promises!"

"You need to know something about me, Luke Kingston. I never break a promise. If you don't believe me, just ask Angie."

In the kitchen, Lucy looked at the table. It looked pretty the way it was set, with patterned Fiesta dishes. Sitting in the middle of the table was a bowl of something that looked and smelled great. "What is it?" she asked.

"Something Mrs. Smith froze just for us. Kind of like that stuff you cooked in your Crock-Pots. Just eat and enjoy it," Angie muttered.

"I thought you were going to start wearing a whistle around your neck," Lucy grumbled.

"I will as soon as I can lay my hands on one. Will you just eat already and tell me what you were doing in there that has left you so cranky?"

"I was getting ready to suck Luke's tonsils out of his throat because he didn't think I could do it."

"That's way too much information for me to handle," Angie said, dipping the big spoon into the mess in the colored bowl. "Way too much."

Lucy offered up a sweet smile.

# Chapter Twenty-one

The Boston Brahmin known as Julian Metcalf removed his ski jacket and tried to settle himself. His three cell phones were within easy reach. Three goddamn cell phones! Who the hell needed three cell phones? He hated them. Sometimes all three rang at the same time. When that happened, he had to fight with himself not to throw them on the floor and stomp them to pieces. Just another hissy fit to prove to himself he was done with the spook business.

He craned his neck to see outside the small window of the plane. A crew was deicing the plane's wings. Twenty minutes. He wondered how icy the runway was. He didn't like flying, never had. If the plane crashed and he died, there would be no one to mourn him. The reason he had never entered into any long-term relationship with a woman, and so had never had any children, was that he was married to his job and refused to inflict the kind of life he led on any woman, regardless of how understanding she would be. So he had scrupulously guarded his heart to avoid the pain that would come from walking away from anything other than casual relationships.

But that day, he was going to do something he'd never done before in all the years of his career. He was going to say the hell with everything, tell the truth, then hand in his resignation, which he'd typed out the night before. His plan was to close up shop and ride off into the sunset, find an island to buy, learn how to strum a guitar, and sit on his ass for the rest of his life. Well, maybe not exactly sit. He'd do some fishing, start drinking those cocktails that came with little umbrellas in them, and eat whatever the hell he pleased. And if some wonderful woman found him, he'd allow himself to be dragged off to her hut. He might even take back the name that was on his birth certificate.

One way or another, he was going to make it happen. Ten years in the business world, followed by another ten as a low-level operative in the agency and another twenty-two years in his current role, was way too long to stay in a job that gave him nothing but ulcers, migraines, and sleepless nights. He was done.

Metcalf sighed. He could see the snow crews moving off. They'd be whizzing down the runway any minute now. He buckled up and closed his eyes. Takeoffs were the worst, with landings coming in a close second. Hyperventilating at thirty thousand feet came in third. He was not flying material in the same way he wasn't marriage material. These days he didn't know what the hell he was. He closed his eyes and hoped for the best.

Two hours later, Julian Metcalf climbed behind the wheel of a Chevy Suburban that he knew was souped up to the gills and was bulletproof. All he really cared about was the four-wheel drive to get him through the snow. He turned on the engine and waited for the heater to kick in. His three cell phones were within easy reach. The special one, the one that the Brightons called on, buzzed. God, how he hated talking to them. But his orders were to call them, orders he hadn't obeyed.

Since he was just hours away from retiring, he decided to get his last licks in and be damned. Let someone else handle the Brightons.

"Metcalf," he said curtly.

"I thought you were going to call us last night," Fritz Brighton snarled. "We sat up and waited. Don't you have any consideration for how we feel?"

**Not one damn little bit.** Metcalf wondered if the kind of attitude he was hearing was part of Fritz's bedside manner. "I was busy, Fritz. I thought I made it clear to you on more than one occasion that my world does not revolve around you. I have a heavy caseload, and as important as you and Helene are, you are still two of twenty-seven. Not to mention that you are retired and safe, which is more than I can say about the other twenty-five agents I have to look out for."

"Every time we call, you're busy. Helene and I want to know what's going on, and don't try bullshitting me, either." Metcalf could hear Helene jabbering in the background, but he couldn't make out the words. And that, he decided, was probably a good thing. "Why do we suddenly have all this extra security? Just tell me that," Fritz Brighton demanded.

**Okay, you son of a bitch, I'm going to tell you.** "Because we're afraid you're going to do something stupid, like try to run. Running is not acceptable. You refuse to believe your doubles died in a tragic accident. Fine. I can live with that. You refuse to believe you are safe. Fine again. But by refusing to believe what we tell you, you become dangerous in our eyes. You made a deal, and you can't change it midstream. We've gone over this a dozen times, and nothing has changed, Fritz, nor will it change anytime soon. Possibly never. That's another way of saying you made your bed twenty-two years ago, and no matter how uncomfortable you now find it, you are going to sleep in it."

"Don't give me that crap. Things have changed. Our doubles are dead. We had to find that out on the Internet. And you're right. We don't believe you. When were you going to tell us? We want to see our daughter. This is the thanks we get for putting our lives on the line for our country. Well?" Fritz Brighton screamed so loud, Metcalf had to hold the phone away from his ear.

Metcalf struggled for patience. **Please, God, just let me get through this one more time, and I swear I will never ask for another thing the rest of my life.** "You were told on day one that there would never be thanks or accolades or favors granted in this line of work. You and your wife said you understood that. You signed papers to that effect. You both willingly, and I stress the word **willingly** here, gave up your rights to your daughter for the good of your country. Our part of the bargain was to see to it that she had a good life. Do I have to remind you it was Helene who came up with that idea, and we agreed? We did our part. Lucy had the best schools, the best medical care that money could buy. She was never out of our sight. She turned into a beautiful, wonderful young woman. She's self-reliant, she's independent, she's caring, she's kind, and she has carved out a life for herself. She buried you and your wife. Actually, she thinks she had you cremated. Let it go, Fritz."

"We will not let it go. She found out, didn't she? That's what this is all about. What the hell did you tell her about us?"

"Nothing yet, but I'm sure being as smart and innovative as she is, she figured some of it out on her own. You sold her out at the age of ten so you and your wife could lead what you thought were going to be the glamorous lives of spies. You loved every minute of it. Don't deny it. Now that you're in the bull pen, you want back what you gave away. Sorry, Fritz. It's too late. That bus left the depot twenty-two years ago, and you were not on it."

"**Glamorous?** Is that what you said? Getting shot in the stomach at Orchard Towers in Singapore! Almost dying. That was glamorous? Getting knifed on Burgos Street in Manila was glamorous? And let's not forget that set-to in Pattaya, Thailand, when Helene and I were jailed for sixty-two days."

"Part of the job, Fritz, just part of the job. You forgot to mention all those lovely state dinners, meeting all those foreign celebrities, living the high life, doing your surgeries on the fly, and let's absolutely not forget all that money you and your wife socked away. You must be right up there with Warren Buffett these days."

"You bastard! We gave up our lives for you people. We agreed to spy for you. We almost lost our lives a dozen times. All we want to do is see our daughter. Is that too much to ask?"

"Well, yes, Fritz, as a matter of fact, it is too much to ask. We never, as in never, never, never, disturb the status quo. You are where you are at the moment. You have a good life, a life people just dream about. You live on a palatial estate. You have servants to wait on you hand and foot. You have a fleet of fancy million-dollar cars. You dine on the best food money can buy. You both wear clothes that cost a normal person's salary for a year. We still allow you to do consulting work in your chosen profession. The medical community still thinks you're top dog in your field. It's not our fault you developed arthritis and can't perform surgery any longer. We arranged it so you could still consult as much as you like. So stop whining and man up to our agreement."

"We will not follow your orders any longer. We're done, finished."

"You will follow our orders. If you don't, I will personally crawl up your ass and chew my way out. Do you understand me, Fritz?" When there was no answer, and Metcalf finally realized he was listening to dead air, he shrugged and pressed the OFF button. He didn't think it likely that he'd be hearing from the Brightons anytime soon. Certainly not before he turned in his resignation and destroyed the cell phone they had to call to reach him.

Metcalf shrugged out of his ski jacket. He was warm now, toasty, actually. He had one more call to make before he headed out to Freehold. He made it, and his message was curt. "Move them now! Don't take your eyes off them and confiscate their passports."

**Ah, how sweet it is,** Metcalf thought as he put the car in gear. **Just hours away from retirement. Hours.** He thought about the Brightons then and wondered again about how they could have just given up their daughter the way they did. **How does a parent do that? How do they justify it?**

They did it for the good of their country was their explanation. But he had never believed it for a minute. They'd been absolutely giddy when they were told by Chuck Carpenter that the agency had come up with doubles to impersonate them back in the States. From that day on, they had never once, as in not a single, solitary time, asked about their daughter. Not until the day they saw that the doubles had been killed.

Metcalf supposed, if the story of the Brightons ever got out, that there would be those who would stand on their side and say they had sacrificed their daughter for the good of the country. But he and Chuck Carpenter knew they'd done it for themselves, because the Brightons were selfish, egotistical people and deserved one another. A sad ending, as far as he was concerned.

Now he was headed toward his last mission. To try to make things right for a young woman so she could make peace with her life.

Metcalf turned on the stereo and cranked it as high as it would go. He was old enough to appreciate and sing along to the words of "Pretty Woman," and he didn't feel one bit foolish.

Forty minutes later, Metcalf turned down the stereo so he could hear what the GPS had to say to him. He winced at the robotic voice. He would be glad when he was on his island and didn't have to deal with all this crap. His two feet would take him where he wanted to go, and if they didn't, then he'd sit on his ass and get a good sunburn. He started to whistle, knowing that with each passing minute, he was that much closer to finding the special island that would finally, finally give him some peace.

"Car's coming," Angie said.

"He's forty minutes early," Luke observed.

"Early is better than late," Lucy said.

When the knock sounded on the front door, and even though they expected it, all three of them almost jumped out of their skins.

"I'll do the honors," Lucy said, leading

the way to the front door. She opened it and looked up at the tall man with the snow-white hair. She thought he looked like an angry lion until she held out her hand and introduced herself, along with Luke and Angie. That was when she changed her mind. He was more like a gentle lion. This was a man with a heart, she decided, and wondered how in the world she knew that. And she had the feeling she'd met him before, or at least seen him somewhere. The wild-looking white mane of hair was what was triggering the memory. Damn, where was it?

That was the moment when Lucy realized she could no longer read minds. Her eyes widened as she tried to remember the last time she'd been able to do that and simply couldn't remember. Her circuitry had righted itself, and she hadn't even known it. That meant she was normal again and clicking on all cylinders. **Yippeee!**

Luke reached for Metcalf's jacket and hung it up.

Angie asked their guest if he wanted coffee. He surprised everyone by saying he would love a cup of good, strong black coffee.

"Then you came to the right place. Is the kitchen okay, Mr. Metcalf? It's where we spend most of our time."

"The kitchen is fine." Metcalf tried to remember the last time he'd actually sat in someone's kitchen, or even his own, and couldn't come up with a time or a place.

Angie poured. Metcalf sampled it and nodded his approval. He looked around the table and knew no one wanted chit-chat, so he got right down to it. "It might be easier if you ask me questions. I can fill you in. Then, hopefully, I can explain everything to your satisfaction." He looked over at Angie. She looked to him like a true loyal friend. His gaze went to Luke, and he decided he was a stand-up guy and in love with Lucy Brighton. And then he really looked at Lucy Brighton's emerald-green eyes and knew he could not tell this young woman a lie of any kind. Anything other than the truth, and she'd see right through it. He wondered if she read minds. **Such a stupid thought.**

"Who did I have cremated? I know they weren't my parents," Lucy said bluntly.

"First things first. You aren't in Kansas anymore, Dorothy. This is as real as it is going to get. You're right. They weren't your parents. They were your parents' doubles here in the States. Who they were isn't important."

Lucy fixed her gaze on Metcalf's. "Now, that's where you're wrong, Mr. Metcalf. They were people. They must have family, who, I'm sure, want their remains. That makes them important to them and to me. Or did you and your people dummy up some ashes and pass them off as the doubles'?"

"I guess I should have said their names aren't important. Their families have been notified. We didn't know about the cremation until after it was done. That's one of the reasons we wanted to talk to you, to ask for the remains so we can turn them over to their relatives."

Lucy digested the words and accepted them. "Where are my parents, my real parents?"

"There are some things I can't tell you, and that is one of them. Suffice it to say that it has to do with national security. I hope you can understand that. Actually, it is the only thing I can't talk to you about. What I will say is that your parents are safe and will remain safe for the rest of their lives as long as no one does anything foolish. Inviting you into their lives will only endanger them, and I am sure you don't want that."

"Were my parents spies?"

"Yes. Very good ones, as a matter of fact. I think they were the best of the best. We gave them both the best legends. Do you know what that means?"

"Phony backgrounds that would stand up against any kind of questioning," Angie blurted out.

"Yes, but they had impeccable credentials to begin with. Both of your parents were doctors, still are, but your father at the time was world renowned. He wore two hats, Lucy. He spied for us as Dr. Fritz Brighton, and then he spied for us under his legend, as did your mother. This country owes them a lot."

"Why did they send me off when I was ten? Is that when all of this started?"

"I think you know the answer to that, Lucy. Yes, they sent you off, and I want you to know that from that moment on, we had eyes on you twenty-four/seven. Your real parents were sent weekly progress reports, pictures that were taken that you never knew about. The doubles were just there as backup. In their reports, there was always a postscript that said they thought you knew they weren't real, because you drew away from them, that there was no intimacy of any kind, not even a peck on the cheek. Is that true?"

"Yes. They were like cold fish. They were polite and cordial, but they didn't want to be around me any more than I wanted to be around them. You were at my high-school graduation, weren't you?"

"Yes, front row, center. I'm surprised you remember me."

"It was the white hair. I've seen you other places, too."

"Yes. You were my responsibility. I cheered every good grade you got. I clapped harder than anyone when you graduated from college and were handed your sheepskin. I applauded you when you got your business off the ground. There was always someone near you, Lucy, someone to jump in if things went awry for you. I know all of us can't make up for a mother's and a father's love, but I want to be as honest with you here as I can. Your parents were never parent material. At least that's what your mother said. Your father was so wrapped up in his profession and in working for us, I always wondered if he even remembered your name. I'm giving you full disclosure here, Lucy."

"And the houses and the safes? I read books. I see movies. Are they safe houses for your other . . . spies?"

"Yes. In a million years, none of us ever thought for a second that you would figure it out, and yet you did. When agents, spies, if you will, get compromised or have to go to ground, we have to have a safe house for them to go to until we can outfit them with new identities. It's that simple. I don't even want to know how you figured it out. All I want is for you to tell me where the contents are. In the interests of national security. If you don't or won't cooperate, then it's out of my hands."

"And if I turn everything over to you, will that be the end of it? Can my friends and I go back to our normal lives?"

"Guaranteed."

"I need a few minutes to think about this and talk it over with my friends."

"Take all the time you need, Lucy. Can I have some more coffee?"

"Of course. Help yourself. By the way, how did you know I'd moved here?"

"Lucy, I'm a spook. We can figure out anything given enough time. We have resources you can only dream about. And we can hide people the same way."

Lucy nodded as she led her little parade into the family room. They all looked at the dying fire and rushed to add more logs.

"We each get a vote," Lucy whispered. "Luke?"

"I say turn it all over and be done with it."

"I agree," Angie said. "In the end, it's up to you, Lucy. I think Luke and I will agree to whatever you want to do. Is it your parents? Do you want to fight to see them? Do you want to play hardball and hold out for that?"

"I'm going to turn it over. I have a few questions, though. And no, I am not going to fight to see my parents. As far as I'm concerned, I was a throwaway. I can never get that back, no matter how hard I try. So, I'm going to let it go. I've gotten this far by myself. Well, obviously, that's not quite true. I had some damn alphabet agency looking after me all these years, but you get my point. Besides, I have you two in my corner now."

Luke swooped Lucy up in his arms, swung her around, and planted a kiss squarely on her lips.

"Well, that's something. You finally kissed her, and it only took some spook from the dregs of Washington to spur you on. Come on, you two. Let's get this show on the road so we can celebrate," Angie hissed. "You don't want him to change his mind, do you?"

Lucy broke away first, a glazed look in her eyes. "God, no. Luke, come on. Get with the program here."

Back in the kitchen, Metcalf correctly interpreted what had gone on. The young man had kissed Lucy, and everyone was happy. He tried not to smile, but he was and always had been a sucker for happy endings.

"We agree to turn everything over, but first, I have a few questions. What about the house in Palm Royal, the house here in New Jersey, and probate? There are enormous insurance policies. I don't want any of it."

"Everything is yours, whether you like it or not. You can sell the houses. You have two death certificates attesting to the fact that Helene and Fritz Brighton are deceased."

"Isn't that fraud?"

"I suppose that would depend on who's doing the asking. The paperwork is all in place. Like it or not, Lucy Brighton, this is the way it has to end. There are a lot of legitimate causes out there crying for help. Look into it. Now it's your turn."

"Angie, give him the keys and the paperwork for the storage lockers."

Angie went to her purse and handed over an envelope. "The keys to the truck are in there. Lucy?"

"I don't want the truck. Raffle it off or give it away. I want your promise, Mr. Metcalf, that the two urns in the back of the Rover will be turned over to the proper people."

"I'll see to it personally."

"Then I guess that concludes our business. By the way, thanks for watching over me all those years."

The white-haired lion smiled, his eyes twinkling down at Lucy. "It was my pleasure.

I will be talking to your parents one more time. I can give them a message if you want me to."

"There's nothing I need to say. Sometimes, silence is golden, or that's what I've been told. But thank you for asking."

"Have a good life, Lucy Brighton."

Lucy smiled. "Count on it, Mr. Metcalf, or whoever you are."

The man known as Julian Metcalf threw back his head and burst out in laughter.

# Epilogue

Lucy had never seen or felt pandemonium, but she felt this was as close to it as possible. She was sitting on the floor in the spacious studio, playing with her real live playmates. For her first ever real birthday party, Luke had shown up with what he considered to be the surprise of all surprises. A dog, a cat, a parrot, and a duck. All with tags on their necks that proclaimed them to be IZZY, BIZZY, LIZZY, and DIZZIE. She'd laughed until she cried, and her sides hurt as she tried to gather all four animals close. To sweeten the gift, Luke had said they were all rescues in need of a loving home,

and what better place than with his beloved.

For the first month, Izzy chewed everything in sight but was especially addicted
to the sofa in the family room. One side
was almost gone. Lucy didn't care. In fact,
she almost went over the moon when the
little Yorkie made his first mess on the carpet in the family room. She loved the big
stain, which she'd pretended to scrub over
and over. It was the stuff her dreams had
been made of. Bizzy spent the first six
weeks being aloof, hissing and snarling
and trying to catch Lizzy, the parrot. It took
three good nips to his head before he settled down and became friends with the
colorful parrot, who learned his new friend's
name in record time. When Bizzy finally
settled down, he claimed his turf, which
was the other half of the sofa, which he
proceeded to shred with his claws. Lucy
pretended to scold him, but her heart
wasn't in it. Instead, she would hug him,
croon to him, and Bizzy would purr so
loud, you could hear him in the next room.
Lizzy, during those six weeks, refused to
stay in his oversize cage and perched on
top of the shower rod or on top of the re-

frigerator. At times, he would swoop down and spit out the few words he'd learned, which were "Good boy" and "Oh boy, good boy," at which point he would dive-bomb Bizzy and Izzy, who snapped and hissed at the parrot's terrorist activities, at which point he zeroed in on Dizzie and claimed her as his own. Dizzie accepted Lizzy's admiration, and the two became inseparable.

Angie poked her head out of her office when she heard Lucy snap her fingers for the animals' attention. Then she blew two sharp blasts on a mini whistle hanging around her neck. The animals scattered to get in line.

Toby, who had resigned from FedEx and was in charge of the IBL+D Foundation, rushed to stand beside Angie so he could see what they both proclaimed to be a miracle of sorts. Lucy got up and fetched the red wagon Angie had given her for Mother's Day. Angie and Toby both had officially proclaimed Lucy a mother to the four animals. Hence, the first ever Mother's Day gift. Izzy hopped in the bright red wagon, followed by Bizzy. Lizzy got behind Dizzie to try to boost the duck into the back and actually succeeded, at which point she swooped in and took her seat next to Dizzie. All four of the **kids,** as Lucy referred to them, waited for another blast from the whistle. When it came, they sat up like they were in a parade. Lucy, grinning from ear to ear, called out, "You'll see us when you see us!" Izzy barked. Bizzy meowed, Lizzy said, "Oh boy!" and Dizzie quacked happily.

Toby put his arm around Angie's shoulders. "I have never ever seen a happier human being."

"Yeah," Angie said softly. "Isn't it great? I don't know how she's going to do, though, when we leave next week for Florida and the wedding. Leaving them behind is going to be hard. I'm glad your brother agreed to come and stay and take care of them."

"Denny's big dream is to go to vet school. Trust me when I tell you those animals will be in good hands."

"I know that. It's Lucy I'm worried about. They're her babies, her kids. You see how she is with them. Remember the day Izzy peed on the carpet and how happy she was to have a stain?"

"I do remember. She called Luke, Adel,

and Bud and was shouting at the top of her lungs. To most people, that would seem beyond stupid, but knowing Lucy's story, I thought it was as great as she did."

"She's getting there, Toby. One step at a time. Like you said, I've never seen her happier. That's all that counts."

"You guys get all caught up?" Toby asked.

"It's all under control. Lucy can go off on her honeymoon with a clear head. Business has been and is being taken care of. The only obstacle that I see is her leaving her little brood. Who else do you know who sleeps with a dog, a cat, a parrot, and a duck?"

Toby laughed. "I just hope there's room for Luke in that big bed."

Angie linked her arm in Toby's. "Let's go up to the house. It's almost lunchtime. Adel and Buddy might need some help packing up the car. I want to make sure Lucy's wedding dress doesn't get all mashed up. Buddy said he wanted to be on the road by one o'clock. Adel is chomping at the bit to get back there so she can help decorate the clubhouse for the wedding. I feel kind of guilty letting her do all that, but she said she doesn't need or want my help. Have you noticed how older people get fixated on things?" Angie said breathlessly.

"Yeah, kind of like us younger ones. Adel considers herself Lucy's stand-in mom, so she's doing what all mothers do, taking charge. Bud's the same way. They want this wedding to be perfect. Adel's also doing the cooking, with Luke's dad helping. A family affair, so to speak. It will all work out the way it's supposed to in the end, and you shouldn't take offense, Angie."

"I'm not. I just wanted to help."

"And you are. You're keeping the artistic side of the business going. That's your job."

"When did you get so smart?"

"When I had the good sense to ask you for a date, that's when. Best decision I ever made in my whole life."

"I'm a good catch, you know," Angie teased as she walked arm in arm with her brand-new fiancé. "I hope Adel made something good for lunch. I'm starved."

"They love driving up here once a month and staying for ten days. Actually, I pretty much think they live for these trips during the summer months. When we're in Palm Royal for the winter months, they just glow.

It's funny, isn't it, Angie, how everything worked out so well for all of us?"

"I think this is where we should all say we're blessed. I was a little worried back then. Since the day Mr. Metcalf walked out the door, Lucy has not once mentioned her parents. Not once. I invited him to the wedding. I didn't tell Lucy, though. I hope she won't be upset. He said he'd be there with bells on. I think we owe him that, don't you, Toby?"

"Actually, I do, and I talked about it with Luke, and he agrees. Lucy will be okay with it, trust me."

Off in the distance, they could hear the sound of a whistle.

"Guess the crew is heading back for lunch," Toby said.

Angie laughed, as did Toby, as Lucy came in sight, pulling the red wagon. Lucy pulled up short and blew the whistle. "Everyone out! Lunchtime! Line up, you guys! Forward march! You're out of line, Bizzy. Move it!" The big tabby obeyed instantly, even though he hissed his disapproval at the reprimand. Lucy looked over at Toby and Angie and grinned. "It's great, isn't it? They actually listen."

Lunch was a quickie, tuna sandwiches and tomato soup. No one cared.

The minute they were finished, Bud had his carry-on bag over his shoulder, and Adel was hugging all the animals one last time before she wrapped her arms around Lucy. Her list of instructions ran to, "There's enough food in the freezer for the three of you to last till you're ready to leave. I did the laundry earlier. All you have to do is tidy up your loose business ends and head to Florida."

"Got it, Mom," Lucy said, hugging her back.

"Just one more week, darlin', and you'll be Mrs. Luke Kingston," Buddy said, hugging her tight. "It will go by in the blink of an eye."

"You promise?" Lucy teased.

"Have I ever been wrong yet?"

"Nope."

"Well, there you go. Shake it, sweetie," he said to his wife. Adel rolled her eyes and waved furiously.

The trio, along with the squawking animals, stayed on point until the loaded minivan was out of sight.

Hands on her hips, Angie said, "Now what?"

Lucy shrugged. "Toby said he wants to run a few things by me. You and I already cleared everything, and the only thing left for me to do is call Henry and make a few other calls I've been putting off. Then I'm free to devote my time to the kids. Actually, we're so under control, we could have left with Adel and Buddy, but I knew in my gut they wanted a head start. So we can play for the next few days. There's a new movie out I'd like to see. And I still need to find a wedding present for Luke. Nothing like waiting for the last minute. I can't think of a thing. The man has everything. I don't want to walk into a shop and point to a gift and say, 'I'll take that.' I need something special, something meaningful. You know what I am saying."

"Lucy, try this on for size. You know that picture Toby took? The one of Luke sleeping on the couch, with Izzy chewing his end of the couch and Bizzy shredding his end, with Lizzy sleeping on Luke's shoulder and Luke's arms wrapped around Dizzie? Why don't you take it somewhere, get it blown up to poster size, then get it framed? He can hang it in his office at the construction site. I think he'd like that better than anything you could possibly buy in a store. The best part is he never saw the picture, because I didn't get it developed until after he left on his last visit."

Lucy grinned from ear to ear. "Oooh, I just love it when you come up with the right answer at just the right time. Find it for me, will you please, while Toby and I go over whatever it is he wants to talk about? We'll meet you down at the studio."

Lucy gave a sharp toot to her whistle, and the kids lined up for the parade to the place where they spent most of the day— the studio, which was full of toys and treats and beds soft as feathers.

In the studio, which Lucy dearly loved, she looked around, knowing she was going to miss it when she went off to Florida. She and Angie had spent weeks making it as homey and comfortable as possible. There were green plants everywhere, real ones that needed to be watered, which was an essential part of Toby's job. The pale pink brick walls were decorated with her original sketches of all the kids. One entire wall was decorated with plaques and awards given to her for innovative contributions to children everywhere.

The bunkhouse, which was now IBL + D's studio, was twenty-seven hundred square feet and was divided into three sections. There was Lucy's area. And next to it was Angie's area. At the back of the building was Toby's office, where he ran the IBL + D Foundation. The furnishings were soft, buttery leather, and the tables were hand hewn from another era. Nothing looked new, but it did look homey, comfortable, and efficient. There was a mini kitchen with ancient appliances that worked, two bathrooms, and a wide central foyer, which no one used. All three loved their own work spaces.

"So, Toby, what do you want to run by me?"

"I'd like to make a sizable donation to St. Jude."

"Okay. What's the problem?"

"If I do that, I'll be dipping into the next quarter. I want to make sure it's okay."

"Absolutely, it's okay. You're doing a super job, Toby. Even my lawyers say you're top-notch. Don't you read the letters that come in from all the organizations thanking us? We've made such a difference for missing and abused children. I think we need to do more. And just last week, more than a dozen letters came in from women who got their lives back because of the battered women's shelters we've funded. Not to mention all those animal sanctuaries that are up and running now, and no animal gets put to sleep. Just keep doing what you're doing. Don't worry if you go into the next quarter. My broker will see to it that he covers everything. The money isn't going to run out, Toby. It is so well invested, we can keep doing this for a very, very long time. And I'm donating a large portion of my dividends from IBL + D, also. We're good to go. Anything else?"

"I don't know how to thank you, Lucy. I really hated driving a truck after I slaved for my degree in business and finance, only to get laid off because of the economy. I also want to thank you for the health benefits. Thanks to you, I'm now in a position to help my brother Denny go to vet school. I love working here. I love the animals, and you know how much I love Angie. I have you to thank for that, too."

"Now you're making me blush. I'm being honest here. I don't know what I'd do without you and Angie. You're my family now. So, it's me who should be thanking you."

"I found it! I found it!" Angie shouted from the doorway. "Time's short, so you should go right now, Lucy, and see if you can get this done. It might take a few days."

Lucy reached for the picture and burst out laughing. "Okay, I'm outta here. Watch the kids, and go easy on the treats. Dizzie is getting addicted to those Froot Loops."

"Go!" Angie shouted.

Lucy scurried away and was back an hour later, saying the poster would be ready the following afternoon.

The days didn't fly by, as Adel and Buddy had predicted, but they didn't lag, either. The trio managed to fill the days and evenings until it was time to board the plane for Florida.

Lucy cried as she hugged and squeezed her kids. Even Angie and Toby had wet eyes. Not Denny, who viewed his responsibility as the ultimate challenge.

"Just keep Froot Loops in your pants pockets, catnip in a bag around your neck, sunflower seeds in your hip pocket, and jerky in your breast pocket, and you'll be okay," Lucy instructed. "They like to ride in the wagon at eleven in the morning and at four in the afternoon. They know when it's time to go to bed, so make sure you go at the same time every night, which is eleven o'clock. They like to watch the news, so be sure to put that on while you're getting ready for bed. Be sure to brush Bizzy's teeth."

"Yes, ma'am," Denny said, his freckles glowing like neon signs on his cheeks. He winked at his brother. There was no doubt in his mind that he could and would control the animals left in his charge.

Wrong.

Five hours later, Luke Kingston was swinging his almost bride high in the air. He kissed her soundly, so soundly, Lucy had to squeal for mercy.

"What's in that big package?" Luke asked Toby as they waited for their luggage at the carousel.

"Something Buddy ordered while he was in Jersey, and it wasn't ready when he left. They delivered it yesterday, so I thought I might as well just bring it with us instead of mailing it," Toby lied with a straight face.

"How are the kids?"

"Well . . . according to this text that just came through from my brother, Izzy is chewing what's left of his corner of the couch, and it's now sagging on one corner. There's nothing left to shred on Bizzy's corner. Lizzy won't come down off the refrigerator, and Dizzie laid an egg in the middle of the kitchen floor. No one knows what to do about the egg. They're circling it and sniffing it. Denny said he is videoing it and will upload it shortly. Other than that, things are fine. Oh, it's raining, so the kids won't go out. He's pulling them around the house in the wagon. Well, he was until Dizzie laid her egg. Now they're all just watching it."

Lucy just smiled.

The clubhouse was packed. It was beautiful, to be sure, with dozens of white roses and white satin ribbon everywhere. Even the runner was white satin. It was easy to see that the residents of Palm Royal had done their best to make this a memorable wedding. Their first.

Luke Sr. and Buddy stood on each side of Angie for the walk down the satin runner. Lucy wanted both of them to "give her away."

Angie, resplendent in a mint-green gown that swirled and twirled, was the matron of honor, and Toby was the best man. Luke's two best friends, Dave and Jack, were his ushers. Emily, Luke's niece, was the flower girl, and his nephew, Benjy, was the ring bearer.

The clubhouse was filled with guests, possibly a hundred in total.

Luke, his eyes glazed, felt weak in the knees when he saw his beloved walking toward him.

"Easy, big guy," Toby said, clutching at Luke's arm to steady him.

"My God, she's beautiful!" Luke whispered.

"That she is. C'mon now, steady as she goes. You can do this."

Luke squared his shoulders. **Damn straight I can do this.** A smile spread across his face as Lucy got closer and closer. Her smile rivaled the sun.

And then it was over, and the minister said, "You may now kiss the bride!" And Luke did.

Congratulations rang through the clubhouse as Luke and Lucy made their way among the guests. When they'd circled the entire room, Lucy felt a tug on her arm. She looked over at Angie. "What?"

"Can you come with me for a few minutes? There's someone who wants to congratulate you."

"Did I miss someone?" Lucy asked anxiously.

"You did. He's waiting. Oh, there he is!"

Lucy gasped when she saw the mane of wild white hair. "Mr. Metcalf! How nice of you to come to my wedding."

"Thank you so much for inviting me."

Lucy wasn't aware that she had invited him, but she wisely kept silent.

"I wanted to be sure I was leaving you in good hands."

"The best, Mr. Metcalf. The best. I didn't think I'd ever see you again. How do you like retirement?"

"It's wonderful."

Lucy bit down on her lower lip. "Helene and Fritz Brighton are not my biological parents, are they?"

Julian Metcalf closed his eyes as he remembered something from Thoreau. **What's the point of having a conscience**

**if you don't listen to it?** Or something along those lines. "No, they are not your parents. How did you figure it out?"

"When you left us back in Freehold, I just had a feeling something still wasn't right, so I took those two baby teeth and had them do a DNA test. I think I knew even before the results came back. I'm glad. Do you know who my **real** parents are?"

"Your mother's name was Paula Kelly. She was one of Helene Brighton's patients. She died giving birth to you. There's no record anywhere of who your father was. The Brightons took you in, but they never legally adopted you."

"Why didn't you tell me that day in Freehold, Mr. Metcalf?"

"It wasn't my place to tell you. Actually, I had been forbidden to tell you. One must obey the laws when one works in the service of the government. Please, don't hold it against me. And please don't dwell on it, either. You're going to have a wonderful life now. Enjoy it. By the way, I brought you a wedding present. It took some doing, but I got it. I'm going to leave now unless you agree to let me have a dance with the bride."

"I would love to dance with you, but I think I should tell you I'm not very good at it. More like I have two left feet."

Metcalf laughed. "That's about how I would sum up my dancing ability. You're okay with what we just talked about, then?" he asked as he led Lucy onto the dance floor.

"I'm very okay with it, Mr. Metcalf. It was the not knowing that bothered me. I want to thank you again for coming. You must have come a long way."

"Halfway around the world, to be accurate. I wanted to be sure you were going to be okay."

"Are you sure now?"

"Yes. Ah, well, we managed not to embarrass ourselves," Metcalf said as he led Lucy over to where her husband was waiting for her. Lucy noticed Luke was holding a small package with a silver ribbon on it. "Your wedding present. Have a good life, Mr. and Mrs. Kingston."

Lucy leaned forward and kissed Julian Metcalf's cheek. She watched as Luke shook his hand. And then he was gone.

"What do you think it is?" Lucy whispered. "I want to open it right now, but that's not the right thing to do in front of all these people. Is it?"

"Who cares? Open it, Lucy."

Lucy's eyes filled with tears, which rolled down her cheeks. "It's the picture Helene took of me with my first missing tooth and the picture of me on my first pony ride. It's all I have of my childhood, that plus my baby tooth. He said . . . he said he had a hard time getting it. Oh, Luke, I don't know what to say or think or do."

"I think you should do what Mr. Metcalf told you to do. Be happy."

"Okay. Okay, I'm happy."

"Atta girl."

Angie nudged Toby. "Tell me that isn't a perfect ending."

"As always, you're right. You and I are going to be just as happy, right?"

"Yep. Forever and ever. C'mon, it's time to dance with me."

Three hours later, the wedding reception was over, and the bride was preparing to toss her bouquet. Of course, Angie caught it and whooped with pleasure.

Just as Luke and Lucy were preparing to leave the hall, Toby came up to them, choked with laughter as he held out his iPhone. Lucy looked down to see her kids clustered in a circle as they all contemplated Egg Number 2.

Tears rolled down her cheeks as Luke gathered her up in his arms and raced out to the car. Their destination, his house, so they could get changed, trade presents, and start their honeymoon.

"You open yours first," Lucy said as she pulled a shirt over her head.

"Oh, my God! This is so perfect, I can't tell you. And I have just the place to hang it in my office. Thanks, Mrs. Kingston."

"Your turn, Mr. Kingston."

"Now, that's a bit of a problem, Mrs. Kingston. My present isn't the kind you can wrap up."

"It isn't?"

"No, it isn't. My present to you is, I'm going to do my best to give you back your childhood. Or at least have you experience what you missed. We have a whole year to accomplish this, with visits home once a month to check on things. For starters, we're off to Australia, because it's winter there now. I'm going to take you sled riding. I'm going to teach you to ski and ice-skate. We're going to roll in the snow and make a snowman. Then, when we're tired, we're going to sit in front of a fire and drink hot cocoa and eat gingerbread cookies. That's what you do after you play in the snow."

"Oh, Luke, really?"

"When we're done with the snow, we're going to Hawaii, where I'm going to teach you to swim, to water-ski, and to ride Jet Skis. We're going to bask on the beach, picnic under palm trees, and eat pineapple till it comes out our ears."

"Oh, Luke, really?"

"Then we're going to head back east to a place I know in upstate New York, Virgil, where they have the best zip line in the world. We're going to go up and down it until we're dizzy. Then we're going to wait as long as it takes for a windy day. Not just any windy day, but a perfect windy day, so we can go kite flying. We're going to walk in the rain, stomp in the puddles, make mud pies, then roll in the mud."

"Oh, Luke, really?"

"Then we're going to head on home just as the leaves change. We're going to rake them, find a way to burn them after we jump in them for hours. We'll go to the Perkins farm and get as many pumpkins as we can carry and carve them and set them all over the place. We're going to have a Halloween party and dress up and scare each other."

"Oh, Luke, really?"

"And then we're going to wait for the first snow on our own turf and trudge through it as we search for the biggest, the most fragrant Christmas tree on those fifty-five acres of yours. I'm going to chop it down, and the two of us are going to drag it home and set it up with all the ornaments I made my mom when I was a kid in school. My sister has them all, and she said she would give them back to me. And you know what else, Lucy? My sister said she's sending me her tiara and her tutu so you can wear them when you go down the zip line for the first time."

"Oh, Luke, really?" Lucy said, tears rolling down her cheeks.

"Yeah, really."